BLUE HORSE DREAMING

Melanie Wallace was born and raised in Manchester, New Hampshire, and now lives with her husband in Myloi, an agrarian village below the Ohi mountain range in Greece, and in Athens. Her novel *The Housekeeper* was longlisted for the Orange Prize for Fiction.

ALSO BY MELANIE WALLACE

The Housekeeper

MELANIE WALLACE

Blue Horse Dreaming

VINTAGE BOOKS
London

Published by Vintage 2009

2 4 6 8 10 9 7 5 3 1

Copyright © Melanie Wallace, 2003

Melanie Wallace has asserted her right under the Copyright, Designs
and Patents Act 1988 to be identified as the author of this work

First published in the United States by MacAdam/Cage Publishing in
2003

First published in Great Britain in 2008 by Harvill Secker

Vintage
Random House, 20 Vauxhall Bridge Road,
London SW1V 2SA

www.vintage-books.co.uk

Addresses for companies within The Random House Group Limited
can be found at: www.randomhouse.co.uk/offices.htm

The Random House Group Limited Reg. No. 954009

A CIP catalogue record for this book
is available from the British Library

ISBN 9780099520474

Penguin Random House is committed to a sustainable future for
our business, our readers and our planet. This book is made from
Forest Stewardship Council® certified paper.

Printed and bound in Great Britain by Clays Ltd, Elcograf S.p.A.

For Peter

One

At first, Lavinia, we did not know what it was we were seeing. From the stockade over which we peered what we saw could have been anything or nothing at all. There was a flare of something, as if dust or smoke, a swirling, but as such things are not unknown in the distances here we watched and wondered whether this disturbance was what it seemed, or whether it was an immense swarm of locusts or a maddened flock of sparrows, an errant windfunnel or a fire of the sort that arises from some surface seam of coal ignited of a sudden and for no reason. As I've written to you before, here brush or tumbleweed can burst into flames, conflagrations of insects can roll across the landscape, winds can kick earth into shapes mistaken for mounted men at full gallop and as suddenly become extinguished, disappear, die away to leave us staring at pure vacuity.

But today what we expected to be nothing more than an illusion became substance, and long before we heard the horses' hooves our eyes discerned the shape of riders in the pale of dawn, and to my relief they rode in a semblance *of formation. I ordered the guards to lower their rifles and together we watched them come on, and I called for reluctant men to open the gates long before we could see their faces; but upon their approach I ordered the guards to hoist their rifles again, for in the immeasurable distance behind our men whose horses we now recognized rode the savages, in a line that stretched long upon the horizon and for as far.*

Our search party rode in, their horses so unruly as to almost stampede toward this decrepit outpost and snorting at being pulled up sharply. As we swung the gates closed after them, the men leapt from their duststreaked, lathered backs, and in those first moments I counted heads and mounts and was relieved that not one had been lost. And then all was pandemonium, Lt. Hastings of the search party yelling orders and the troops calling out and the two civilians, Smith and Buwell, men I dislike and who I described to you previously, bellowing demands no one heeded, and the savages without renting the air with their inhuman cries at a distance beyond our range. Of the two redeemed captives who rode in with the search party, Constance Smith threw herself instantly from her pony and was almost trampled, while the other woman sat her magnificent horse like a statue. Men ran to and fro, saddles and blankets were stripped from the horses, reins were grabbed, and the hostages were quickly readied. I made myself heard above the din and ordered a volley of fire, and the signal roar from the rifles stilled those within and the savages without, and only then did a hush fall over all, so that when the guards cried out that one of the savages was riding forward with three riderless ponies, their voices were heard. The three savages we pulled from the makeshift prison—as you know, this was once upon a time a chicken coop—blinked in the gray light as their ankles and wrists were unbound and they were pushed ungently forward, stumbling at each step, as the gate was once again opened. And then I was amazed: for no sooner had they reached the gate than they found their legs and sprinted madly, and with sudden and inexplicable agility reached those riderless ponies and bounded onto their backs and then to great whoops and cries galloped away, the entire line of savages turning and racing toward the very ends of the earth.

Lt. Hastings saluted me smartly then, but the others—those troops of the search party and those troops who remained here—respected no rank and instead led the blowing, spent horses away, or dropped onto the ground in exhaustion or lit cheroots or slapped their hats against their thighs or greeted one another with grunts and feints and jabs. The Smith woman was crying and laughing and grabbing at the waists of the standing soldiers, swinging herself about in a crazed dance as the men pushed her away, and then she threw herself at the washerwoman and then at her own husband, whose response was to hit her hard with the flat of his palm and raise his hand to her again, though the blow almost knocked her to the ground. Somehow I managed to place myself between them, ordering Smith to tend his mount and telling Maria—strange how all washerwomen in military camps seem to bear this name—to take his near hysterical but now subdued wife with her, and Constance Smith was led away, her hand covering the corner of her mouth and cheek where she was struck.

Only James Buwell, the brother in law of the other redeemed captive, remained then, holding the reins of his mount and the tether of the massive horse upon which his brother's wife sat, not looking at him nor at anything. When he caught my eye he said one thing and one thing only: Pull the stinking bitch off.

I don't take orders, I told him. And at that he threw the tether line at me and walked away.

The woman did not dismount. If she heard his words, or mine, she gave no acknowledgment. But when he was out of earshot, I heard her say clearly, without looking down at me, as if she were speaking to the sky: I will not live among you.

Major Robert Cutter pauses, for there are things he cannot write. Of the constriction in his chest, the hollow twist of surprising pain he inexplicably feels when he first looks at her face. Of her distended belly, full with child, of her broken and dirty nails half-mooning long, beautiful fingers, longer elegant hands. Of the perfectly painted red circle upon one cheek, visible beneath the streaking of dust and sweat and grime. Of the translucent color of her eyes, soft as wild sage, of the light within them and of their haunting clarity as she stares at nothing at all. He cannot write these things, not to anyone and certainly not to his wife, because he is deeply disturbed by them and because he does not understand why he was so struck, so moved by this woman's impassivity, by the chiseled structure of her thin face and by the sign drawn upon it, by her dignified and dismissive countenance, by the majesty of the blue roan she sat.

The knock on what serves as a door, with its ill-fitting planks nailed to slatted pieces of wood that betray the shape of branches, interrupts Cutter's pause. Because the planks are imperfectly sawed and the door hangs unevenly from its hinges, he can see the boots of Lt. Hastings, who stands on the other side. Cutter blots the words that have not dried, then puts the letter beneath the daily logbook that is the sole object on the writing table but for the inkwell and a stand of pens and tips, a wax seal, a candle stub.

Come in, Cutter says.

The door swings open, and the tall lieutenant ducks into the small room. Sir, Hastings says, straightening with a salute. Only then does Cutter wonder for an instant at the impression he must make, unshaven as he is, as he passes a palm over his grizzled face and sparse, uncombed hair.

At ease.

Hastings drops his salute and pretends not to notice Cutter's disheveled appearance, his grimed and undone collar, soiled shirt, and threadbare jacket—unavoidably patched in places, Hastings knows—whose brass buttons have hardly been rubbed, let alone polished, for what must be ages. He watches Cutter rise stiffly from the improbable writing table, improbable because the table, like the bookshelves against one wall, is from another world, one difficult to remember and one the lieutenant finds oddly disturbing, as he does all enchantment, to recall. Every time he enters Cutter's quarters Hastings has, quite against his will, a fleeting impression of his own childhood, of promenades and well-turned ankles, the scent of perfumes, a view of an apple orchard seen from opened parlor windows, gloves laced at the wrist, the small waists of young women, the laughter of gentlemen, appointed dining rooms, bouquets of hyacinth, impressions of things long lost, scarcely recalled; and then those impressions too disappear, dissipate into the chinked walls, the cracked plaster, the beam-and-slat ceiling from which insects and worse drop, the hardpacked dirt floor covered by a grimed rug.

Cutter extracts a bottle of cognac from behind the worn volumes of Shakespeare and, turning, motions the lieutenant to sit. Hastings drags the only other chair in the room from against a wall and places himself in it before the writing table, glad that he will be able to brief Major Robert Cutter like this, wearily but with the aroma of fine liquor in his nostrils and with its taste redolent upon his tongue.

There is much to tell. Of the insubordination and near-desertion of two enlisted men. Of the lack of water sources to the northwest. Of the difficulties with Jonas Smith and James Buwell, who demanded that the horses and men be pushed beyond their limits in their search for the savages with whom the now-redeemed captives were found. Of the savages themselves, who were—Hastings thinks fortunately, but does not say this—breaking down their pitiful and makeshift homes, about to move on to other grounds to better weather the coming hard season; of their flea-bitten dogs, their comely horse herd, their ugly women and children and of the stench of these, of their numbers, which can only be estimated, and their weapons. Of the dangers of being so few, the search party having consisted of twenty, including a designated cook and the two men,

Buwell and Smith. Of the negotiations between Hastings and the savages, held not with words but with signs, of the utter futility of trying to communicate with palms and fingers held in mime and with stick figures drawn in the dust. Of the manner in which Constance Smith and Abigail Buwell—fully savage, that one, Hastings opines—were finally remanded to the search party. Of the return journey, with Hastings wary of the savages trailing them; of the doubling of sentries, the fitful watches, the exhaustion, the dwindling supplies, the lay of the land, the brackish water in their canteens, the hollow-flanked horses suffering from dehydration, the viability of using mules should further forays be necessary.

Lt. Hastings has hardly slept during the fortnight he and the search party have been gone. The tin cup he holds is refilled and the liquor flows through him, numbing his gut and loosening his weary body. He stretches his long legs and studies for a moment his filthy cavalry boots, then looks up and finds that Cutter's face seems not so lined, so haggard or drawn, not so aged as when he first came through the door. No, Hastings does not think the savages will return: he thinks them, oddly and for reasons he cannot explain, to be men of their word. And a trade was made.

In three days, he says, wondering if Cutter can hear the slur that has begun to soften his speech, all traces of them will disappear. And then the lieutenant shakes his head, as much to clear it as to reveal his incredulity, then continues. The savages can and do simply vanish, sir, he admits, then leans forward confidentially. I find it's as though nature conspires with them. I mean, one day they are there, and the next all signs of them have been erased. Their encampments, even their trails.

Well. It's a damnable place, after all, Cutter remarks slowly, a godforsaken place. Hastings does not know whether Cutter's words are to be taken as consolation or irony, looks at him as sharply as he can, reads impassivity in his expression. As a matter of fact, Cutter adds.

Hastings feels suddenly unhinged. He pushes back against his seat, raises the tin cup with its last draught of cognac, swallows, tables the cup.

Lieutenant, Cutter says, you should get some rest. I'll see to Smith and Buwell and their women myself. You've nothing more to do.

There's the matter of the report.

Cutter waves his hand, resisting an urge to counter that reports are useless. He lets his hand drop and says instead, You've been as detailed as any report needs.

Hastings' eyes stray to the logbook on the table, and then he looks away. He suspects that nothing has been recorded in it for a long time, and he knows that the dead quartermaster's ledgers are still within the quartermaster's now uninhabited quarters, untouched and unwritten in since the man's death. He hesitates to ask whether the log is up to date, whether the quartermaster's ledgers should be retrieved; he is afraid Cutter will think he doubts him, which he does, though Cutter is correct: this frontier, this outpost, seems godforsaken, and a daily log and supply ledgers are probably useless in view of the fact that all contact has been lost with the rest of the world anyway.

Cutter does not offer to refill their cups. The lieutenant realizes he has no other reason to stay. He rises and salutes. Dismissed, John, Cutter says, then watches him fit his lanky frame through the doorway as Cutter thinks: An officer who appreciates a good glass of cognac likely makes a fair officer. Then thinks: What a waste.

Two

He shaves ineptly, unable to catch his reflection in the worn mirror hung beside the basin, and when finished he runs his hands over his hair, buttons his grimed collar, brushes the dust from his breeches and jacket. When Cutter finally steps out of his quarters the whiteness of the day blinds him momentarily and he squints into the light, the squat darkness of the buildings shadowing into a blur before slowly coming into focus. Disgust hits him, there's a twist to the pit of his stomach as though there's a tilt to the earth: these things he feels every time he leaves his quarters to confront—or, more precisely, to be confronted by—the hellishness of this place, its disarray, and his visceral reaction to the stupidity of his superiors who without foresight or hindsight thought to reman what had once been a fort, abandoned during the war and left to rot for years thereafter, in order to secure a frontier without boundaries for settlers who never materialized.

Almost from the beginning Cutter saw this outpost as an ill-fated ship, one with its sails rent, its men spent, its hull irreparably leaking, anchored upon some vast and damning sea. He has tried to shake himself of the simile, but finds himself foundering within it each and every time he faces the improbable and useless quadrant someone once conceived of as a parade ground, the buildings surrounding it in various states of disrepair, the stables with their collapsing roofs, the ramshackle barracks without glass or waxed paper in their gaping windows, the pokeweed pushing through broken porch planking, the leanto coverings of grainsack canvas tearing here and shredded there, the fallen and un-replaced clapboards and shingles warping and rotting. The detritus is everywhere: strewn among the myriad firepits dug into the ground are discarded wagon rims and broken wheels, stands of empty barrels, haphazard kindling stacks, unprotected charcoal heaps, dirty pots and pans, washbasins, rotting boots, piles of discarded clothes worn thin and for too long, one cannon and scattered cannon balls and two rusting if mounted and undoubtedly useless Gatling guns, emptied powder kegs, men (yes, yes, Cutter has come to consider even the troops as part of the disorder) so immobile as to appear drunk or dead. They lie about here and there, some sprawled facedown in the dust, others sleeping in the paltry shelter of the leantos or sitting with their backs against the walls on sentry duty, the lucky ones in the decrepit barracks, all passing their hours dreamlessly or fitfully until duty shifts change, until the grazing and wood details come or go, until hunger or thirst or their need to use the open latrines motivates them. Dreadful this place, Cutter thinks, unable to shake himself of his vision that he and these men are wrecked upon the doldrums, powerless to return from where they had come, unable now even to imagine what current led them here, cast them adrift, left them futureless and dwarfed by a landscape as treacherous and inhospitable as the sea: beyond the stockade the world spins away forever, into infinity, its daunting immensity as incomprehensible as the span of any ocean. Dreadful, he thinks again, swallows bile, takes a deep breath, almost as dreadful as the war. Which, now long receded like a spent tidal wave, stranded them here—these troops, himself—like living flotsam spun from its murkiest, darkest depths. They, Cutter reflects, we, this, are nothing but the war's aftermath. This dreadful place but an afterthought.

And then he steps into the aftermath, into the afterthought, into the light, fighting the pain in his shoulder and in his knee and making an effort to walk without limping or hunching. Across the way a rat-tailed brindle cur rises, shakes itself, and stiffly makes its way toward him, head bowed, backend swaying. No one remembers when or where exactly on the journey to this outpost the dog joined them, and no one has given it a name. Cutter waits for the dog before crossing over to the sutler, whose store by all logic should be closed; the men as well as the officers, after all, have not received their pay for months, but Ezekiel Pace still freely and greedily extends credit at exorbitant interest on already exorbitant prices to any and all except the black smithy named Cole.

The sutler fears and despises dogs, Cutter knows, so he takes small if perverse pleasure now in approaching Pace, who in another time and place—certainly during the war—Cutter would have imprisoned on the slightest pretense whatsoever, though here and now he can do no more than request from an unresponsive and distant general headquarters the sutler's removal from the outpost for the sale of moldy, weevily staples, rancid lard, green-sided bacon, moth-eaten blankets and clothes, old tack, flimsy belts and the like the men yet find superior to anything the military has issued or, rather, failed to issue. Pace backs into the storefront doorway at Cutter's approach and spits, then wipes at the tobacco juice on his bottom lip with the back of his hand. The cur sniffs at the wad of tobacco slime, looks up in disappointment, wags its tail.

That dog's not allowed in here, Pace says.

I'm not coming in.

The sutler crosses his arms over the pouch that is his stomach, sniffs the air as if scenting Cutter's animosity, tries to conceal his disappointment. He believes that Cutter has money, and Cutter knows this; he also knows that Pace keeps track of time and that time is running out for the sutler, now that the troops' pockets have been emptied. Well, Pace says, as I'm sure this ain't no social visit, you might wanna tell me somethin' I don't know.

Such as.

Such as, your supply wagons are on their way. Such as, you're about to cover your troops' debts. Such as, you're in need of whatever I got, and that you'll pay for it.

The supply wagons are on their way. As for what's due you from the troops, you might consider moving on.

Ha.

Take my advice.

That ain't no advice. I'm owed a great deal. Besides, your men would hardly eat if it wasn't for me.

They'd manage.

Ha. G'day to you, Major. 'Less there's something you want to buy.

Actually, I'm requisitioning today. Maria will be along for garb for the two women the search party brought in. And seeing whatever you've got you've scavenged from the emigrant trail, no one's paying for it.

You can't requisition nothing. I ain't military.

I don't care.

It cost me to collect what I got. Time for sure. And I bartered some.

I know as well as you do what the emigrants threw away.

Then let those women go scrounge for themselves. This ain't a free store, and I ain't in the charity business. Not even for white women that's been living with savages against their will.

If you had a heart, Pace, I'd have it cut out, Cutter says. The garments are free of charge.

You got a whole bunch of men to order around here. Whyn't you go do that.

The dog sidles over to Cutter and noses his hand. Cutter would like nothing better than to set the cur on the sutler but realizes the futility of such a thought—the dog is too old, harmless—and turns his back on the man in frustration, then picks his way across the disarray of the quadrant. He tells himself that tomorrow he'll give orders to restore this place to some semblance of a military camp, maybe appoint an adjutant though Cutter has no need for one, even retrieve the dead quartermaster's ledgers that must be lying about in a corner, as unclaimed and untouched as the quartermaster's place itself, for the troops believe that what killed the man still lingers there, embedded in the timbers, the planks, the dirt floor. Cutter tries to recall how many supply convoys had arrived and departed—two, three?—since the quartermaster died of meningitis, finds himself unsure, feels distressed at not having kept track; and then he wonders when it was that he lost touch with his responsibilities. Wonders how it is he has come to feel so old.

He also wonders whether Pace will give Maria anything for the Buwell and Smith women to wear. The dog rubs its head on Cutter's leg, and suddenly Cutter realizes he has stopped dead in his tracks, that he is standing on the edge of the ludicrous parade ground, that he does not know how long he has been there.

Around him, men stir from where they lie unsheltered, rouse themselves up onto elbows and bony behinds, crane their heads at the din from behind the stables and stay where they are or gaze vacantly at nothing at all, ignore the calls from beyond the stockade gates, the yells of the sentries to open the gates, so that it is the sentries who have to descend from the stockade's narrow, rickety ramparts and push the massive crosspole free and swing the gates inward for the returning wood detail. Some troops walk beside the harnessed mules and others ride on the timber, the mounted guards preceding and following, and all pass Cutter by without a salute, without so much as a nod. The old dog barks twice, convulsing with the effort, and Cutter absently touches its head to quiet it. Several soldiers silently rise and, without dusting themselves off, saunter over to the wagon and begin to pull the wood off as the mules are unharnessed, the jinnys and jacks nuzzling and nipping one another. Cutter limps forward and flags three tired-looking, mounted guards and orders them back out, to where the emigrant trail begins, to scavenge for female garb. Just in case the sutler proves incorrigible.

When Cutter finally humps around the stables, the dog padding at his heels, what he sees makes him break stride, forget the soreness in his knee, leave the cur in his tracks. Dust surrounds the handful of jeering troops standing a crescent about the horse on which Abigail Buwell rode in, taunting it as it turns frenzied circles, kicks out viciously, rushes at James Buwell as he tries to get past it. Beyond the circle of dust the horse kicks up, Abigail Buwell crouches impassively, her back to the stockade. On the edge of the fray Maria is yelling and pulling at Constance Smith, who with her husband is egging James Buwell on and shouting invectives at Abigail Buwell. The troops weave and feint at the horse, heckling the creature and mocking one another's cowardice; and then Cutter hears his own voice, muffled as if in a nightmare, cry out for them to disperse as he stumbles at a run, his breathing ragged, through what seems to be pure solidity. And then he is upon them. Cutter pulls the first soldier he reaches about by an arm and pushes him away as he now bellows *Disperse!*, whereupon the other troops step away, out of reach, glaring at Cutter in dull surprise and sullen contempt, for his command will return them to nothing but their listless boredom. They walk backwards and at a distance from one another, grumbling, and then become silent. Cutter yells at James Buwell to stop, grabs the back of Jonas Smith's shirt, sends Smith spinning. Abigail Buwell's horse rushes Buwell at that moment, and in his scramble to get out of its way Buwell puts himself within Cutter's reach, and Cutter hauls him rearward and swings him about so clumsily that Buwell loses his footing and falls heavily, his arm folding underneath him in an awkward way and crunching with a sickening sound.

And then it is over but for the agitated circles the magnificent horse continues to turn, but for the unearthly howl—odd to hear from a man, though the sound is familiar to Cutter and to anyone who has been in battle—that comes from Buwell, who rolls to his knees and then collapses onto his side, rolls again, howls the louder. You fool, Constance Smith cackles, she ain't worth it, she ain't worth nothin', and Cutter suddenly notices the bruise about Constance Smith's caving mouth, her scabrous, milkwhite eye. C'mon, Maria mutters, pulling at her, c'mon, you're filthy, we got things to do, but the woman tries to bite Maria's hand, prompting Maria to swear at her with those words taught the washerwoman by roughriders and soldiers and whoremongers, and the troops laugh at Maria's curses, grin and nod and elbow one another as they begin to saunter away. Jonas Smith comes to stand over Buwell as Smith's wife, still trying to wrench free from Maria, drags her toward Cutter. Let her go, get Matthews, Cutter tells Maria, and she unhands

Constance Smith and, still swearing, disappears at a run and returns with the doctor in what seems to Cutter to be no time at all.

Dr. Thomas Matthews opens his bag as he kneels by James Buwell, who suddenly quiets and pales as Matthews takes his arm in both hands, runs his fingers from elbow to knuckles, speaks to Buwell in a low voice. Cutter tells Jonas Smith to back off and, to his surprise, the man does, with Constance Smith following suit, Maria at her side. After a few moments James Buwell nods his head at something Matthews says, and the doctor pauses before snapping the bone into place, lickety-split, ignoring the fierce scream that comes from Buwell—one that becomes a prolonged wail—as Matthews splints the wrist and wraps it with the same swift motion other men use to tie the legs of a roped calf. When Matthews gets Buwell to his feet and begins to lead him away, Constance Smith turns and hawks in Abigail Buwell's direction, then shrieks at her in a tongue Cutter has never heard before.

Jonas Smith wallops his wife into silence before Cutter can reach him, push him away from her. That's enough, Cutter fairly growls, placing himself—once again, he reflects—between the two. Constance Smith turns her back, hunches over, drools blood and spits a broken tooth onto the ground. And then Maria is beside her, one arm about the woman's waist. Get her inside your place, Cutter says, and Maria gives him a sideways glance at which he frowns.

I told her I don't want her speakin' that lingo, Smith mutters as Maria leads his wife away.

And I don't want you here, Cutter says. When your

friend's arm is set, leave. Both of you.

We ain't military, Smith retorts. You can't order us around.

Cutter feels his temper rise, is reminded of the sutler.

We got rights here, Smith insists. And our women.

You can exercise your rights on the other side of these walls. Your wife will be fed, she'll be given clothes, she'll have a medical examination. You'll be able to be on your way tomorrow.

Smith stares at Cutter for a long moment, looks down and toes the ground, swivels his head, cracks his neck. And then he turns wordlessly on his heel and walks away, landing a kick to the old cur straggling in Cutter's direction. The dog lets out a pitiful yelp. Abigail Buwell, behind her now stilled, lathered blue roan, covers her face with her hands at the sound. When Major Robert Cutter looks in her direction, only the horse meets his gaze, then pins its ears, snakes its neck, and snaps its teeth.

At day's end, fires burn beneath the messes cooking in soot-blackened pots while men wait, lounging in the dusk, smoking, whittling, picking at their fingers. The sweeter smell of manure mixes with the stench from the latrines and the odors of spoiled bacon, boiling beans, frying dough, ignited coal, burning wood. From the doctor's quarters, a mean planked affair with a rotting porch, a yellowish light spills from the only window.

Cutter hesitates before stepping onto Matthews' porch. His reluctance is genuine, for he knows that

Matthews' sallow, feverish wife will hardly appreciate his visit at this hour; but he needs to know if the doctor has examined the two redeemed captives before Cutter speaks to Jonas Smith and James Buwell—now camping outside the walls, the devil take both of them—in the morning and sends them on their way with the women. When Cutter steps onto the porch, Matthews opens the door of his own accord, motions for Cutter to stay where he is, glances back inside, then nods at the major and comes out, closing the door gently behind him. I only need a few minutes of your time, Cutter tells him. She's sleeping, Matthews says, so I've nothing but time until she wakes.

They sit on the edge of the chairless porch. Matthews tells Cutter that he, indeed, examined Constance Smith. But for the loss of several teeth, a bruised mouth, the milky—and, he thinks, sightless— eye, the scars on her back, a healed puncture wound on one thigh, the doctor found nothing remarkable about the woman except her thinness. He remarks that the probable blindness, the condition of her gums, might be attributable to a curious kind of starvation, perhaps self-imposed, perhaps not. He also notes that Constance Smith's memory, in contrast to her body, seems unimpaired.

She certainly remembers English, Cutter notes.

In a vitriolic way, the doctor acknowledges.

And the Buwell woman?

Matthews shakes his head. Her, he says, I don't understand.

You couldn't approach her.

I wouldn't, more like it, not with that horse standing

21

guard. I stood at a distance and spoke to her for a time, but got no response. They say she doesn't remember English.

They?

Lt. Hastings. Others in the search party. James Buwell, not that he's to be trusted.

What does Constance Smith say?

She says to hang her from a gallows.

Cutter raises his eyebrows, looks over the outpost, watches the smoke rising from the fires, then glances at Matthews. The doctor is half his age, Cutter finds himself thinking with a poignancy he seldom allows himself, struck now—as he often is—by the fineness of Matthews' flawless features made finer by some inner kindness; half Cutter's age, with a consumptive, dying wife even younger. Matthews' expression momentarily betrays the slightest hint of self-consciousness, and Cutter suddenly fears the younger man has read his mind. Cutter does not want to demean him with pity: after all, they are both men who have chosen professions in which death is commonplace, pity unacceptable.

How soon will she give birth, Cutter asks without inflection, for he already knows the answer.

I'd say she's overdue.

That's my impression.

I wouldn't expect the child to live. Or her.

Something tightens in Cutter's chest. She's a young woman, he says to Matthews. She looks strong.

The doctor shakes his head thoughtfully. This uprooting must be taxing. And there's the shock of return. He feels Cutter's eyes on him and shrugs. And I don't know, Matthews muses aloud, what it is she's being returned to. Civilization excepted, of course. But her husband is dead. The man who brought her back is his brother, but I don't find him sympathetic nor do I understand why he thinks he has a right to her. Needless to say, she's obviously carrying a savage's child; I'm going to assume by choice.

That remains unclear.

Lt. Hastings told me she was forced to leave another child behind, to which she seemed very attached.

The lieutenant had not told this to Cutter, who ponders it for a moment, suppresses a sigh. So much in this world, he finally says, always seems to remain unclear.

It is the doctor's turn to glance sideways. In what sense, Robert?

Cutter feels unexpectedly grateful for this quiet, unassuming intimacy. He wants suddenly to bare his soul, to say: What is unclear is what we are doing here at all, at this awful outpost, at the edge of this appalling frontier, here on earth, but he refrains from doing so and simply shakes his head. I was just thinking, Cutter tells him, that I'm not sure our mission here is to redeem captives, to be at the mercy of strangers like Jonas Smith and James Buwell, who wander into the outpost with savages as prisoners and demand we take them at their word, assign troops to them, send men out to face unknown dangers and possible death. I was just thinking that I'm not sure I acted correctly.

There isn't always a book of rules to follow.

No. Perhaps I'll mention that in my report. In which I'll be relieved to state that no one was lost or injured.

For that, I'm sure everyone is grateful.

Most of all, me.

From inside the room the two men hear a wracking cough. Susan, Matthews says.

How is she?

Not better.

Well, go on in. I've kept you too long.

Not at all, Matthews says as both men rise.

Sorry to say, Cutter mentions, I'll need a statement of examination, when you've a moment, to accompany my report.

You'll have it, Matthews says.

Cutter finds Maria where he always found her after dark, in the area behind the sutler's. Here, somehow, the washerwoman managed over time to construct a walled leanto of sorts sagging against the back wall of the store, with two makeshift rooms on either side of a roofed entryway. Her place faces onto a swept yard inhabited by barrels and poles, a boiler cauldron and firepit, a useless and unused butter churn, discarded barrels and barrels of lard, overturned pails and pails of charcoal, cakes of lye, and yards upon yards of rope. Two faded blankets hang, in lieu of doors, at the entry to each side room; there are no windows. The cast iron stove in the entryway is unlit, as it mostly is until the deeper cold begins. Cutter can well imagine the favors Maria cast upon those who helped build this odd structure, for he has more than once turned a blind eye and deaf ear to such. Especially as, four times in moments of profound loneliness, Cutter too came to Maria, though the memory of those visits makes him flinch with great embarrassment, having met her feigned passion with an unfeigned lassitude that only deepened his sense of guilt and weariness at having grown old. Since that last time, Cutter has treated Maria with a cold formality and allowed her to stay without a hint of condemnation, aware of her sexual trafficking and outrageous rates, suspecting also that she charges inflated prices to troops too fatigued or listless to boil water and buy soap to wash their wretched clothes, too unfamiliar with the art of patching and sewing to mend, or make from scraps, shirts, underclothes, pants.

Cutter does not call out her name, his tread is enough. Maria appears from one blanketed doorway, lantern in hand, then disappears within. The second time she appears, Constance Smith is with her, and Cutter is startled to see that the woman has donned righteous dress, a worn calico retrieved from some-where, as well as a bonnet and shoes. Constance Smith stumbles, grins a partially toothless grin, looks witchlike in the flickering light with her white eye. These are lamin', she says, pointing at her shoes. But civilizin'.

Good, Cutter replies, making an effort to be polite, though he hardly feels disposed to civility with her.

Maria looks at him triumphantly. The clothes will cost money, she says. Just this one's. The soldiers brought me rags for free, but they're for the other one.

Cutter shakes his head.

In dollars.

My husband ain't got money, Constance Smith says.

I'm sure Maria will reach some accommodation with the sutler then.

And my husband, he wants to be with me, Constance

Smith adds. He don't understand why he can't.

He knows damn well why, Cutter tells her. This is a military outpost, not a hotel. And if Maria were to put you both up, you'd have to pay her double. More, for breaking the rules.

In dollars, Maria says.

Oh.

You'll be on your way home tomorrow, Cutter assures Constance Smith. And I take it your needs are met.

I'm clean, I got clothes, and I ate, if that's what you mean.

That's what I mean. And your friend?

She ain't no friend to me. Or me to her.

Go back inside now, Maria says to Constance Smith, giving her the lantern. Go on. I'll be talking to the major now, while you get yourself to bed.

The woman turns, walks a pinched walk back, disappears behind the curtain. Where is—Cutter begins, but Maria steps forward and takes him by his elbow as though steering an errant child. He stiffens at her touch, steps away from her reach, nods at her to lead the way. Maria puts her hands on her hips and walks in front of him, tossing glances over her shoulder that make him realize how long it has been since he approved of her, that make him understand Maria knows blackmail like her own name and that he has reason to fear; for she is bound by no law and no word not to reveal his inadequacies, she could shout from the center of the derelict quadrant the news of his betrayals, his impotency, his descents into temptation that left him unfulfilled, embarrassed, frozen.

When Maria halts for a moment, Cutter stops behind her, takes a step back. Roberto, she says teasingly, turning to him, you're not such an old man as you think.

If it's money you want for taking in the Smith woman, Maria, show some respect.

They circle a part of the corral, and the horses within raise their heads in the dark, then move slowly away, their haunches and backs and necks and manes barely distinguishable one from the other in the mean starlight. At the far end of the corral and beyond it, Abigail Buwell's horse stands as if carved from bluish alabaster.

She's over there, Maria says. They say she can't speak gringo no more.

What do you think?

I think the same.

Cutter knows better.

Thank you, he says. Go on back now.

Watch that horse, Maria warns. It's crazy. I'd hate to have to warm up to some spanking new commander younger than you. And handsomer.

Cutter attempts to smile, grimaces in spite of himself. If Maria notices, she shows nothing, for she turns on her heel and with a toss of her long hair is gone. And then he walks slowly toward the horse, which as Cutter approaches moves to face him, ears back, neck arched. An evil bite, Cutter decides, and stops short.

I only wanted to know if you needed anything, he eventually says to Abigail Buwell.

The figure on the ground rocks slightly, stills, then resumes rocking again. He feels as though his legs are hollow, but there is no tightening in his chest, for which he is grateful. He cannot see her features in the dark, though he can make out that she has wrapped her arms around her knees and bent her head over them. He considers the position must be painful with the belly she has.

Cutter stands for a long time, hoping to outwait Abigail Buwell's silence and the blue roan's vigilance, but the horse never loses interest, never relaxes or lowers its head, never moves away. Abigail Buwell never stops rocking. His legs are tired, he is tired, the pain in his knee and shoulder baleful. There is shrapnel in him yet.

Good evening, he finally says.

Three

That which haunts Major Robert Cutter does not appear this night. He makes his way slowly back around the corral, apprehensive now that he is alone with the dark, hating the lack of moonlight. You have become ridiculous, Cutter tells himself edgily, but he is terrified nonetheless by the boy—ephemeral, material—who steps from the depths of night or sits in the mouth of an overturned barrel, plays in the remotest corners of the outpost, lurks on the stable roof, and is then gone, a shade melting into shadow. Cutter does not believe that the boy is a figment of his imagination or the offspring of his overwrought anxieties, but something purely other-worldly—and Cutter has never believed in other worlds. Not one man from the hundreds Cutter saw killed and knew by name in the war had ever come back after death, not even his own brother, with whom he had made a pact: if one of them died, they'd promised each other, and there was life beyond, the dead brother would return to his beloved sibling with a series of signs—a certain word written upon a blank piece of paper, a candle lighting by itself, a code tapped lightly upon the living's shoulder. But there had never been a sign, nor a visitation, not in all these years, though Cutter had waited, though he had slept upon his brother's grave more than once despite the fact that there were troops and officers who thought him macabre or much deranged at that time. Cutter was neither, he was simply patient. He was patient too with the absurd and costly séances, patient with the shuddering of tables, the rattling of windows, the tinkling of unseen chimes, the disembodied tones in the medium's voice; but there was never a word he would have recognized as spoken by his brother. There was nothing. In the end, Cutter's patience gave way to an unshakable disbelief in the afterlife. Which disbelief had recently been shaken.

Cutter draws near the pitted embers and pauses, looks about him. The faces of the sleeping men who lie here and there about the waning fires are indistinguishable, one from another, as are their blanket-shrouded shapes. None stir. Beyond them, the dark takes hold, and Cutter skirts its boundaries, picking his way cautiously through the sleeping troops until they are behind him and then, keeping his eyes to the ground, he steps onto the useless, littered quadrant and takes a deep breath. He wills himself to look at nothing and certainly not into the night that lies between him and his quarters. The throbbing sear in his knee hobbles his gait as Cutter breaks into a painful run until he is there, lunging for his door, stifling the cry in his throat and terrified at what might be at his back. And then Cutter is inside, with the sound of his heart in his ears as loud as any horse's gallop, with a pounding in his chest as he fumbles for an oil lamp and lights it with trembling hands.

The room seems warm despite the chill that presses against its outer walls, seeps in from under the ill-hung door. The flicker of the yellow light, the closeness of these walls, the passing of the minutes calm him. Eventually, Cutter pours water from the pitcher into the porcelain basin and rinses his hands, his face, wipes them. He stands for a long time thereafter—for how long, he doesn't know—listening to the night, hearing nothing.

He lowers the lamp's flame and thinks to sleep, but he cannot bear the thought of undressing, of the sight of his thinning shanks, his wilted sex, of the puckered, purplish scars he will find below one shoulder and about his knee, of the whiteness of his ankles and feet and stomach and wrists. He sits instead at the writing table, takes up his pen, and removes several sheaves of paper from under the logbook, rustles through them, selects a blank sheet. *Ah, dearest Lavinia,* he writes, *it was wise of you not to accompany me to this outpost, for were you here you would have to make allowances for a husband who has become ludicrous, not only in appearance but in mind and in the same careworn manner, for both are frayed. I find that my edges are no longer distinct; perhaps something in my brain bleeds, perhaps some embolism erupted and drowned logic, or perhaps age is a mean thing, returning us from whence we came, to something not unlike child-hood, which only children can survive because they hardly understand its frights and have not a presentiment of fragile mortality. Whatever the cause, the dark now holds great terror for me; I, who always loved best those moonless nights made deeper by canopied clouds spread like a thick black shawl across the heavens, am now paralyzed when in its clutch. In the dark I tremble, cries catch in my throat, my legs become leaden; I am deafened by the sound of my own heart. I fear to see things. I fear things that cannot be seen. It was wise of you not to accompany me to this place.*

I so burden you with the goings-on here and now with the lunatic within me that you must think I have not a tender heart; to the contrary, you are in my thoughts always, you are my beacon, my way. I find the distance between us both incomprehensible and irksome, incomprehensible when I wonder whether I have become like the blind, unable to recall the curve of your smile and a world I've not seen for far too long, irksome because I am, without you, so utterly, so perfectly, alone. I have no one to read aloud to me at night, as you know, and no one to read to; never does a word of sweetness fall upon me, and those words of sweetness within me are locked deep inside and will remain unspoken until you hand me the key. I charge you to remember me, your loving husband. I promise to join you soon, though when I cannot say. Yrs truly, Robert Cutter. Postscript: I have had no news of our dear Henry. Perhaps you know more than I of our son's whereabouts.

Before he pulls off his boots and lies fully clothed upon the narrow bed in the back room of his quarters, Cutter tears what he has written this night into small pieces. He wants to add nothing to his wife's distress, and he thinks his words, himself, distressing. The thin cornhusk mattress rustles with his every movement, and he moves about a great deal, not only because the mattress has its own topography, one that resists him, but because he is sleepless. *To sleep, perchance to dream,* he recites, trying to remember Lavinia's touch—were her hands cool, were they soft as water running over mink?—but Cutter cannot summon the lightness of her stroke upon his wrist, nor see the shape of her hands, the lines about her mouth, the crook of her elbow. *To sleep, perchance to dream,* Cutter recites again, trying to remember the cadence, the lilt, the tones of his wife's voice. Which he cannot.

Four

Report to Comdr First Army
Re: Redemption of two captives, and on the prevailing
conditions at Outpost 2881

Sir:

*We have at this outpost two redeemed female captives,
whose names are Constance Smith and Abigail Buwell.
They had been captured by savages and lived among them
for some four years. The following is the account of their
redemption.*

*Several weeks ago, two men named Jonas Smith and
James Buwell arrived here, having in tow three savages
who were bound hand and foot upon their mounts, their
mounts being likewise bound one to another tail to neck.
The men are sodders who were unacquainted with one
another until four years ago, when their homesteads were
raided by savages. At Jonas Smith's place the savages killed
several cows, set fire to his home, and captured his wife
Constance, all on a day when he was some miles distant,*

gathering wood. James Buwell stated that the savages stole from him one horse, but his sod house was left intact; when the savages espied him and gave chase, he managed to outgallop them on his best horse. Upon losing them, Buwell headed for his brother's home, but upon arriving found his brother slain in the most horrible manner in a field he had been plowing. His brother's wife, Abigail, was missing, as were two horses.

Several days after the savages were last seen in the area, Smith and Buwell met and attempted to trail them. The men wandered for many days before their horses were badly spent, and they eventually relinquished their pursuit. Nothing more was heard of Constance Smith or Abigail Buwell or of their captors until a group of savages recently revisited the very same territory, passing close to Buwell's place. Upon recognizing a piebald with distinctive markings as being one of the same horses ridden on that fateful raid some years before, Buwell rode hard to Smith's, and the two men armed themselves and set out after this band in the hope of trailing them to their encampment, and in the hope that the women were still alive and among them.

The savages were again raiding horses, and the number they had gathered made for easy tracking. However, some days after starting out, Buwell and Smith saw from a crest that the savages had come across a wagon of emigrants that they calculated almost two days' trek from here. I cannot fathom why this wagon was traveling alone on the now unused emigrant trail and at this late date in the season, and no one survived the savages to tell. Buwell and Smith, however, managed to attack the savages, several of whom were dismounted, killing two. The others rode off, stampeding not only the herd but also the ponies of the three savages who remained on foot, whom Buwell and Smith captured. They made their prisoners dig the graves of the seven people who were murdered, including four small children, and they were buried beside their wagon, which was ill provisioned, but from which the men managed to take some hardtack and dried meat. Fearing a retaliatory raid, Buwell and Smith decided to head with their captives to this outpost, which lies in a southwesterly direction from where the massacre took place. They mounted the savages on the horses that were still tethered to the wagon, leaving the yoke of oxen free.

Upon arriving here, Buwell and Smith told their story and demanded that a search party return to the massacre site with them to pick up the trail of the savages. They were fully convinced that the band was the same that had taken Jonas Smith's wife and James Buwell's sister in law. I assigned Lt. John Hastings to gather men, mounts, arms, provisions, and what articles of trade might be useful to prove goodwill, and to accompany the civilians on their quest. Buwell claimed that he knew sign language, though this proved untrue. Both Smith and Buwell were convinced that the savages would trade the women for the three prisoners the men had taken, for the savages' numbers are dwindling and their need for males is terrific, as these are the hunters and raiders, and upon them depends the life of the band.

Lt. Hastings reported that they picked up the savages' trail at the site of the massacred emigrants' wagon. Wild animals had dug into the shallow graves and pulled body parts to the surface, making evident to Hastings that the emigrants had been hideously murdered and mutilated, *their scalps being gone and their bodies punctured by many holes, some the marks of being eaten but many yet recognizable as ghastly wounds. In the wagon there was nothing that would identify the names of the people and children murdered.*

Lt. Hastings' search party finally located the savages many days after leaving here. That night the search party camped far from the savages and lit no fire, so as to surprise the savages just before dawn. As the savages' encampment was spread on both sides of a stream bottom that erupted from a deep ravine, Lt. Hastings and his men set out in the moonlight before daybreak, with twelve men positioned above the savages and within good shooting range; and at the first sign of light, as they were instructed, they volleyed. The savages stumbled naked from those conical homes that were still standing, for some had been broken down and packed onto travois, and met with the sight of the lieutenant, accompanied by James Buwell, Jonas Smith, and several soldiers, riding into their camp. Lt. Hastings said the savages were so dumbstruck and frightened that at first he could not imagine that these were the same as had brutally murdered the emigrants, but then a woman began to run toward them, screaming, until she was pinned down and dragged away by two other women, and that this woman was, to his mind, white, having skin much lighter than that of any savage he had yet seen.

Jonas Smith, who heard his wife's screams, grabbed his rifle and was like to begin a massacre, which undoubtedly would have resulted in a horrific scene but for the wits of the lieutenant, who knocked Smith's gun away and threatened to shoot him. The savages watched this and thereafter would not negotiate with Smith, though the lieutenant immediately requested that Buwell tell the savages that they had come to make a trade. Whatever signs he made were incomprehensible to the savages, one of whom pelted him with a piece of manure, to the great delight of all, in spite of the tension. Eventually, Lt. Hastings stated, he made it clear to the savages that Abigail Buwell and Constance Smith could be traded for the three savages Buwell and Smith had captured and brought to Outpost 2881. The savages insisted they had only one white woman, the one who had been espied, Jonas Smith's wife; but James Buwell was dissatisfied with the savages' claim, and he demanded that all their women be brought forth, and so they were. Among them he recognized his brother's wife, though she looked very much to be one of them and had at her side a child of about two and was herself with child. She made no indication that she recognized James Buwell, and when he pointed at her she was much frightened and in the savages' tongue made much protest. But Constance Smith said that yes, this was Abigail Buwell, and that she had been captured on the same day as herself, and that she was now a heathen. Lt. Hastings felt himself incapable of doing less than returning the woman to civilization, and so negotiations continued. Before Abigail Buwell was reluctantly handed over to the search party, the savages separated her from her child and gave her a fine horse.

Within minutes of the search party's return here, the three savages held as prisoners were released from their confinement and, once freed, joined their fellows and rode away. They have not returned.

Dr. Thomas Matthews has examined Constance Smith, and his medical report is appended. She says she *was ill-treated by the savages. She remembers the English language and feels herself saved. Her hatred toward her captors is all consuming, and her attitude toward them is unforgiving; and though she readily admitted to Dr. Matthews that she had not been violated by them, she is unwilling to count that as a sign of their humanity, as she is of the opinion that they are not human.*

Constance Smith will return to her former life with her husband.

James Buwell, who has a broken wrist, insists that Abigail Buwell be left here, in our care, until after she gives birth; he further demands that the infant be taken from her or killed. Neither demand regarding the infant, I needlessly add, will be met. Buwell says that he will return for her in good time; according to Lt. Hastings, she is to become Buwell's wife, for she was his brother's wife and is now (in James Buwell's mind) wedded to him through the murder of his brother. As Abigail Buwell has refused, even if she is so capable, to acknowledge where she is, I am at a lack of words to describe what indeed will be the outcome of this. She did not speak to anyone during the journey to our outpost and seems much distressed in her mind, and she seeks the companionship only of her horse. She has proven inaccessible, for none can approach her. I can only hope that James Buwell's leaving, and the birth of the child, might bring her to regain her senses.

As to the conditions here, I must stress that the nonappearance of supply convoys over a substantial period of time has now begun to make life unbearable and any semblance of order less and less possible. I use these words reluctantly, for I understand it is my responsibility as commanding officer to see that provisions are made for the troops under even the greatest duress; yet I cannot now imagine how I can fulfill that responsibility. The men have not been paid in months. What is left of their uniforms is in tatters, and they have been forced to search the old emigrant trail for remnants of clothes and pieces of cloth with which to cover themselves. As this outpost is dependent upon supply lines for rations—the frontier yields little, and most wildlife has been slaughtered—our food stocks are greatly diminished, and a hard season is fast approaching. We are so few and so involved with gathering wood so we will not freeze, and with grazing the horses and mules, that there is little time to repair, never mind set in order, the dwellings and stables; and were it not for the ingenuity of the smithy who is constantly reforging the horses' shoes and saving every scrap of metal to turn into hinges and bolts, nails and the like, as well as repairing our sorely used axes and hammers, chisels and saws, we would be in dire straits indeed.

At present, there are 67 soldiers left to man this outpost, including myself. The fevers of last spring, as I previously reported, killed 13, and 16 men have disappeared. Their names are recorded, but we are unable to go after deserters for fear of losing others, as the troops are dispirited. They are beginning to complain that this is less an army unit than a scavenging operation, and their morale is fast deteriorating with that reality. They claim that the supply wagons are but phantoms, and they know the sutler's goods are rotten and unaffordable. They buy from him what they can on what credit he extends, however, which will leave them penniless if they are ever paid.

The soldier who last rode out with an official report from me, as well as with the troops' mail pouch, returned without having delivered either to Fort H, for he reported back that the place was no longer manned. To be more precise, and to use his word: deserted. Which explains, I am sure, why we have heard nothing from Fort H in many weeks, but, of course, explains nothing else. Outpost 2881 is now separated by a fortnight of hard riding—something neither my troops nor mounts are capable of—to the nearest garrison beyond the defunct Fort H, should that garrison still exist. The telegraph lines, which were destroyed by the savages, have not yet been replaced. I fear we are harshly isolated.

As the last outpost before an endless frontier that is more our enemy than even the savages, our mission is now, in my mind, unclear, especially as the emigrant trail is no longer used and the railroad being completed far distant from us. Given our precarious situation, it seems to me incongruous that Outpost 2881 should remain.

Please advise.

He hesitates before signing his name. What Cutter has written concerning the conditions of the outpost is but a barely veiled criticism, and the report—if delivered—will not be met pleasantly. He knows he alone will be blamed for the deteriorating conditions, as well as for the desertions that represent nothing less than a lack of morale, which Cutter's commanders will assess to be a reflection of his own lack of moral fiber: this much is certain. He knows they will say, as was once said, that it was a mistake he was ever given a posting at all after the war.

At that time, there was an entire military—two, if one were to count the defeated, and one had to count them—to be dismantled, soldiers to be released rather than fed, generals and colonels and majors from within the officer corps to be decommissioned rather than kept; the government was near bankruptcy, the economy in ruins, towns and villages destroyed, farmlands wasted, docksides emptied, people displaced. Cutter knew what his few friends, fellow officers, told him in confidence then: that rumor had it he'd lost his nerve after his brother's death, that Cutter's superiors questioned whether he was ever quite the same commander thereafter, that it was remarked in unofficial conversations that Cutter took fewer chances with his men after he lost his brother, that he led patrols senselessly far from the range of action to keep them from harm, and that only out of pity—and, of course, his friends' loyal connections—was Cutter demoted, but kept, and then assigned to the farthest frontier. His friends said he was among the lucky, lucky to be given the rank of major, lucky to be given any rank at all. He now barely remembers that he had ever been a brigadier, and he hardly considers himself lucky.

What will to live Cutter had mustered after the war he feels is now draining away, suppurating from his soul as though from a wound that cannot be healed. Lavinia seemed as dazed as he by the war, by life then: she buried three children without him, the ten-year-old twins, dead of typhus, and their oldest, a daughter, later stricken by the binding colic; and Cutter at times considered their youngest as good as dead, given Henry's nervous constitution, his incomprehensible manias, his mercurial depressions that—at times—took him away from life and locked him behind barred doors or placed him among the mad in quiet places. Their first reunion after the war, which took place in the house of Lavinia's parents, was bitter. Of it, Cutter has only the impression of sitting for hours in a gloomy parlor, of Lavinia's hand lying cold and unresponsive in his, of their only remaining child's strange babble, of being trapped by grief, of feeling that he and Lavinia had become estranged by too many deaths, by too many years apart, by the grievous losses war and those years of separation had wrought upon them. When his commission came and he was summoned, Cutter left his wife to the genteel poverty allowed by his salary, pretending that time would heal what he knew it could not; and he knew without asking that Lavinia had not the fortitude to withstand the frontier, knew without her saying it that the graves of their children were closer to her heart than the bed of her husband.

From their lives, Cutter took with him to the frontier a writing table, a case of cognac, bookshelves, his favorite books, a small portrait of Lavinia and none of Henry, and the letters Lavinia had written to him, tied in packets with blue ribbon. Left behind were likenesses of his dead children and dead brother, which he could not bear to gaze upon.

Major Robert Cutter signs the report. It will later be placed in evidence against him, testimony of his mental and moral state, an indication to some members of the court-martial of what they will determine to be his pitiable decline. Cutter, after signing it, doubts it will ever arrive at its destination.

Five

I t is Cole who selects the horse to be ridden to what Major Robert Cutter must assume is the nearest manned garrison beyond Fort H, for no one better knows the conditions of the mounts. The bay gelding stands patiently, the smithy trimming and filing its hooves, nailing on new shoes, as the major watches. The shoes Cole has fashioned cover the entire frog; on the front feet the iron ends in an inverted V at the back of each hoof. The horse oversteps himself, is his only problem, the smithy says. This'll keep him from cracking himself good.

Cutter wonders who Lt. Hastings has assigned to be the courier. Someone, he hopes, who can manage the long, precarious journey without ruining the horse, someone who will return. The bay is worth a good deal.

Bean's your man, Cole says.

The major wonders whether he wondered aloud.

Bean had no problem going it alone to Fort H and back, last time. And he knows how to pace a horse, the smithy continues.

That counts for something.

It does. He'll be back, and neither of them will be spent.

You think so.

Yes sir, I do.

Well, Cutter says, that counts for something too.

The smithy lets go of the hoof he has just shod, looks over at the major, nods. With his black skin and eyes, Cole is the only other man on the post more isolated than Cutter, the major reflects. Though he is quick to think that now more isolated than either of them is the redeemed captive who slept beneath the belly of her horse throughout the night.

That woman got a name? Cole asks.

Cutter is brought up short, as he always is, by the smithy's curious telepathy. Abigail Buwell.

Abbie, for short, must have been.

Probably.

That's a mighty fine horse she's with.

He wonders if Cole has spoken with her.

I ain't, Cole says, been close or nothing. But I watched her—you understand, without troubling—walk it about this morning. She's got a way with that horse few people are born to. Makes you humble, if you know what I mean.

No one told Cutter that Abigail Buwell had been about.

She was up before the sun. Moved around like a ghost, like to have scared me to death. If I hadn't seen the horse behind her I probably would have jumped right outta my skin.

You weren't asleep.

Nah, I do my sleeping in the afternoons mostly. I get too spooked to sleep good most nights.

Bad dreams?

No, sir, I don't suffer those, Cole tells him. Bad premonitions, more like it. They're mostly stronger in the dark, if you know what I mean.

He does.

Well, Cole, I should find Bean.

It'd be better for him to start tomorrow morning, sir. Let the horse stand a night in the new shoes.

It's too late for him to ride out today anyway.

The smithy nods in agreement. One black hand strokes the bay's withers, and the gelding turns its head and gazes at the smithy with a kind eye. Bean's patching on his saddlebags in the leanto closest to the doctor's, Cole tells the major. He's assuming the mail weight will be substantial.

Cutter has forgotten to inform the troops to ready their mail.

Lt. Hastings let it be known that Bean'd be riding out, Cole says.

Lt. John Hastings will testify at the major's court-martial that he found Robert Cutter to be a fair commander, though one occasioned to symptoms of forgetfulness that could be, Hastings was pressed to admit, mistaken for neglect. He will not be able to shed any light on why conditions at the outpost worsened so after the redeemed captives were brought in, but he will go to great lengths to persuade the court that the hunting party he led thereafter was so delayed in its return, and the supply wagons so tardy, that conditions could not but deteriorate. The court will not be persuaded.

Bean and Lt. Hastings stand in Cutter's quarters and watch as Major Robert Cutter places his report and the doctor's addendum in a piece of burlap, folds the cloth, seals it with wax, then places it in the mail pouch. The men's letters have been collected, but the major has waved off the suggestion that he censor them, and they are already in Bean's saddlebags. Cutter hands Bean the mail pouch and thinks the man looks young, younger than any soldier could possibly be. Bean swears he can ride by the stars.

You'll leave at dawn tomorrow, Cutter tells him. Try not to wear out that horse.

I wouldn't think of it, sir, Bean replies.

You're under orders to rest two days at the garrison when you arrive there.

Thank you, sir.

The men are depending on you to bring them their mail. As am I.

Yes, sir.

Cutter decides not to say anything else. He doesn't want to speculate on what Bean should do if he finds the garrison empty; he doesn't want to plead with him not to desert, to return with the bay; he doesn't want to let his desperation show. Dismissed, he concludes.

Both men salute Cutter and turn on their heels, the lieutenant preceding Bean. The door swings shut, then opens again to reveal Hastings.

Lieutenant?

Sir, I just considered, perhaps you've overlooked enclosing something, well, personal.

No, I haven't overlooked that. The letter I'm writing is a long one.

You're sure, sir?

I am.

Hastings hesitates. Thank you anyway, Lieutenant, the major says.

Cutter thinks it is the lieutenant again, though the knock on the door is somewhat heavier than Hastings', and he looks up from nothing, from holding his head in his hands, buttons his collar and says, Come in. But it is Jonas Smith.

Me and the missus, we can't be goin' yet, Smith announces.

Cutter had assumed Smith and his wife gone, James Buwell gone. His interviews with each of them that morning had been cursory, and then he had written his report. He hadn't given them another thought.

Smith nervously fingers the hat he holds, his close-set eyes darting into the corners of the room, the doorway to the other room, everywhere. There is something about him Cutter finds weasel-like. He does not invite Smith to sit, waits out a silence, watches him squirm.

A newspaper man's just rode in, Smith tells him.

That anyone has ridden in strikes Cutter as ludicrous. He looks at Smith as though the man has lost his mind.

Alone?

Yep. Says he was down our way and heard we went lookin' for our women. And now he's here, and he wants to write up a story. He'll be needin' some time to talk with my wife.

Perhaps he'd like to do that while accompanying you on your way.

Smith looks as though he is about to laugh, as though the major is making a joke, then realizes Cutter's seriousness and fidgets instead. I don't know about that, he whines. He's come a long ways to be goin' anywhere just now. He—he's tired, I'd say.

You would.

Smith shifts his weight from one foot to another, discomforted. Look, he tells Cutter, dropping his voice conspiratorially, there's money in it.

Pardon?

The newspaper man'll pay for the story, sure. There's money in it.

Maria will be glad to know she'll be compensated in that case, Smith.

The man's mouth opens wordlessly. The brindle cur pads into the open door and, lowering its head and wagging its tail, pushes past Smith and settles into a corner.

I told your wife this is a military outpost, Cutter says, not a hotel. I'm telling you the same. I commandeered troops for you; your wife and Abigail Buwell were brought back, and now you want hospitality so you can make money. You have twenty-four hours, Smith, and then you and your wife are to leave. Camp outside the walls, set up along the emigrant trail, go to the devil, I don't care. And take your friend Buwell with you.

He's not my friend, Smith protests. 'Sides, he's already gone. I ain't the one who made trouble.

Twenty-four hours.

Cutter pushes his chair back and stands. Smith leaves without a word, spitting as he steps outside and then again when he passes Hastings, on his way to the major's quarters to report the journalist's arrival.

Reed Gabriel is not yet a journalist of note, but he has an easy way about him and a laconic confidence, and he knows a story when he comes across one. He also knows that his greatest qualities—a feigned equanimity that will later become second nature to him and an instinctive, uncanny ability to listen—inspire people to reveal themselves to him as ridiculous or as tragic as they are, and he is already persuaded that most human beings are born to the tragic. Riding the frontier has only steeled him in that belief, for the hard lives he has witnessed and the stories told to him by rail-thin women and men aged long before their time have convinced him that the one experience that binds most of displaced humanity has something to do with the utterly sad nature of interrupted dreams, which seem to him the only ones that exist beyond the reach of civilization.

A tale of captivity is exactly what Reed Gabriel needs to become famous, and he sits with a sense of tiredness and relief now that he is at the outpost, for the story is his. Cutter and Hastings find him chewing the end of an unlit cheroot, resting on a makeshift bench he's pulled—from where? the major wonders—before the doctor's porch, out of the way, listening to the wet, choking coughs of the doctor's wife in the quarters behind him, observing the sutler sitting morosely before the closed door of his store, surveying the general disorder, watching the ragtag troops begin their end-of-day routine, dragging wood and coal to the firepits and cooking, or lounging or playing cards or just slapping away the chill, and leering at Maria as she makes her way among them.

One look at Reed Gabriel as he contemplates the scene and Cutter knows: This is a man who misses nothing. Knows: In another time, another place, he would have made a great sniper.

Reed Gabriel gets to his feet at the approach of the officers, smiles warmly, extends his hand, takes in the major's lined face and unkempt appearance, the lieutenant's unshined boots, nods with the handshakes, introduces himself. Yes, Gabriel has untacked and watered his horse, it's tethered behind the stables, and Cutter knows without asking that Gabriel has already seen Abigail Buwell and the blue roan, Maria's leanto, and probably counted every mount in the corral, assessed the smithy's workplace and perhaps Cole himself, and noted the poor condition of the stables and barracks, of the troops' uniforms, of their messes, of the littered and useless parade quadrant. They make small talk, and when the doctor comes out from his quarters at the sound of their voices, Gabriel introduces himself, inquires tactfully as to what ails the woman inside, commiserates with Matthews for a moment, then pulls a flask from the saddlebag that lies on the bench and offers it around. Sour mash, Gabriel says. Matthews takes a polite swig and shakes his head at the liquor's bite, swallows and wipes the sting of tears from his eyes, seats himself on the porch edge.

The lieutenant does the same.

Reed Gabriel engages Matthews on the course of curious fevers found on the frontier, of diseases unknown beyond the reaches of civilization, while Cutter remains standing and refuses a drink from the flask. There's more of this, Gabriel tells him, but the major declines again and, without asking Gabriel how long he intends to stay, bids them good evening. Cutter is inexplicably and, he realizes, unfairly irritated by the journalist's easy way, his effortlessness, his natural assumption of familiarity; and he tries not to limp as he leaves, consciously straightens his back, peers beyond the first glow of the fires, then passes the men illuminated by them. He makes his way beyond the stables and beyond the washerwoman's place, trying to ignore the gnawing ache in his knee and the deep pain in his shoulder that are taking his breath away. The dusk is suddenly deeper, the horses barely distinguishable in the corral, as Cutter touches the corral rails and walks around to where the magnificent horse stands ghostlike in the first wash of night.

When he finally manages to make out Abigail Buwell's shape, a clammy hand seems to squeeze his innards, and he freezes at the sight before him. Abigail Buwell does not look up at him from where she sits cross-legged beyond the horse, her back against a corral post, though the roan flicks its tail and flattens its ears in warning, stamps a forefoot, then paws at the ground. Instead, she keeps her head bent and continues to shear her hair from her scalp, heedless of piercing it with the knife she holds, heedless of the pain and the stickiness, the warmth of trickling blood. The metal blade glints dully in her hand and the horse turns a full circle before her, two, before she pauses, the knife held in midair, and raises her eyes to Cutter.

He stands helplessly some distance from the roan, meets her eyes, then watches her lower her head once again, scrape at her scalp with the blade.

Stop, stop, Cutter finally pleads, with desperation in his voice, stop. Think of the child.

Abigail Buwell steadies her hand above her head, holds the knife still. She does not look at Major Robert Cutter again, and for a moment she does not move. And then she shears another piece from her scalp. His heart feels the rip.

Long after the major recedes into the darkness, Abigail Buwell wills the child within her to remain unborn and hunches against its kicks, against the movement of its fists, against its slow revolution within so as to position itself head downward, nature knowing the flow of gravity. From where she sits, now beneath the blue roan's belly, she can barely distinguish the hooves and hocks and pasterns and knees of any horse beyond those of her own, which stands sentinel over her. She clasps her forearms about her knees, trying to fold into herself, trying to fold into the unborn infant.

She is aware of many things, of the universe of minutiae, of the blood that courses in her veins, of its rhythmic pulse, of the breath of the horse above her, the scent of it, the gurgling in its gut, of the dung beetles pushing their worked, rounded balls of manure through the sand, of the fine dust that hangs in the air and, on the slightest whisper of a breeze, spirals about the horse's hooves and fetlocks, blows gently about its knees and into its mane and into her eyes and into the eyes of the corralled horses, causing them to shake their heads and necks and roil their skins, cowkick, swish their tails. She is aware that there is no moon, that it sleeps elsewhere, and that with its reappearance a new cycle will begin—has, with its disappearance, already begun—and that it will be true to what it is called by the savages: this will be the moon of devouring dustblow, for which the savages have one word, and in this moon, Abigail Buwell knows, the winds will howl and the dryness of the earth will scatter itself, and the insects will come. Already there is dust in her nostrils and on her face and hands and on the wounds of her scalp and on her robes and on the doeskin leggings that cover her feet, and by morning the coats of the horses will begin to dull with a covering of grit so fine as to be mistaken for sullied dew. Eventually the air will thicken and become white, the horizons blur and then disappear, and all things become indistinguishable. Except the body within her.

She wills the child to remain unborn and her hunger, her thirst, to abate. She takes from an amulet about her neck three pebbles and places them in her mouth, rolls them with her tongue, feels the saliva dampen the back of her throat, then rests her head upon her knees, whereupon the darkened bloodstains are already disappearing under a layer of fine sand. Her scalp is dry, and the nicks and cuts and puncture wounds itch sorely, but she does not touch her shorn head nor grope for the knife that lies beside her. From time to time she raises her head to gaze into the dark that obscures the stockade, studies the faint shape of the corral railings, the washerwoman's leanto and the blankets that bloom and blow from her doorways beyond the fire that spirals upward. She hears the sounds of men calling to one another and the voices of Maria and the sutler, who sit like weirdly undulating apparitions between the flames of a bloodorange blaze and the washerwoman's quarters.

Abigail Buwell does not know that James Buwell, with his cast wrist, has left the outpost, that he has taken his peculiar horse—unmistakable with its lopped gait, a four-beat canter—and ridden off in the direction of his homestead. When she comes to realize he has gone, she will consider his absence a sign that the universe has swallowed him whole. She will think nothing of tomorrow, for she is living only within her body, in the present, and so will not consider that he might return for her. She does not think of Constance Smith, who hardly looked in Abigail Buwell's direction today as she practiced walking to and fro in spastic arrhythmia, her feet too large for the shoes she was given; though at one moment, when Maria was elsewhere, Jonas Smith snuck toward the washerwoman's place and, reaching his promenading wife, cornered her with a cry against a wall, hoisted her skirts, groped her. At that moment, Constance Smith locked eyes with Abigail Buwell across the distance; and it was Constance Smith who broke their stare, pushed her husband away, smoothed her skirts.

Abigail Buwell does not think of the major, the man

who wears brass buttons, the one who knows that she still speaks his language. She thinks of nothing, knows nothing of tomorrow; and she fears nothing but the birth of the child and the future that stretches darkly before her. She wills the child to remain unborn, she wills her future to remain blank, she plays with the pebbles upon her tongue, feels a kick. The child within her blinks, unfurls a fist, clenches it, rolls ever so slightly. Its head pressing against her bladder.

Sometime later in the night, after the breeze has grown bolder, Abigail Buwell will watch the sutler across the way get up and disappear, watch Maria furtively follow him. The fire they leave behind will be but a bed of glowing coals. She will feel a sudden chill, pull the robes closer about her, and lay on her side, knees curled toward her chest, as the man who is as dark as the depths of a high mountain lake comes toward her. He is humming softly, and as he approaches the blue roan does not move other than to raise its head and prick its ears as it follows his movements.

Cole doesn't speak as he puts a piece of jerky and a tin of water near her, he does not cease humming as he passes close to the horse, so closely that he reaches out and touches it lightly, passing one dark hand along the curve of its neck; and then he is gone. Abigail Buwell does not stir, for she knows that only a harmless soul could have passed so near as to run a hand over the roan, would have left such an offering. The horse whinnies softly as the man disappears into the deep night; and from that moment on, Abigail Buwell will always think of Cole in the language of the savages, she will always think of him in their one word for people of his color:

They-Who-Wear-Their-Shadows.

But for now, she sucks at the pebbles still in her mouth, bears a spasm of her unborn child willing itself to be born, and breathes deeply into the dust.

Six

The brindle cur shifts its position from before Cutter's door and corners itself, flopping to the floor, and the sand that has ridged in the shape of the dog's curl scatters into the room where Cutter has sequestered himself throughout this day, disheartened by all that must be done and by the sheer impossibility of doing anything at all, overcome by a despondency that has left him morose. The pain in his shoulder and knee have become unbearable for reasons he cannot understand, as unbearable as the ceaseless wind and the blowing sands that scratch at the outer walls. Hastings, who at daybreak reported the departure of Bean, found Cutter out of sorts and chafed at being brusquely dismissed, but Cutter was ashamed and irked at being seen as he was, unwashed, unshaven, in a state of undress. Cutter's soiled undershirt was untucked, his breeches undone; and then there was the stench of his innards, the unsightly, stinking chamberpot Cutter had left uncovered. He has yet to empty it, though night is now creeping into his quarters; it will certainly overflow,

Cutter knows, if he uses it again. And so, slowly, stiffly, he rises, runs his hands over his hair, tucks in his shirt, buttons on his collar, pulls on his jacket. He takes the chamberpot, opens the door against the wind and, closing the cur within, hobbles into the dark to empty it beyond the several shacks that suffice as the officers' quarters, none of them inhabited by anyone except Cutter and Matthews.

As he passes Matthews' quarters, Cutter thinks he hears voices from within, though he cannot be sure because of the wind. But as he retraces his steps, his chamberpot emptied, he catches the unmistakable sound of Constance Smith's high-pitched cackle, which stops him in his tracks. He strains to hear more, hears nothing, sets the pot down, and steps onto the doctor's porch. When Cutter knocks at the door, Reed Gabriel opens it.

The Smiths look up in uneasy surprise at the major from where they are sitting on the floor, their empty plates resting on their laps, as Reed Gabriel shuts the door behind Cutter. Matthews rises from his wife's bedside, but Cutter motions for the doctor to stay where he is, nods at Gabriel, and moves across the room to greet a pinched-looking Susan Matthews. She is propped against two pillows, her thin wrists and hands, face and throat ghostly, bloodless, her dark eyes hollowed and feverish. Mrs. Matthews, Cutter says, taking her hand. Major, she responds, managing a wan smile.

Cutter declines a plate of salt pork and beans, realizing that Matthews has shared his mess with the Smiths and Gabriel, and knowing the doctor will be grateful for leftovers at breakfast. Gabriel watches

Cutter carefully and, noting his polite refusal, instantly regrets that he imposed on Matthews to feed three extra mouths, regrets also that the doctor—reluctant to admit any hardship or insist that his ailing wife hardly needed the strain of company—kindly obliged Gabriel and the Smiths. Gabriel is already aware that provisions are in short supply, that the troops are sopping gritty baconfat with pieces of moldy hardtack, that there is no fresh bread, that only a few messes are lucky enough to have small amounts of flour that the men make into dough and fry in lard. He has seen no rice except at the sutler's store; candles seem nonexistent; and there is no evidence of soap except at the washerwoman's, who surely trades (what, Gabriel can easily imagine) with the sutler.

Cutter releases Susan Matthews' hand, stands uncomfortably in her gaze, considers that he should leave and return with cognac—surely, he thinks, a sip might stir Susan Matthews' blood, bring color to her cheeks—but he has few bottles left and he is loath to waste good liquor on the Smiths, who show no sign of leaving Matthews' quarters at the moment. Gabriel, still standing, finishes the mouthful of food left on his plate as Cutter takes his leave of the doctor's wife and turns toward the Smiths and Gabriel. Sir, Gabriel says then, I've managed to have a good look around the outpost.

That the journalist has addressed Cutter as though he were a respectful subordinate strikes the major as odd, for Cutter can certainly imagine what Gabriel must have seen, must think. Tomorrow, Cutter tells himself, as he told himself the day before, and every day before yesterday, he must reclaim his command, have the lieutenant hold morning parade drills, provision a hunting party, rotate troops from the grazing detail to the wood detail, from the wood detail to sentry detail, and from the current sentries select troops to join the grazing detail, have others fill in the old latrine and dig a new one, send several troops with mules and a cart to ride the old emigrant trail, where surely there must be something salvageable—clothes and bedding that have somehow not rotted, unspoiled barrels of pickled tongue or corned beef, discarded tack, boots. Cutter finds himself wondering how many troops he can spare, for the outpost needs to defend itself in case the savages attack, as ludicrous as Cutter finds the possibility.

It's quite large, Reed Gabriel comments.

I'm sure you've been most impressed, Cutter remarks, one way or another.

Gabriel is taken aback by the irony in the major's tone, but before he can say anything Hastings knocks, then opens the door. Join us, Matthews says from across the room, and Hastings closes the door behind him, salutes Cutter, declines the doctor's offer of a plate of food. Take a seat, Matthews tells him, but Hastings shakes his head and approaches Susan Matthews instead, bows to her. It's good to see you up and about, Mrs. Matthews, Hastings tells her.

Thank you, lieutenant. I'm hardly either. But are you sure you won't eat? Or at least sit?

I'm fine, Mrs. Matthews.

Have you an officers' mess? Gabriel asks with strained innocence.

Not at the moment, Hastings replies, turning to him.

And the officers?

The lieutenant glances at Cutter, who remains

silent. We lost a number of men to fevers and meningitis earlier this year, Matthews tells Gabriel. Among them a captain, the major's adjutant, our quartermaster, two sergeants, and a corporal.

Gabriel whistles through his teeth, then looks at the major, who watches as Smith studies his empty plate and his wife works her mouth oddly with its missing teeth.

I expect, Cutter interjects, looking at the Smiths, that you'll be leaving tomorrow.

The major wants to discuss anything but this place, the conditions here, the deaths, the past.

It is Gabriel who speaks. If it's not inconvenient, Major, I'd like to persuade the Smiths to stay another day. I need Mrs. Smith to go over parts of her story, and I'd like to try to speak to Mrs. Buwell as well. Of course, Mrs. Smith would have to act as my interpreter.

I doubt Mrs. Buwell would appreciate being disturbed. Or that she has any intention of speaking to anyone.

I'd like to try. One day will suffice.

She ain't gonna talk, Constance Smith says, least of all to me.

There's your answer, Mr. Gabriel.

Gabriel throws an exasperated look at Constance Smith. I thought we'd agreed to speak with her.

I'm willin', but that don't mean a thing.

I don't want Mrs. Buwell distressed more than she already is, as she's in our care, Cutter tells Gabriel. She's given every sign of wanting to be left alone, and she should be allowed to adjust in her own time.

Constance Smith caws. That heathen ain't gonna

adjust to nothin'. She's one of them, Major, through and through. She became savage by her ownself, she ain't spoke English since a long while now, and one look at her, sittin' underneath that horse, should tell you she's plumb lost her mind.

I wouldn't begin to assume she has lost her mind, Cutter retorts disdainfully. She appears, quite simply, to be suffering.

She should suffer. If it was up to me, she'd suffer worse than death. All of 'em would. They should all be tortured and got rid of. And that's what you should be doin', if you don't mind my sayin', these soldiers lollin' about shameless-like should be killin' off those savages instead.

The major glares her into silence. Matthews turns to his wife and helps her into a more comfortable position. That's right, Jonas Smith concurs.

It does seem curious, Major, that you don't seem intent upon—to use an official term—suppressing the savages.

Why curious, Mr. Gabriel.

Well, it's my understanding that all units on the frontier are at the moment engaged in carrying out a set policy of suppression. Not to be applied, of course, to those savages who can be persuaded to give themselves over to civilization on the lands we have reserved for that purpose.

Cutter raises his eyebrows. That may be your understanding, he says slowly, but you may be misinformed.

I doubt that.

We know of no such policy, Lt. Hastings says.

I find that hard to believe, Gabriel replies incredulously.

The major shrugs. In the silence that descends, Cutter can sense Hastings' resentment of Gabriel's tone; he feels the lieutenant's eyes on him, knows that he is waiting for Cutter to respond. Cutter cannot let the silence speak for itself; he does not want to foster doubt in Hastings' mind, for doubt leads to insubordination, and Cutter needs his lieutenant to trust him, to remain loyal.

There are harder things to believe, Cutter finally says. The isolation we suffer here, for one. The fact that the savages have done us no harm since we arrived here, and seem indeed to be in pitiful condition themselves. When we first occupied this outpost, they even traded peacefully with the sutler, and with those who still traveled upon the old emigrant trail.

All I know, Smith says, is that four years ago they took my wife and sorely used her. And I saw what they did to those emigrants we stumbled on.

Cutter says nothing to Smith: there is nothing he can say. Instead, he says goodnight to the Matthews, to Hastings, and nods a curt farewell at Gabriel as he makes his way to the door. The Smiths do not so much as stir at Cutter's exit. Outside, Cutter stands for a moment and watches the silhouettes of men passing to and fro beyond the firepits. The outline of the stockade is softened by the windblown sand; even the dark seems obscured by it. The strains of a harmonica being played inside the barracks carry, dissipate. Cutter retrieves his chamberpot and ducks into the wind, tastes the dust in his mouth, feels it line the back of his throat, fill his nostrils.

No written order, or any copy of such, to wage a war of extermination against the remaining savages will be found among the major's papers. Lt. John Hastings will testify at Major Robert Cutter's court-martial that Hastings knew of no such policy, and that he did not know whether Cutter had ever received such a directive. Hastings will also, quite reluctantly, admit that the final order given to him while under the major's command was to not, under any circumstances, engage the savages in warfare. It will be the court's assessment that the order was indeed delivered, based on the testimony of the military courier who delivered it. It will be the court's opinion that the directive was ignored by Major Robert Cutter, and the document itself destroyed.

The wind is full of dust and sand and grit this day and has not abated, though it is now the dead of night. I feel with a dreadful foreboding the shift of the earth's axis; if I could see the constellations above, or the planets, they would surely be more distant and colder than just a week ago. This night is interminable, and there are longer nights to come, Lavinia. I do not sleep well, I suffer a restless despondency, and it is not difficult to ascertain why: though I wonder if you were here, would I be more consoled, or more concerned? Perhaps, I think, both.

But you are not here. Would that you were, for the redeemed captive I mentioned, the one who said she would not live among us and has not spoken since, will give birth very soon, and there is not a woman present to comfort her, for Susan Matthews is dreadfully ill and the washerwoman, I believe, is truly useless. The other redeemed captive and her husband, an unpleasant couple full of spite and bile, will leave tomorrow if I have my way, and it is a day too late as far as I am concerned, for as long as they remain they only do the poor woman more harm than good. Men, as you know, are hardly fit to be companions to women on the eve of birthing; and as I write this I am seized by shame, knowing that I was not present at the births of three of our four beloved children, and useless— indeed, removed from the house by the midwife—at our dear departed daughter's birth. But when I think of how beautiful you were in your ripeness, I am held breathless even now, at this age, by desire. And beset with woeful memories of all we have lost, for these overlay the past further beyond, one that I can only summon by much will, of the halcyon days of frenzied courtship, of our passionate and youthful union, of our early married life. If someone had said to me then, ah, but wait, you will eventually discover life to be a destiny that leads only to loneliness, that you will bury your loved ones and wish it was you who were laid to rest, that you will age having seen the most horrific of horrors, I would not have believed him. But now, with you far away and me imprisoned at this distance by despair, I cannot think otherwise. Pitiful, this.

I do not know how you bear me, my dear, or the laments and complaints of an aging man who is yet your husband. Perhaps as you read this you are laughing, as you were always quick to do when we were young, before the adversity of it all defeated us. I have had too much cognac, and the flame flickers as the lamp's wick shortens, and the spirits are all but evaporated. I kiss you goodnight, and write only to caution you that you must write or appear to me soon, for without you I am utterly lost.

The child remains unborn. Abigail Buwell, who thinks of herself only by another name in another tongue, rises in the darkness from beneath her horse's belly. Her scalp is raw, sore, her hunger painful. She allows herself a moment of longing for the taste of curdled milk taken from within a slaughtered calf's belly, then stems her longing, as it is born of memory, and she does not want to remember. Memory is the province of the living.

She raises her hand to the roan and the horse remains where it is as she wanders silently through the dustblow. She can smell the unwashed men, smell their sleep, their soiled odors and their dreamless slumbers repulsive to her. She whispers to the stabled horses and mules, drifts ghostlike past them, and pauses by the smithy's forge, liking the odor of damped coke and unburned coal, of burnished metal, of horse sweat. She lingers there, touching the curved horseshoes, an anvil, the bellows, Cole's tools, the walls, the corners of the stall, then glides away, passes by the old chicken coop, and makes her way to the outpost's gate, which she gropes as though she were blind. The crosspole holding the gates closed takes three men to manage, and she cannot lift and slide the pole nor open the gate nor see the endless beyond through the cracks between the gate's timbers. There is no starlight, no moon, no planets, and the windswept heavens are black, obscure. Abigail Buwell stands for a long time at the gate, her long hands and longer fingers upon the crosspole, as the sand and dust blow through the night, through her soul.

And then she follows the outpost's inner circumference, touching its walls, slipping into the undershadows whenever a sentry passes above her, follows her belly. It leads her from the walls to several abandoned shacks and before Matthews' quarters, where she tilts her head slightly and catches the scent of death, then passes by. Beyond the doctor's place, she sees the boy.

He stands in front of Major Robert Cutter's door, fluidly swaying from side to side, making circles with his knees, rolling on his feet. As Abigail Buwell raises a hand to her forehead to shield her eyes from the dust, the grit, as if unsure of the vision, Cutter opens his door and stands within it, a black form outlined against the pale light behind him. The boy becomes motionless, as unmoving as the major who stands bootless, hatless, without his jacket, his suspenders hanging, his sleeves undone, in dark relief before the apparition. And then the boy takes one step sideward, another, turns three sluggish cartwheels with great precision—hand, hand, foot, foot, each coming down separately, deliberately, through each revolution—and is gone.

At that moment, a chill runs through Abigail Buwell, for she knows the boy to be unreal, from the place of the undead, and the man who stands staring at emptiness— now that the boy has disappeared—to be uncommon. For Major Robert Cutter is someone to whom visions appear, and in the world from which Abigail Buwell has been uprooted, this counts for much, and sometimes for everything. The savages know that visions—even and especially when their meaning is not revealed, even and especially when they seem incomprehensible—are sacred. For which there is a gesture—two hands gently touched palm to palm and then opened flatly to the heavens, like the capture and release of smoke—but no word in her adopted language.

Seven

Reed Gabriel, upon waking, senses a change in the air. There is a density to it, a whiteness, as if an entire layer of desert were suspended in its gusting whorls. Its thickness is in his nostrils, his tongue is coated and feels like sandpaper, and from where he lies upon the hard ground he is amazed to see that the thickness of the air has obscured the edges of all things, the stockade and the rickety stable roof, the sutler's, the barracks, the old chicken coop, even the movements of men. And the men are in motion, their voices catching on the wind, their words and cries buffeted about. Gabriel pulls a piece of hardtack from the saddlebag he used as a pillow, sits up and narrows his eyes, ponders the activity before him— the horses being groomed, their tails pulled, the tack being dragged out and soaped and shined, the bridle bits and reins being checked, the wood detail leaving, the corralled horses being moved out and those under night guard in the grazing fields being herded in, saddlebags being packed, rifles cleaned. He chews the hardtack listlessly and dislikes its taste of grit, then rises fully clothed and works his blanket into a bedroll before wandering beyond the quadrant in the hope of finding a pot of boiled coffee with something left in it. When he does, he takes a cup from among many discarded, rubs it with sand before dunking it into a trough of water he hopes is clean, then walks over to the mess and pours himself the dregs, lets the hot liquid burn his tongue, the back of his throat, and gulps again as he listens to the soldiers, picking up bits and pieces of conversations regarding the orders they have been given. There is a good deal of grumbling, and the soldiers hunch against the wind and move about reluctantly, as if already wearied; and Gabriel considers that his species is truly one given to habits, indolence among them, and finds it unsurprising that, having had far too little to do for far too long, the troops are now resentful at being assigned new duties.

The sutler has dragged a long table from somewhere and backed it against his store, and the major inspects the goods he has placed upon it. Gabriel knows that the piles of bacon and hardtack, coffee and sugar, rice and beans must mean that troops are being provisioned, and his curiosity is stirred. Gabriel walks slowly toward the store, wondering whether Cutter indeed received orders he has until now ignored, wondering whether his presence—and his own knowledge of the government's policy—has spurred the major to act. He finds Cutter running his hands through a sack of dirty rice, letting the grains pour through his fingers, saying, There's more pebbles than rice in this, but the sutler replies with a shrug, Take it or leave it. The major argues the price with him until the sutler throws up his hands and goes inside, returning with salt, pepper, candles, matchsticks in tins, tobacco.

I take it a detail is going out, Gabriel offers by way of greeting.

Cutter stiffens, studies Gabriel as if trying to make up his mind whether to give the journalist the time of day. That's right, the major finally says, turning back to the goods and then, as if in afterthought, adding: If you could finish what it is you need to do with the Smiths, they can be escorted out. In about two hours' time, I'd say. You're welcome to go with them.

I'll do my best, Gabriel returns. I'll need to get provisioned as well.

He has mistaken or—since Cutter thinks Gabriel is much cleverer than that—twisted the major's meaning. Cutter does not clarify that he wants Gabriel to leave with the Smiths, nor retract the offer: a civilian riding with the hunting detail's troops, and a journalist to boot, might serve as a deterrent to desertion.

Add another man to the list, Cutter says to the sutler.

I'll pay for my share of the provisions, Gabriel says.

Of course, the major replies.

Gabriel goes in search of Constance Smith and finds her arguing with the washerwoman. Maria is standing, hands on her hips, less than a handlength from the woman. She is shouting about the money Constance Smith owes her as if the latter were deaf.

Gabriel asks the amount and pays it to Maria, and

Constance Smith looks disappointed: what he gives the washerwoman, she knows, will be deducted from what he has promised her. Maria takes the coins and shamelessly stuffs them into a pocket sewn on the inside of her skirts, revealing a comely calf and knee, then walks away. The uncovered boiler cauldron on the firepit steams, the scum of dust and fine sand on its surface forming a bubbly crust.

You're packed, I take it, Gabriel says to Constance Smith.

I got nothing to pack.

And your husband.

He's gettin' the horses ready.

I'll be riding along, he tells her, so we'll have time to go over your story once again. Until you and your husband go your own way.

Disappointment crosses her face. The longer Gabriel is with them, the longer her wait for the money. She thinks maybe she should raise her price, but he interrupts her thoughts. We need to talk with Mrs. Buwell, he says. We don't have much time.

Constance Smith thinks about the money again, then shakes her head.

What?

I said I'd do it, but it ain't part of our deal.

He takes in her bony cheeks and hollow mouth with its missing teeth and the milkwhite eye. She meets his stare with her good eye, shakes her head again. It ain't, she says, crossing her arms.

How much?

Fifteen dollars more.

Ten.

Fifteen. And like I said, no matter if she don't talk.

Ten. And your husband doesn't have to know I'm paying you extra.

Give it to me now.

After.

He'll be around here any minute.

After, Gabriel repeats. She hesitates, then shrugs. Deal, she says. When they head toward the back of the corral, he follows rather than walk beside her, watches her limp in her ridiculous shoes. The blue roan raises its head and eyes them as they approach, then cautiously steps away from Abigail Buwell, who is sitting cross-legged on the ground.

Constance Smith yells something then, the guttural, explosive syllables a cacophony that astounds Gabriel, who lunges at her and swings her about. Stop, he tells her, and don't say anything I don't tell you to say.

Abigail Buwell does not raise her head from her arms. The horse beside her flattens its ears and snakes its head at them. Gabriel and Constance Smith stay beyond striking distance, though Gabriel knows the roan can cover the yards between it and them at breakneck speed and kick out in the blink of an eye. They stand for a few moments in silence, waiting for the horse to relax.

Now, he tells Constance Smith, but at the sound of his voice the horse rears its head, snaps its teeth, grinds its jaw.

Ten dollars.

You'll have it. Tell her that I want to help her.

There's no word for help. They ain't got one. 'Sides, she don't need help.

Then tell her I want to speak to her as a friend.

Hard sounds fly from Constance Smith's mouth. Abigail Buwell does not look at her.

Well, Constance Smith comments to Gabriel after a moment, I'd say you're bein' stupid. She don't want no friends.

Tell her I'm her friend, Gabriel persists. Tell her I want to hear her story, from the beginning. That I want her to tell me about her husband.

Which one?

He is taken aback. He means her true husband, not the savage who must be father of the child she is carrying. He reconsiders.

The savage.

Constance Smith speaks for longer than he would have imagined it would take to say such a simple thing. Abigail Buwell does not react.

She ain't gonna speak.

Try again.

Constance Smith says something that makes Abigail Buwell raise her head and stare at the two of them as if they're mad.

What did you say?

I said if she don't look up you'll shoot the horse.

Good lord.

Well, she looked up, didn't she?

Tell her I have no intention of shooting anything. That I'm speaking to her as a friend, that I want to hear her story. That I will write what she tells me. That I'll write anything she tells me.

When Constance Smith finishes speaking, Abigail Buwell remains motionless, and the blue roan drops its head and nuzzles her shoulder. She reaches up with a hand and strokes its nose without taking her eyes from them, and then she makes a gesture with both hands that Gabriel has never seen before and does not understand. She raises her hands palm outward and spreads her fingers, then snaps her wrists inward and drops both hands into the dirt with a slapping sound. Constance Smith utters an aggressive monosyllabic bark, then turns on her heel.

Hey, Gabriel says.

You keep your money, Constance Smith tells him over her shoulder as she walks away.

Abigail Buwell watches him. Wait, he yells at Constance Smith, who turns to face him. There ain't nothin' to wait for, Constance Smith says.

What did she mean by that? With her hands?

She just disappeared us. We ain't here.

She's looking straight at me.

Through you's more like it.

Tell her to tell me why she's done that to herself, why she's cut off her hair.

She won't speak. We ain't here, far as she's concerned. And I don't have to ask her nonsense. I know why she done it.

Why?

'Cause she's mournin', Constance Smith answers, turning away again.

Come back here, Gabriel says angrily. Constance Smith halts, faces Gabriel once more, kicks at the ground, shakes her head. She doesn't return to him, but she goes no farther. When he looks back at Abigail Buwell, he is struck by the stoic dignity of her face, the sorrow about her eyes, the set to her mouth. Something about her bloody scalp and sheared hair—akin to disfigurement, self-mutilation, a sign of internal distress—seduces him.

He does not take his eyes from her when he speaks. Tell her, he instructs Constance Smith, that I want to know why she's mourning.

Constance Smith looks at him contemptuously and says nothing. But Abigail Buwell raises one hand, touches the circle upon her filthy cheek, and holds his gaze before dropping her head onto her knees.

She ain't gonna talk, Constance Smith says.

She touched her cheek.

She's got nothin' to say that the circle don't say for itself.

And what is that?

Constance Smith spits. There is dust in her mouth, her nostrils, her eyes. That she is well loved by him. By the savage who painted it on.

She understood. She heard what I said, and she understood.

Go to hell, Constance Smith says to Gabriel. I done told you her story along with mine. And with that she leaves him standing there. As she strides away in the ill-fitting shoes, she tosses a look over her shoulder at Abigail Buwell and screeches, Whore!

If Abigail Buwell understands, she gives no sign. Reed Gabriel stands his ground for what seems an eternity, speaking to her, but she does not raise her head, and the horse does not leave her. Only after Gabriel's voice becomes hoarse, his mouth dry, does he give up. When he finally turns around, he starts at the sight of Cole standing behind him, feels the hairs rise on the back of his neck. You could scare a man to death, Gabriel tells him edgily.

And you might be tiring that poor woman to death, the smithy says in return.

Eight

Long after Major Robert Cutter has come to consider Reed Gabriel to be a sympathetic man, long after Cutter has been disgraced, had his command stripped from him, worse, and long after Abigail Buwell has been committed to Clearwater Asylum, Cutter—his memories of the outpost still raw—comes across the published account of Constance Smith's captivity. He will read it aloud to Abigail Buwell during a visit to her, sitting beside her upon the manicured lawn of the asylum grounds, with the late afternoon sun slanting through the day's stillness. Remember, he will say before commencing, Gabriel told me that he felt he had to stay true to Constance Smith's words.

My Life Among the Savages

A narrative of the trials and sufferings of
Constance Smith,
who was kidnapped from her home and husband

by savages
and who survived the hardships and horror of
life among them for four terrible years, during which
she witnessed torture and murder and mayhem,
and from whom she tried to escape and was recaptured
only to be sorely used.
As told to Reed Gabriel,
who took no liberties with this tale of captivity
but to write it in more proper English
than was spoken, and who did so in the first place
because of the captive's desire to assuage
the consciences of those who believed
the brutal extermination of the savages to be warranted,
there being no other way to make human
these creatures that were less than human,
proven by their lack of respect for life
and all living things.

I am not sure of my date of birth, but when I was given in marriage to Jonas Smith he was told by my parents that I was of marrying age, that being about eighteen; and he knew me to be of hardy constitution, for we had met upon the emigrant trail where he had taken a fancy to me and me to him. Some two months upon it he announced he had decided to go no farther than this point where the prairie seemed to stretch endless and that he could see no sense in either turning back or keeping on, his few cattle being worn and his horses and oxen in bad need of rest as were all of ours. He asked my father and mother to be married to me, it being uncommon that a man should begin a life in the middle of nowhere alone, and he promised them we would stray no farther south than a week's ride from the emigrant trail and at this spot, which he marked with some spokes from a discarded wagon wheel, that they might find our direction if they turned back. My parents were glad of his proposal, having seven other children and not knowing how their provisions might hold, and said if I was willing he could have me, for it seemed he would make a providing husband. It seemed right I should be married to a man I had a liking for, and so a man who could read from the Bible married us the next day. Thereafter my parents, their eyes full of tears, and the wagon train departed, leaving me with a chest with some clothes and bedding in it, and Jonas Smith and I went south for some days and near a creek began our hard lives, without benefit of neighbors, for there were none close by. Our home is now not as isolated as it was then, for more sodders came to settle about after my captivity, and two days' distance from us there is now a small town, which was not there when we first passed this way.

I was just over a year married to Jonas Smith, and we were homesteading in a poor way, though we had a few cows and a makeshift house of a cavern and a room, which had timbered and mud-plastered walls and a sod roof and dirt floor. It was early autumn when days are much the same, the weather being clear and constant, and my husband had taken an oxen pair and his horse in search of wood. He had to ride out a half day to find timber, for trees were sparse in the place we had settled in and are sparser today. I am not sure which date it was, for we kept time by the moon, but on that hateful morning some hours after my husband was gone came a group of savages, walking their horses nicely as if meaning no harm. I was in the garden, and I made as if savages came visiting all the time, though my heart was pounding. I walked the distance to the house very calmly, but just as I got to the door they made an unearthly howling and whipped their ponies to a run, and I was so taken afright that I grabbed our infant, just two months of age, who was fast asleep, and tried to flee. I did not get far before I was grabbed by the bonnet and scalp and fairly pulled off my feet and then dropped to the ground, and the baby went flying. I got to my knees and crawled to him, and hovered over him praying all the while as the savages rode around me at a terrible pace, screaming and hollering and hooting. Through the dust from their horses' hooves I could see that some of them had dismounted and were running in and out of the house with what few clothes we had, scattering our belongings, one of them putting the only petticoat I owned over his head. The cows were lowing and huddled in the field beyond, and some of the savages rode hard at them and chased them down and shot arrows into them so that the poor things were killed, and hardly had they fallen before the savages were ripping open their stomachs and tearing out their guts to eat their livers raw. The brutes smeared themselves with blood, so that their arms and faces were red, and rode back with the quivering meat in their hands, having torn the animals to pieces; then they made a fair game of joining those who were circling about me and the babe. When the savages tired of that they set fire to the house, and as it was burning they put a rope around my neck and tried to take the infant from me, but I would not give him up and they laughed and threw me onto a thin pony, one that was riderless, for they had a number of riderless horses that ran with them. I fell off and near choked to death as soon as they kicked their horses into motion, and only for the savage holding the other part of the rope was I not killed, though there would be many a day from that time on when I wished I had been, then and there. Some of them dismounted and kicked me until I got to my feet and then they threw me onto the horse with the savage holding the rope, and I held on for dear life, my babe crushed between us, as we went flying across the plains. Every time one of the other savages would gallop near he would strike me, the blows so hard as to take my breath away, and by the end of the day I knew my back was bruised and bleeding, for I could feel where the gingham had run with blood and stuck to me.

They didn't stop until almost nightfall, and by that time we had fallen in with a second group of savages, from the same band, who had with them several very good horses they had stolen and another captive. I could not see her face, for she had been hit hard in the head and they had thrown her, unconscious, over the withers of a piebald horse ridden by one of the heathen. Her arms and hair hung down, and whether she was dead or alive I could not tell. By the time they stopped to camp in the mouth of a well hid ravine, my baby was crying endlessly and was blue in the face, and I was half dead from thirst and fear. They slid the other woman from the horse and let her hit the ground without catching her, and she rolled onto her side and then I saw that her hair was bloody near her forehead, and that she had a gash in her scalp. They took me off the horse and again tried to take the babe from me, but I fought back as best I could until the brutes were much amused. After that they pulled me by the rope around my neck and tied me tightly to a tree, by my throat, and I could not have taken apart their knots if I had tried. I kept the babe in my arms and would not put him down. They dragged the other woman close by and tied her hands and her feet together, behind her back, so that she lay in an awkward way so painful as to cause her to moan something pitiful.

The savages made no fire and gave us no water or food, but took good care of their horses, for they led them to the small stream that pooled at places farther up the ravine. That evening, we neither drank nor ate. My babe would not take the breast, but quieted with a dazed look in his dear little eyes, and as the night grew cold I kept him pressed to my bosom, hoping to keep him warm and preserve his life. The other captive came to sometime in the night, and she groaned and cried out for water repeatedly until a savage came over to her and kicked her twice, very hard, and silenced her. At dawn she lay on her side, her eyes wide open, watching me clutch the babe. I was afraid she would speak again and bring upon our heads the wrath of the savages, but it was the infant who—oh, misfortune of misfortunes— did this, for the babe was inconsolable. I tried to suckle, but his bawling only worsened, and then one of the savages came over and crouched before me, watching me try to quiet the babe and give him my breast, and then he took the babe from me, gently but firmly, pulling him out of my arms. Some distance from us, the brute swung him in a circle and dashed him against a large boulder, and my babe's brains were splattered and his lifeless body flung to the ground and kicked away.

I could hear myself screaming and screaming, and I was screaming even as they untied me and took the rope from around my neck, but I had no strength to stand and so they threw me onto the pony and tied my ankles together, passing the rope under the creature's belly. As I was still screaming for my dead child, one of the savages came over to me and put a knife into my thigh, and when I felt it and looked down I was so stunned by the blade handle sticking out that I fell silent, and he grunted in satisfaction as he walked away. I am sure I fainted, and though I must have returned to consciousness long before midday, I remember nothing else before realizing that the sun was high overhead and that the knife was still in my thigh. I must mention here that I do not know where my babe was murdered, and it still grieves me deeply that I could not give his small remains a decent burial.

For a second day and night we went without water. The other captive had recovered sufficiently to be mounted with a savage on a broad-backed horse. She often lost consciousness or slept, I could not tell which, but she no longer asked for water though her lips were parched and her face and wrists and hands were like mine burned by the sun, for she was fair though raven-haired. I felt no thirst or hunger. I no longer wished to live and prayed only to be delivered from this life to the next that I might join my hapless babe and, for all I knew, my husband, whom I presumed dead. The third day we were joined by even more savages, and these were herding a large group of horses and a few mules, all of which had been stolen on raids, and as we now went more slowly through the immensity of the land it was evident that the savages were wary of being discovered, by whom I could not imagine, and they suffered themselves to be quiet and pushed the herd before us with a singularity of mind. I must add that before being dismounted the second evening, the same savage who had stabbed me recovered his knife by pulling it out of my thigh, and that I had not even the strength to scream at the blinding pain that began at that moment; and though there was little blood the wound festered so that by the time we reached the savages' encampment, four days after being taken, an old woman had to apply poultices to it for some days before the stench and the swelling went away. These poultices were made of moss and bark and feathers and I knew then not what else, though I later learned the savages had also mixed in the blood of snake with horse dung and dirt and spit; and I think it a wonder to this day I did not die from their ministrations.

I must describe something of the way the savages appeared. They wore little clothing, and what they wore was made of animal hides softened in a most disgusting manner—by chewing. The women always scraped the fat from the inside of the hides, for this was among their duties, and pegged them a day or two, smearing them with the scraped fat, before pounding the hides and chewing on them; the old women had teeth worn down to nubs from having done this all their lives. Each male savage had a loincloth of sorts, and some had leggings as well, though few covered their feet. Their chests and shoulders and backs they left bare for the most part, except for articles of clothing they had stolen from the emigrants and settlers, and these might be ladies' bodices or vests or even shirtwaists from which they ripped the arms. One or two of them had bone or quill vests, well worked and beaded, and sometimes decorated with buttons they had ripped from the bodies of those they massacred, for they were always careful to remove the clothes from the dead before mutilating them for sport. They decorated their hair with colored string and feathers, and they wore in their ears the teeth of bear and lynx, or sometimes colored stones strung on hoops of sinew, and they took much time with their toilet, combing and greasing their hair and sometimes plaiting it in one long braid down their backs or over one ear. They colored their faces on occasion, or painted them with symbols. They had such a fierce appearance that I wonder how I did not die from fright in the beginning, though much worse than their appearance awaited me.

At the end of the third day we came across a cow and calf that had somehow wandered far from the old emigrant trail or from some hapless homesteader, and the savages slaughtered both. They gutted the calf immediately and opened its stomach to pull out the curdled milk that was in its belly, which they ate with their hands. They took us from the horses and brought us to the kill and motioned for us to eat, and though I could not, the other captive thrust her hands into the stomach and ate several mouthfuls of the nauseating stuff, and at that they seemed quite pleased. When they had finished with the curds they set upon the raw liver; and then they cut out the ribs from the cow and carried them with us some distance, for we rode until after dark, reaching the foothills of a mountain range, where we camped in a good place, with a small river cascading through, and they made a fire for the first time and of the cooked meat I ate, and we were given water to drink. That night they did not tie us, but set us in their midst so it was impossible for us to escape. It was on this night that the other captive, whose name was Abigail Buwell, and I managed to whisper a few words to one another, though when the savages heard us they hit us with sticks on our heads and much hurt and frightened us. On the dawn of the fourth day we were again placed upon the horses, but for the first time Abigail Buwell was left to ride by herself. She had rubbed some of the dried blood from her scalp and face and appeared to be recovering from the blow to her head, which had left her with badly bruised eyes.

The horses they drove before them as we climbed higher and higher, and the foothills gave way to a much colder clime as we continued now into the mountains. (How they knew the way without any trails that we could see I do not know, but the savages had a skill for remembering the lay of the land at all times, and they always found their way to their last encampment without difficulty. If the camp had been moved while members of the band were gone, raiding or hunting, bones and rocks were left behind in patterns the savages understood, and these directed them to where the next encampment could be found.) Abigail Buwell seemed very alert this day. I saw that she looked about her often by simply shifting her eyes to the right and left, and I tried to do the same, hoping to remember landmarks we might follow later should we be able to escape. Finally

we came to a high meadow, at which time the savages'
ponies began to neigh, and they were answered at a
distance, from the depths of a high canyon, by many
others. At this the horses we rode began to prance and
buck, and I was much tossed about and had to hold onto
the mane of the pony that carried me so I might not slip
sideways and be dragged to my death, for my ankles
were bound. But the savages kept their mounts in check
and only when we heard the howling and barking of dogs
and the cries of the women, raising their voices in an
ungodly fashion, did they let go and race toward their
homes, my horse galloping among them.

Their homes were what we call wickups; they were
conical in shape and made of poles and skin, and they
could be easily dismantled and moved upon travois.
Here there were close to forty such wickups, and in
each many savages lived, along with their dogs and their
fleas and as many possessions as each family had, plus
the little food they stored, for they thought not of the
future but lived from day to day, unlike people. The
savages threw their horses' tethers to the women and
children who greeted us, and amid great jubilation they
unbound and pulled us from our ponies and we were
surrounded by a multitude of stinking, ugly creatures
whose unearthly whoops and cries much frightened me.
All these monsters touched and pinched us and hit us,
pulled at our hair, put their fingers into our mouths and
ears, and the children poked us with small sticks and
threw rocks at us, all of which we had to endure without
complaint, for we had learned in those few days that any
show of weakness only spurred the savages to beat us
mercilessly.

I was given to an old woman who had no children and whose husband was dead. She was so poor that she lived by begging, which the savages allowed among themselves, in a manner of speaking; for while they had no patience with those who could not provide for themselves, and were greatly irritated by them, the savages would not suffer one of their kind to die from hunger or cold. Why I was given to her is this: being a crone and alone, she was a burden to others, and I was to gather wood and forage food for her, and break down her wickup when necessary and harness it to myself and her dogs, of which she had many—mostly large curs, infested with fleas. The savages seemed joyous when I was pushed in the old woman's direction, but when she grabbed me by the hair and tried to pull me about, I knocked her hand away and kicked at her. She screamed something at me and a good many savages laughed, and then she disappeared and returned with a club, with which she hit me repeatedly, until I covered my head, and then she went to work on my back, and when she finished she led me away by the hair without any resistance.

I did not see what had happened to Abigail Buwell, though I later understood she had been given to a family who had lost a son and who had never had a daughter. The savage she had ridden with was the only brother of that son. It was her duty to tether his horse after he returned from hunting or thieving, and she had little to do otherwise than to help with the cooking from time to time, for she had a way with horses and was soon entrusted to care for the herd, as was her wont. And so, whereas I had the misfortune of being enslaved to a horrible old woman who beat me ceaselessly and used me mercilessly, Abigail Buwell was from the start, if such a thing could be said, treated well. She was dressed almost immediately in savage garb, for though a few days passed before we next saw one another, when I did see her she was wearing doeskin leggings and a tunic, and her hair had been plaited, and her head and face were beginning to heal from her wounds and the bruising. I was left to wear the dress in which I had been captured until it fell into tatters, and I suffered half-naked from the cold that winter until I learned to beg for pieces of discarded skins in order to clothe myself.

In the first days we could not move about the savages unnoticed, and if we strayed to the edge of their encampment those hardhearted women and vile children, who were brutal by nature and knew not the meaning of tears, would drive us back, beating us with sticks or pelting us with stones. We did not understand their language and I was beaten severely and often for not knowing what was being said to me by the old woman and others, but I learned quickly the words for wood and water, and for various foods. By and by, however, as it became clear that we had no means of escape, we found ourselves allowed to wander the encampment and sometimes we met as if by chance to say a few words to each other under our breaths before going our separate ways. In this manner Abigail Buwell and I long planned our escape, and we both squirreled away what we could, in small pouches that we hid and would carry with us in that event, pine nuts and dried berries and the like. Abigail Buwell was learning their tongue much faster than I, having kinder teachers, they being her adoptive family, and she was learning their ways as well. Some months after we were taken captive she told me that many of the savages would leave to hunt the following day, and that the night thereafter we must somehow make our escape.

By this time she often stayed with the horses at night, for she had a way with them, as I said, and was trusted to keep good watch over them; and though there were others who watched over the herd they were dispersed and, being lazy, quite given to sleep, so it would be possible for her to slip away. I, however, was obliged to sleep in the wickup of the filthy old crone, and her dogs growled at my slightest movement. The night we were to escape, I mixed into a bowl of slop for the dogs some sap the savages often gave to colicky infants, and I mixed the same into the old woman's food. She wrinkled her nose at the taste, then sniffed at it for some time before partaking of all; when she bedded herself at dark, she fell into a deep sleep. I sat at the wickup opening and waited for all to quiet, and then, without closing the flap, managed to crawl away slowly. Though the wickup was on the edge of the encampment, it seemed a lifetime before I was able to stand and run. I was shoeless, and as soon as I could reach the stream that ran along the encampment and far down the mountainside, I stepped into it and slowed so as not to splash, and in the half-moonlight suffered the cold water and rocks so as not to leave a trail. At one point, at a deep pool below a small cascade, I waited as we had planned, and soon Abigail Buwell appeared and we began our flight from our captors.

We spoke then, in whispers, only as to what we

must do, for we had agreed that we would travel by night and rest, hiding ourselves, during the day. Abigail Buwell proposed we should walk in the stream as long as it might flow so as to leave no footprints and no scent of ourselves. We reckoned if we traveled downstream for as long as we could, it would take us far from the way we had originally come, for when the savages brought us to their encampment we came across this stream only a short distance from it. And so we abided the cold water, the rocks, the deep pools into which we sometimes fell and in which we floundered, terrified, for I could not swim and the doeskin robes worn by Abigail Buwell weighed her down. Several times during that first night I thought we would drown, though I was happier with that fate than with the thought of continuing to live among those brutes. By the time it dawned we were far downstream, but wet and cold, and when we came upon some bushes along the stream's bank behind which we might hide ourselves, we took to them. To our delight, we discovered a small cavern hidden by the shrubs, wherein we could both lie down. We stripped away our wet things and lay them on the bushes before us, certain the thickness of the bushes would not reveal them, and, shivering, lay side by side and slept as best we could.

Late that afternoon we huddled together, ate a handful of nuts and berries, and were much refreshed. We were thirsty; but we did not dare to go out to the stream for fear of being seen. We heard nothing—no voices, no horses—and were much relieved, believing our plan to follow the course of the stream, which was ever widening, to be a good one. On that afternoon, Abigail Buwell told me of her captivity. She said that on the morning of it, she heard her husband's shouts from a distant field, where he had gone to plow, and that she ran and hurriedly threw a bridle onto an old mare and, riding bareback, kicked the horse into a canter, not knowing what it was that was making him cry out so. He was beyond a depression and a stand of trees, so even as she rode toward him she could not see him, and his incessant screams much alarmed her. But, oh, even the greatest imagination cannot conceive of the tortures these savages delighted in! Her last visage of her dying husband was of a naked man scalped alive and disemboweling, for the brutes had incised the man's belly and extracted a piece of intestine and pulled this out and tied it to a horse's tail, and they were making merry as they made the horse buck and romp farther and farther from where the poor man lay on the ground as his guts were pulled from him and the savages hacked at him with their hatchets. Abigail Buwell said that she was too terrified to faint at the sight, and that she turned her old horse abruptly so as to escape with her life, but not before being espied by the savages, who pursued her and in no time were riding alongside her, whooping and hollering. She remembered nothing after being struck at by one of the heathens, causing the wound to her head and her to fall. She told me she was very sure her husband was dead, and I told her I was not certain that mine was alive, but that if he were he would surely never stop looking for me. She told me that her husband's brother, who lived some distance from where this atrocity took place, was quite possibly alive; but she said that if we made our escape she would not return to the homestead she and her husband had made for themselves, for the brother was of bad character and she would not abide him. Such unkind words for the good man who would one day seek her release from captivity!

After this she spoke no more of her travails, or of her husband's brother, who went in search of her as my husband did for me, and to whom she should be beholden. By the time we were redeemed, Abigail Buwell had become a savage herself, and she had long treated me as the other brutes did, though not quite as harshly. She did not wish to leave the savages and to all appearances had forgotten or forsaken the English language, and from the moment she was redeemed she never showed anything but regret at her removal from that ghastly life we led in their midst; and as far as I know she never spoke to her husband's brother, who was the cause of her redemption. I will say no more about her except that during our captivity she became godless, and that she bore one child and was carrying another when we were rescued from the savages. What has happened to her I do not know, and care less.

However, at this time, in the cavern, we had but one objective, our liberation, and we were like sisters at that moment. When night fell we pulled on our damp clothes and immediately became wet and chilled again. Our feet had been torn and bloodied on the previous night, but the coldness of the water numbed them, for which we were grateful. As we made our way downstream, woe of woes, we found we could no longer ford the depths, and we were forced onto the banks to make progress. When morning came, alas, we found ourselves without shelter, for the land had begun to roll away from the mountains and the hilly expanse was quite treeless, so we lay as best we could in the grasses, hoping their height would cover us. That day we heard horses, and we knew the savages were on our trail; they were riding in the stream, crossing it back and forth, searching for us. By late afternoon they had come quite close to us twice. We were much afraid of being captured again, and at dusk we could wait no longer. We agreed to crawl as far as the grasses afforded cover, then run as fast as our feet would fly, always in a downward direction, for the hills certainly rolled to the plains, though we could not see these. We had not heard the savages for some time, but they must have decided to wait far from us; they were always devious when tracking and hunting, and had wily ways, as the reader will discover. For though we crawled a great distance under cover of dusk and finally managed to get to our feet and run, we were discovered, not by the savages per se, but by a colt that was much attached to Abigail Buwell. The colt had been used like a hunting dog, to track our scent; and when it caught wind of us, it galloped toward us, whinnying and neighing and thus signaling to the brutes that it had found us; and we knew our freedom was at an end the moment it came upon us. And so we were taken again, having enjoyed less than two days at liberty. We were then forced to trot back on foot, in the midst of the mounted savages, the entire distance, all the while stumbling and losing our balance; and once we arrived at the encampment we were severely beaten, though we were already half dead from exhaustion.

Thereafter the savages took great pains to keep us apart. I never again had another conversation with Abigail Buwell; and, after a certain time, as I have mentioned, she stopped speaking our language altogether. But even in the language of the savages she never addressed me, though I sometimes went to her adopted family's wickup and begged for the scraps that were tossed at me as to a dog. The more savage Abigail Buwell became, the less I thought of her as human, and so I did not miss her company.

The savages moved their wickups from place to place several times each year, sometimes according to season and, in my opinion, more frequently according to whim. They were a shiftless lot who thought nothing of moving here and there, for no reason whatsoever, whenever the urge touched them. My life was dreadful, for I was used as a slave; the old woman was ruthless and beat me at the slightest provocation or none at all. During the first year, of which I kept track by notching the number of moons that had come and gone on a stick I used for walking, it fell to me to gather berries of all sorts, and to dry them, and to gather and leech and pound acorns, from which we made a poor flour, as well as to search for edible roots and bitter wild greens, to gather firewood and kindling, and to beg meat from those who returned from their hunting laden with kill. After a time my clothes were ripped and torn, and as I have recounted I almost froze to death that first winter, for I was sent out to gather wood with the younger girls, who kept a watch on me and who were not responsible for carrying such large loads on their backs as I was. One day one of them gave me a large piece of an old blanket that had surely belonged on a horse, from which I fashioned a cape of sorts and leggings, and I wrapped my feet with grasses and wound animal skin around them, and thus was I attired. Later, I managed to beg or find discarded things, and so clothed myself, but, oh, the sight I must have presented! My hair sometimes fell out in clumps, and the old woman had knocked several of my teeth down my throat with her club. One of my eyes went blind; the orb turned white, a condition not dissimilar to mooneye suffered by horses, though I had no mirror and did not know at the time what had happened. I prayed to die, but was not delivered, though I knew not why: and I lived in such a miserable state that I could no longer imagine the past would ever be recovered, and I believed miserably that my husband was as lost to me as my dear, dead babe.

As I said, we moved several times a year. Sometimes we came across other savages or trappers or mountain men, with whom trades were bargained; but at those times I was kept out of sight, bound and gagged. Once, in the second year, a raiding party returned with other captives, comprising three white men and a boy, as well as several stolen horses, one of which they gave to the old crone and which made my life more wretched, for now I had to provide feed for the creature even in winter, which meant cutting and stripping cottonwood, though at least I no longer had to haul the travois with the dogs thereafter, the horse doing the work. The three male captives had killed several of the savages upon their raiding, and they were handed over to the families of the dead to decide in which manner they wished the captives killed. All three were murdered in the most heinous ways. One was stripped naked and bound to a tree and used as target practice by the children, who laughed as they pierced and punctured every part of him as he slowly bled to death; they plunged knives into his eyes and ears and cut his nipples from him and worse. This happened on one day, and the other two captives were made to watch, though their fates would differ. For the second captive was murdered by being stretched upon the ground, his legs and arms spread and bound to stakes; after he was eviscerated the savages brought their dogs to him and encouraged them to feast while he was yet living, which they did. The third man lost his mind at the sight. His screams would have filled the whole of the universe, but the savages stuffed his mouth with dirt and then gagged him. I believe the poor man, in agony, tried desperately to choke himself to death by swallowing the dirt, but he could not, being hung by his ankles from a tree. He died, however, almost immediately thereafter, before the savages could do him more mischief; they intended to build a fire beneath him and roast his brains, but found no amusement in it once the man was dead. The boy, however, was given to a family who had lost a grown daughter. He died the following year, having been thrown by a vicious pony. By that time he had become a savage, and his death was much mourned.

The old woman died about the time of the boy, being taken by pains in the stomach one night and the next morning being cold as a stone. Her meager belongings were distributed among those who had less than others, as was their custom; even the horse was given away. I, too, being her property, was given to a poor old man, his son and the son's wife, and their two children, and though I was given food by them, for the son hunted, I was tossed the scraps and the worst pieces of meat or fat. But my life was not so harsh as before. The son's wife did not beat me, and at times she gave me things she no longer wanted, and so I went better clothed and more appropriately than at any time since my captivity. I gathered wood and took care of the brats, who were, like all savage children, expected to do nothing but play and brawl until a certain age, and there was nothing they were not allowed, including biting and kicking and stabbing and whipping me. But I persevered, and as from the beginning remembered my prayers, which I said with great constancy. In this way passed my years among the savages, whose way of life fast deteriorated; in my last year with them their hunts had not been successful, and we moved more and more often; what we managed to gather and dry was less plentiful, and hunger became a constant and cruel companion. I resigned myself to not surviving another winter, and I had long been ready to meet our Maker by the time many of their dogs had been eaten, for there was very little food, though why the savages would not eat horses I cannot say, as they always had more of these than they needed.

Just as the situation was becoming more and more desperate, a group of savages rode out, ostensibly to hunt; they returned with no food and had with them instead some stolen horses, but they had lost three of their number. From the lamentations, and the hysterics, I assumed that the three were dead, and at some time thereafter, when there was almost nothing left to eat, it was decided to move once again. Many broke down their wickups that selfsame day, and there were many travois readied. The next morning the savages were surprised by soldiers. Shocked to see the bluecoats riding in, they came stumbling out from the remaining wickups half naked and clapped their hands over their ears as the troops around and above us fired a terrible volley. In the pandemonium I was forgotten long enough to run toward the soldiers, screaming, before being dragged away by the son's wife and pulled back into their wickup, where I was gagged and bound. I knew I had been seen, and prayed I would not be left behind, though I feared no one could have recognized me for the woman I had once been—someone who was not a savage.

I did not know my husband was with the soldiers, or that he had seen me.

When the son's wife finally took away my gag and unbound me, she fed me and combed my hair and righted as best she could the rags I was wearing. I had never known such attention from this family, and as the smallest children watched with their thumbs in their mouths I felt myself trembling with fear, thinking they were readying me for a terrible death. When they finally led me from the wickup I was stood before a pony of poor condition and then mounted upon it, and only then did I hope to think I might be led to the soldiers. I was dazed and could not speak, so overjoyed was I, and it was only when I saw my husband that I began to carry on like a crazy woman, blabbering and sobbing, which the savages found amusing. Then they pulled me from the pony and laughed to see me fall to the ground and throw my arms about my husband's knees. It was a good while before I could understand what he was saying to me, and longer before I could stand, but when I was finally sensible the lieutenant leading the soldiers asked me whether a woman named Abigail Buwell was among the savages, and I said there was. The lieutenant seemed distressed by my response; later I learned that the savages had tried to persuade him there were no other captives among them. The savages had been caught in an outright lie and would now lose face unless the lieutenant bargained hard, which he did. He told me to tell them he did not wish to return with only one captive—me—but if he were forced to do so, one of the three savages to be exchanged for us would be put to death instead of being freed. The savages wanted to know the manner of killing, and the lieutenant said the savage would be hung by the neck, which the brutes considered a shameful way to die. At that I begged the lieutenant to say nothing more, and not to use me in this way, for I was seized by the terror of being abandoned to these wretches on account of Abigail Buwell; but he was adamant, and I had no choice and so related to the savages what he had said.

After that the brutes left us and took a long, and for me agonizing, time in deciding. When Abigail Buwell was finally brought to us, she was mounted on the very horse that was responsible for finding us when we escaped, her favorite, and a red circle had been painted upon her cheek by the savage with whom she had so shamelessly consorted. If she recognized her brother in law, she gave no indication of such.

Thus ended our years of captivity.

I never forgot my civilized tongue nor my prayers, and for this I remain to this day grateful. I know not why I was singled out for such a trial and for such punishment, for I was too young when I was taken to have committed any grievous wrong, and I have no idea why my babe was so cruelly murdered, his brains dashed out, and denied a decent burial. I have never found it in my heart to think at all kindly toward the savages, for I never witnessed any act of kindness among them. The years I passed among them, the reader can be assured, I would sooner forget than remember. Let those who think the savages were wrongly hunted down and exterminated be reminded by what I have recounted as the truth: the savages were worse than vermin. They had none of the ways of people, and they could never be civilized, despite their resemblance to us, which was only skin-deep. Since my deliverance, I have been gladdened by the righteous policy of our government, which has succeeded, by confinement or by killing, in clearing the last of the savages from the face our land. We can finally sleep peacefully and wake without the dread that we might be stolen from our homes and loved ones. For this, I, who suffered at their hands, say: God bless the nation.

The major will silently drop the journal onto his knees after he finishes reading, then study Abigail Buwell's profile. Her head will be bent in the reddening glow of late afternoon, and she will absently raise one hand to her cheek that was once painted with a crimson circle, then drop her hand atop the other in her lap.

She had no infant, Abigail Buwell will say then. Nor were there ever other captives. And then she will rise and without saying goodbye to him make her way back to the entrance of the asylum, her shadow long behind her.

Nine

Reed Gabriel delays the hunting detail from leaving, for his horse has tossed a shoe, and Gabriel now stands patiently, listening to the smithy hum a song as he trims and files the hoof. The horse—a high-strung if honest creature that dislikes being shod—is, in Cole's hands, remarkably still.

The detail has been provisioned for three weeks, Gabriel has been informed by Lt. Hastings; with it goes a wagon, one of three remaining at the outpost excepting the sutler's. Gabriel surmises they might be gone for longer than three weeks if the hunt goes badly; he has a sense of the lieutenant's seriousness, and he has seen enough to realize that the outpost's survival may well depend on the detail's success. He listens to the smithy hammering, counts twenty-four readied, riderless mounts; another ten troops and a mule-drawn cart with provisions have already left to scavenge the old emigrant trail. They will, Gabriel knows, have to ride a long way before finding anything of use, for he followed the trail on his way to the outpost and for many miles saw only marked gravesites, the crosses in places averaging four to the mile, as well as abandoned wagons, broken barrels, heaps of decayed clothes, discarded cast iron stoves, rotting chests, broken wheels. He wonders how long the scavenging detail will be gone, given the meager provisions carried; at the most, he calculates, a week. With these two details gone, the outpost will have only half its men; and on any given day half of those will be on wood and grazing details, leaving the place defenseless in the face of attack. Gabriel wonders whether Cutter is apprehensive, but finds it impossible to read the man who, across the dismal quadrant, appears to be arguing with the sutler again.

It is only later that Reed Gabriel is told by the lieutenant that the troops' pay as well as supply wagons have not arrived for months, and realizes that Cutter must have emptied his own pockets, or compromised his future salary, to reimburse the sutler for both details' provisions. Gabriel will think it a munificent, if desperate, last gamble to fend off what would otherwise be certain starvation during the harsh winter months to come. But for now, he leads his shod horse to where Jonas Smith and his wife stand before their mounts, the condition of her pony more pitiful than the day they rode in. There is no tack for it, and when Constance Smith mounts she sits on a worn blanket girthed with a rope, cutting an inane figure in the bonnet and dress and shoes she insists upon wearing, even to ride.

The major breaks away from the sutler when he hears Hastings give the order to mount. He limps over to the troops and to Hastings, who leans from his saddle and listens to Cutter, whose words—Under no circumstances, he tells the lieutenant, are you to engage the savages—Gabriel cannot hear. When Hastings straightens, he smartly salutes his haggard commanding officer and gives the call to open the gates.

Gabriel climbs into his saddle with an easy swing and pulls his horse up short, allowing the troops and the Smiths to precede him. When he casts a last backward glance over his left shoulder, he sees Abigail Buwell through the swirl of dust, standing behind her swollen belly beyond the stable's far edge.

Abigail Buwell, her angularity and protruding roundness softened by the dustblow, watches as Lt. Hastings and the troops and the Smiths and, in the rear, the man of questions ride out through the gates. It is not the men nor Constance Smith who interest her, and not even the windscoured landscape beyond them, but the horses. She can tell those that are backsore even at a walk, for they pull with their front legs, and those that are lame, for they jerk their heads or flick an ear ever so slightly, and those that are fresh and eager, for they can hardly stand still, and those that are criminal, for they gnash their teeth and snap at being girthed and refuse to move forward. She knows which mounts will throw shoes and which will buck at the transition to a canter, which will stumble when put to a trot, which will play with their bits until they lock them between their teeth and then shy at their own shadows or the flap of a neckerchief, any excuse to leap sideways, to falter, to balk, to pull the reins out of careless hands, to unseat the rider.

There are horses with kind eyes and horses whose madness and spirit shines from them. She does not know whether the wild look in a rolled eyeball, the white showing, is something she first noticed as a child on the streets, where beaten drays dragged wagons and the few well-to-do pranced their purebloods, or in the first home she remembers, where newspaper and magazine pages with their etchings of mounted riders were pasted onto the walls to hold back the drafts and chinked plaster in the best of times and tore loose in the worst. The leaders of the country were always mounted on horses with crazy eyes and flared nostrils; men in uniform also rode such creatures, as did ladies on sidesaddles, and those fox-hunting, the eyes of the dogs rounder and even more lunatic than those of the horses. She would fall asleep under their mad gazes and awaken to the same; she would sit on a stool beneath them, quietly watching her mother smear her mouth with color and rouge her cheeks; and she was always bathed, standing in a basin, under their unabashed stares. Or perhaps she first saw the shining in their eyes the one time she was taken to the circus.

The freaks frightened her and made her cry, for they were immense, sitting in their cubicles above the crowds: the toothless and bearded crone, her tongue lolling; the corpulent man whose fat rippled over the sides of the stool he sat; the boy with the distended and bony head that grew in barnacled hives; the midget geek, who stood on bowed legs with a bloody and headless pigeon in his hands. She was more frightened by the things in jars, in an ill-lit, makeshift chamber of horrors: an almost full-term, two-headed fetus with four arms plucked from a dead woman's abdomen; feathered chicks in cracked eggshells; an albino snake with two black eyes and seven black penises; a human brain sprouting worms. She was so small that the man with her mother had to stoop slightly to hold onto her hand, and it was he who slapped her bawling into silence as her mother's reddened mouth rounded itself into a pout and bent toward the child, whispering that she would see the ponies only if she stopped fussing. Abigail swallowed her tears and gulped and tried not to look at what it was that made her mother and the man who accompanied her laugh. When they finally entered a broad tent, she could smell the bodies seated hip to hip, smell their breaths, the reek of damp clothes, unwashed sweat, cheap pomades and cheaper perfumes. She suffered clowns and their violent antics, scantily clad women suspended from bars that swung from the tentpoles, tightsuited jugglers and acrobats, the man's fingers tight about her wrist, before the white horses raced into the ring. Their eyes shone bloodred in the flickering torchlight, their ears were flattened and their nostrils flared, and as they galloped about men and women lithe as moonlight leapt onto and off them; at that moment all else vanished for her, the crowd disappeared, as did the man's viselike grip and her mother's beautiful mouth. And with a precocity instinctive only to children, she understood that it was the circle that mattered, that its perfection alone meant that even the most insensible and intractable horses could be ridden, gaited, controlled. She cried once again when the white horses were made to bow and then were trotted away, she wept for them to return, cried to be allowed to follow them, and again she was struck, this time harder than before. And then she bit the man's hand viciously.

She doesn't remember if she ever saw him again. But she knows that she most loves horses with a wild, mad look in their eyes, for these are the ones that will suffer no blows.

The child within her rolls and drops low into her abdomen, and she staggers slightly, wills it to wait. She knows it will not be born with a wildness in its gaze, but with dust in its eyes. She does not want it to be born at all.

The major watches Abigail Buwell from where he stands, also in part obscured by the whirling dust. The troops left to the outpost, other than those on grazing and wood and sentry details, have already sought shelter in the leantos and barracks. The sentries peer over the stockade, their shapes thinned in the blowing sand, and stare at a world that has lost its horizons, its sun, its clouds, to an impenetrability into which Hastings' troops and the civilians have not so much disappeared as been swallowed by, and even though the sentries can still faintly hear the horses, they can no longer discern them or their riders. The sand fills their nostrils, leaves them cottonmouthed, and though they duck their heads their eyes tear and streak fine, wet lines down their faces. When Cutter finally turns his gaze from Abigail Buwell to the stilled sentries, he sees them as dead men propped against some ship's rails, frozen in place, their bodies stiff, their grip unrelenting against the violent blow of foamy winds. A shudder quakes through him at the perception, and his knee and shoulder ache as badly as in those first moments after the bullets had torn into his flesh. He stands rooted to the spot and thinks: There is nothing I can do. There is nothing to be done.

He knows without thinking, in his bones, there is much to be done. Across the quadrant, Ezekiel Pace sits before his store, a bandana pulled halfway up his face, a ludicrous, bell-shaped figure hunching against the wind. The major looks from the sentries to the sutler, tells himself to go over to Pace and demand a bill of lading, tells himself he should immediately enter quantities and amounts into the dead quartermaster's ledger before he forgets the weight of the provisions and their costs; but he is loath to speak to Pace again this day, the man is too difficult, his greed too transparent. Besides, the sutler strikes Cutter as oddly moribund, sitting stupidly in the dust, the blowing sand, the grit; any other storekeeper in his position would be preparing to make the long journey back to civilization to restock and reoutfit instead of waiting to become just another mouth to feed, though Pace will starve more slowly than the rest, the major finds himself thinking, being able to live for some time off his own fat. Cutter decides that the sands can blow until they bury the man for all he cares, he decides the accounting can wait. He decides that everything can wait.

Everything, that is, but the child waiting to be born. Cutter does not see Abigail Buwell turn, and she vanishes. There is nothing but wind and sand where she had stood, and he feels a sudden, erratic beating to his heart and a whittling away at his insides, so that what is left of his soul drains from within him and seeps into the ground at his feet. He fights the pain in his shoulder, his knee, leans into a gust of wind and, turning toward his quarters, squints against the dustblow, sees that a small dune has piled against the doctor's door, wishes that Matthews would appear, would join him for a cognac—for what else is there to do in this infernal situation?—and reassure Cutter that normality might be reestablished at any moment, that the wind will die, that the animals will be watered and fed, the wood unloaded, fires built, suppers cooked, harmonicas played, details safely returned, that supply wagons and the troops' pay will arrive. The doctor does not appear as the major walks toward his quarters, and Cutter does not know how he will stay sane until the evening, until the next morning, until the day he retires.

Perhaps Matthews will pay a visit later, the major thinks as he opens the door and slams it shut against the wind, then thinks perhaps not. The sutler certainly will not. Maria, he realizes with an odd, almost embarrassed sense of disappointment, most certainly will not, though she will be visited in the dark to come by one or two of the men, the most foolish or the loneliest, and surely by the sutler for trade in kind. Bean will not return, if at all, for many days to come. The supply convoys seem like figments of a malign imagination, and the enemy without, those unfettered savages who are left—the reason for this outpost's perilous existence—roaming the inhospitable beyond, are purely, perfectly, nothing less than inconceivable.

Even in the beginning, even at close range, the savages were, to Cutter, inconceivable. There was their startling, and to him unnerving, appearance, the men half-naked and certainly men, if of a color he had never before imagined, with lean bodies, long muscles, hairless faces, and flowing, feather-decorated hair, the skins of wild animals or improbably colored cloths about their loins. With their fringed leggings and beaded slippers, their triangular teeth, their oval eyes, they sat their saddleless horses as though they had sprouted from their backs, centaur-like and yet different. Their horses were painted with handprints and circles and stars in what seemed to Cutter to be hieroglyphic storylines, and their manes and tails were streaked with colors: ocher, yellow, blue. None of what he had read about the savages, nothing in the likenesses he had seen, prepared Cutter for their actuality, the immediacy of their otherness; for what he had read and seen were static, and the reality of them was not: they were fully alive.

At the beginning of the long war, when it seemed it would not last, there were arguments among Cutter's fellow officers as to the future fate of the savages, to whom they would surely turn their attention after they tired of killing one another. Some mimed the musings of philosophers who claimed that the savages, living without the concepts of sin or property or privacy, were the noblest among earth's peoples; others railed that without such concepts the savages were not people, and that they should be herded like animals and penned and the males gelded, or that they should be hunted down like game, their heads mounted as trophies, their few belongings left to scatter, to rot. The sides, of course, could not be resolved, and the arguments proved but a specious pastime before the real business of slaughter. The war did not end quickly; indeed, it did not end until after the blood of a million and more had seeped into the ground; and after that, when Robert Cutter found himself posted to the back of beyond, to a place the savages still claimed as part of their world, he was as stunned to perplexity by them as he was by the war's consequences and his mission.

The bleakness of the savages' existence negated, for him, the very notion of nobility. The harshness of the land was too overwhelming to afford anything but a primeval, animal-like dignity to those who managed to survive it. Their babies never cried. Stories abounded: that the savages could not shed tears because they had no emotions, and thus were capable of the most outrageous tortures, of inhuman mutilations; that they faced their opponents with an insane bravery that meant certain death, for they went into battle holding magic pouches before them and incanting secret words to stop bullets that would not be stopped. When the savages died at the hands of troops, they were dismembered, dissected like specimens: Cutter had seen soldiers wearing dried scrotum sacks as snuff pouches and dried ears as decorations on belts and pared teeth strung in necklaces. But the savages the major and his troops had encountered seemed pitiable, even shy; they rarely appeared, and when they did they mostly roamed the old emigrant trail, scavenging as Cutter's troops were now doing, or trading with the luckless or the ignorant who had chosen to follow the long-unused trail, heedless of its silent, admonishing grave markers.

The savages, after Cutter and his troops first arrived at the outpost, sometimes encamped outside its walls, set up their wickups, lazed about, and traded with the sutler, who took pelts from them and in return gave them glass beads, corncob pipes, moth-eaten blankets.

Cutter had an interpreter then, a mountain man of indeterminable age who had ridden into the outpost one day and remained for several months, bartering his skills with an axe and his knowledge of the savages' tongue for whisky and food. Together, Cutter and the mountain man sometimes walked among the encamped savages and were greeted by their shameless, bare-breasted women, by silent babies, by gaunt men mounted on painted ponies. The major saw that some of the savages were pockmarked and others rickety. He did not understand how they could take such delight in trading for worthless articles. The interpreter translated small talk for the major, but never framed the questions Cutter felt were important; indeed, the man on one occasion laughed derisively at him. They don't have words for what you're telling me to ask, the interpreter told Cutter. They got no words for faith, or history, or time. Ask them about rain instead. Or hunting. Or the shape of the hills seven days' ride from here.

The major wanted to know the savages' beliefs, their past, their customs. He argued with the interpreter. They must, Cutter insisted, have some notion of how they came to be, who their ancestors were, who they are.

Go look at their wickups, the interpreter replied dismissively. You'll find what they know drawn on them. There's mountains and stars. The moon and clouds. Grass and trees and horses. Lightning. Dogs in abundance.

Cutter found the drawings—stick figures and animals, circles, squiggly lines, arrows, mountain peaks, spirals, leafless trees, handprints, eyes—incomprehensible.

They must believe in something, Cutter insisted.

Who cares, replied the interpreter.

Dr. Matthews does not visit Cutter that evening, or the next, and the dust storm does not abate, though it wanes, then gales, then wanes again. The troops have to be threatened before forming details now, the sand is blinding, the men wrap anything they can find about their faces, their necks; they rip apart rotting trouser legs and shirtsleeves and undergarments and wind these about them so that all that can be seen are their eyes, and sometimes even these are covered. The sutler has disappeared, the washerwoman as well; the smithy's fires go unlit, Abigail Buwell is forgotten. The major loses track of time, of days, the nights, he neither undresses nor dresses; the cur urinates in the corners of Cutter's quarters unless pushed outside, then paws the door and whines; the blown sand blasts the walls, forms dunes on sills and porches and against doorways, floats like scum atop the water in the basin, sinks to the bottom of Cutter's water pitcher, irritates his gums. Cutter pores over the quartermaster's two ledgers, one complete and one not, both of which were brought to him, unasked, by Cole; and the major does not know which surprised him more, the man's unnerving way of anticipating him or his fearlessness, for Cole had gone into the dead man's quarters. Which no one else would do. Since the quartermaster's death, the troops have refused to enter the place, make it habitable, secure the roof, the planking, roll the dirt floor, erect bunks; they refused even to pilfer the quartermaster's, being of one mind that what had killed him was embedded in the walls, the beams, the ceiling, in dust and mold, and unable to forget the horror of his screams, his ravings, the extraordinary violence of his solitary end.

Even Cutter found himself leery, opening the ledgers and turning their pages, felt himself shrink from touching them. But more disturbing than the thought of contamination, and far more fascinating, were the quartermaster's entries, and not just those from the end of his life, during his illness, but those from months before: on almost every page, among the more sensible entries—lists of supplies, their cost, their distribution, their weight, and the names of the troops, their dates of birth, ages, the childhood illnesses they had suffered, the length of their service, their hometowns, and the dates of their burials, notations of desertions—the quartermaster had inserted drawings, doodles, and fantastical accounts. The major tries to recall the quartermaster now, tries to remember if he ever had an inkling that the man was capable of entering a receipt for five thousand ladies' silk scarves, a hundredweight of knitting needles and several top hats, or a ton of green hock bones (inedible, the quartermaster had recorded, for the lack of peas with which to cook them). These imaginary entries were summed at the improbable cost of three dollars and sixty-five cents and accompanied by several drawings of otherwise naked women wearing scarves—some knitting, others punctured by knitting needles—as well as sketches of a hock bone crowned with a top hat; and Cutter studies these in amazement, for he cannot remember the quartermaster as anything but serious and competent, if a bit dour. Cutter peruses over and again the quartermaster's lewd drawings of animals copulating, of men leering at women raising their skirts, turns over entirely blank pages under the heading "Penmanship" and other pages filled with childishly drawn stars. There are accomplished caricatures as well, of Matthews sawing at limbs, of Hastings kissing a mule, of Cole hanging from the gallows, of Cutter perched upon an island as large as his buttocks and no larger, staring at a half-sunken ship. Under which was written: *'Twas not Crusoe who said no man is an island.*

The quartermaster's last entries fill only a few pages of the second ledger: by the dates recorded, the major knows, the man was then ill. His handwriting, previously neat, begins to sprawl, to curve, to rise and fall, in disregard of the faintly drawn lines the quartermaster could no longer follow or see; the letters become disconnected. He writes thirty times: *Fear green eyes, for through such prismed glances curses befall.* And a dozen times: *The wounds of murdered men perforate and bleed again when their murderers pass their graves.* And once: *Appalling this all-encompassing darkness, wherein blacker thoughts loom.*

It is the last cogent entry, for on the following pages are incomprehensible words, perhaps entire phrases, made up of letters that together bear no meaning: *Sktlwe gnoot 3btowq ecwqibbd.* And: *777 mbrs lkmbeeee.* On several pages there are nothing but question marks, some written backwards, some upside down, some large, others small. And then there is nothing but for one page on which appears a series of intertwined spirals, on the bottom of which in the tiniest letters imaginable is scrawled *Aaaaaaaaaagggggghhhhhh.*

Cutter thinks to burn the ledgers.

It is against regulations.

He turns the pages backward, forward. Let them see this, he decides, let my superiors take a look lest they forget what happens to a man's mind when it is severely strained. For it has been a long time since the war. He flips to the quartermaster's last page of spirals, turns it, takes up his pen and writes: *The foregoing page marks the last entry of Quartermaster Josiah Hendricks, d. of spinal meningitis, date unrecorded. Buried in uniform one-half mile from the west wall of Outpost 2881, may he rest in peace.*

Cutter puts the pen down, thinks to close the ledger, stares across the room at the brindle cur that seems more dead than alive in repose, turns another page, takes up his pen again. *In memoriam,* he writes as a heading. And then, below that: *Outfitted and dispatched today, 24 troops including Lt. John Hastings, on hunting detail, with provisions for three weeks. Also provisioned in like manner 10 troops, for scavenging the emigrant trail, for a maximum of eight days; as there are no other officers, appointed Gerald Spillway as acting sergeant. The following per diem, except where noted, accorded each man for the number of days noted above:*

8 oz bacon
16 oz hardtack
2 oz coffee
2 oz sugar
3 oz peas or rice
Salt
Pepper
Vinegar
3 candles per man, for entirety of mission
1/2 bar soap per two men, per entirety of mission

Hereinafter recorded, to the best of my knowledge, are the sundry holdings of Outpost 2881, as of this day, including those mounts provisioned to the hunting and scavenging details.

78 horses
14 mules
50 saddles and girths
56 complete bridles, with bits and reins
8 hackamores
39 halters
5 sets of double traces
2 sets of quadruple traces
Two wagons and tongues, for double traces
One wagon and tongue, for quadruple traces
44 empty barrels
Uncounted metal pails
4 iron stoves
Cooking cauldrons in various states of repair
1/2 ton nails, various sizes
10 ton cordwood
4 ton planking
c. 80 pr horseshoes, unfitted
15 saws
34 hammers
29 large axes
35 small axes
2 rusted Gatling guns, inoperable
1 inoperable cannon
27 cannon balls

Several rotting piles of clothing
More rotting piles of discarded & soleless boots
Army issue uniforms: none but those being worn
24 boxes hobnails
30 boxes brass buttons

Unconfirmed / whereabouts unknown:
5,000 silk scarves (ladies')
A hundredweight of knitting needles
Several top hats
1 ton green hock bones

The cur whimpers in dreamsleep. Cutter pauses at the sound, looks at the dog and then at the door, the walls, for he is suddenly aware the wind carries with it a sound he has never before heard, a hushed but ominous drone, and then he hears a voice calling and a shout in return, both as though from a great distance. The dog stirs and gets to its feet, shakes itself, then curls its tail between its legs and cowers. For a moment he is unsure whether he has imagined the voices, but Cutter puts his pen down and closes the ledger and pushes his chair back, wiping at his eyes—the dog whining now and turning a circle and then another—and stiffly shuffling to the door as he hears the now unmistakably frightened calls of men, the panicked neighing of horses. He pushes open the door and, dragging his leg, painfully steps out into the whiteness of blowing sand, the cur at his heels inexplicably loping off and disappearing. Cutter squints and humps beyond the barracks, his knee sore, sees the sentries in the swirl above him, pointing, shouting. The fear in their voices confounds him as much as the flies do, for there are flies everywhere bandied about by the wind, and he swipes at them and climbs the ladder and gains the walkway along the stockade, shields his eyes with his hands.

What he peers at in the distance, what the men are pointing at, is a darkness spilling over the endless horizon with the solidity of a breaking wave. For a moment Cutter is reminded of a tornado twisted upon its side, and he becomes as terrified as the sentries, for their panic is contagious. The blackness does not right itself, it broadens, as if far beyond and riding at an ungodly pace toward them are the savages, thousands of them, mounted on galloping horses that are kicking up vast clouds of coal dust; but then the major realizes that the band of darkness is purely airborne, for deeply slate-tinted stains discolor what he knows must be above the earth. It is as though the flaps of the grim reaper's flimsy garments were extended vastly across the sky; and, indeed, the gloom has already begun to take on ghostly shapes. It's the end of the world! one of the men yells into the wind, and the sentries scatter, half-flying from the walkway, dropping to the ground and running for shelter, flailing their arms against the onslaught of flies. Bugler, bugler! Cutter wants to cry out, but the outpost no longer has a bugler or—as far as he knows—any bugle. And then he spins around, amazed to hear a bugle's peal, to see Cole below, braced against the wind and blowing the old horn, his cheeks distended with effort. Cole blows the distress signal again, and Cutter turns back to look over the stockade at the horizon, hoping for a sign of the wood and grazing details, hoping the troops beyond the oupost have seen what is coming toward them.

They'll hear the bugle if they're near, Cole yells up at him, trumpeting the notes once more. And then the doctor shouts into Cutter's ear, for Matthews is beside him. Good lord, Matthews cries, get inside! What is happening, what is this? Cutter screams into the wind, but the doctor is already descending the ladder. When Matthews calls out something from below, the major cannot distinguish his words. Cutter's knee almost folds under him, he barely manages the ladder; on the ground, he steadies his legs and stands, surveying the seemingly deserted outpost: the sutler is nowhere to be seen, the troops have barricaded themselves within the barracks— crushed, surely, in that mean space—the leantos are empty, Matthews has disappeared. Only Cole remains, yelling that he needs help to open the gates. Cutter heads for the barracks, butting his head into the wind, flailing his arms at the flies. When he bangs on a door the men inside open it only a crack, and Cutter orders someone, anyone, to come help open the gates, and finally someone obeys, squeezes through the door, and he and Cutter manage to make their way over to Cole, heave the crosspole, and let the gates blow open. From beyond them comes the sound of racing horses, and Cutter and Cole and the soldier jump back as the animals materialize, wild-eyed, frightened, bucking. The grazing detail troops scream to one another to leave them uncorralled, leap from their mounts, push the gates closed, and put the crosspole in place before running for shelter, leaving the milling, frantic horses and Cutter and Cole to fend for themselves.

Take cover, sir, Cole yells at Cutter, and is gone. The

major fights his way through the wind, the flies, and when he reaches his rooms he struggles with the door. Inside, he pushes his weight against it, latches it, and realizes he has no idea where the cur is. A droning vibrates in the room, flies are crawling in through the cracks, through the opening at the base of the ill-hung door. Cutter tells himself to forget the dog, gets a blanket from his bed, kicks it into the space between the door and floor as best he can as the droning grows louder, now accompanied by a pelting sound not unlike hail thudding upon soft earth.

Cutter finds that his hands are trembling. He is drenched in sweat. By the time he uncorks the cognac, the flies are pushing into the cracks he will not be able to seal, working their way through the slatted ceiling, the badly chinked walls. He slaps at them with a neckerchief and ties a rag around his head and keeps the open mouth of the cognac bottle covered with a palm. He thinks of Lt. Hastings and the hunting detail, somewhere beyond the horizon; he tells himself they are days away from this plague of insects, as is the scavenging detail—whose whereabouts he can only surmise—and unlike the unreturned and unprotected wood detail. The flies thicken in the room, and Cutter corners himself on the floor, the rag on his head, bottle in hand, letting the cognac dispel the raging pain in his knee and lessen the fear gripping his insides. He waits, listening for the dog.

I begin, Lavinia, to despair that we are removed beyond the rational world: here even nature acts in the most unpredictable, unnatural of ways and in the most destructive, and I can hardly hope to fully describe or give meaning, if there is any, to what we yesterday beheld and suffered. I found myself wracking my brain to recall incidents of pestilence from the past, remembering naught but those that mention locusts; of flies I could think of no examples.

Lest you think I am quite mad, the air, my dearest, was yesterday fairly screaming with the sound of buzzing, and the horizon was scaled black with flies. The pests came like an evil fog lying over the land, and for what seemed an eternity they drowned out even the sound of the wind, which was surely howling. Everyone barricaded themselves behind shut doors, even the washerwoman who, I later learned, managed to gain entry to the sutler's place and hid within his store: I've seen hide nor hair of either since. The doctor and his wife shuttered themselves as best they could, and I stuffed a blanket under my door so the creatures would not invade, but they were relentless and crawled through the cracks in the walls, penetrated by way of the ill-chinked ceiling, and were everywhere, so that I had to bear their crawling over all of me. They came so thickly as to layer one upon another, crushing themselves; I have never seen such a thing before and hope never to witness it again, for the sound was dreadful and the millions of these creatures terrifying. If you were here, you would have surely died from fright: Mrs. Matthews, being compromised for so long, is now contending with the shock of it all, and the doctor fears for her life. Dead flies littered the grounds of the outpost inches deep, and those near death continued to buzz loudly; we could hear them inside the lungs of the horses and mules they had suffocated, drowning in the liquid filling their lungs. Would that it had rained, or been freezing; either, I believe, would have weakened the pests, diluted their onslaught.

I feel my own inward spirit growing weak. Winter is not yet upon us, but the frost of old age is not quickening; of this you would not know, being younger than I, being eternally young. I could barely bring myself to leave my quarters after this plague swept over us, to face the consequences of it, and the dulling pain of my old wounds bears no comparison to the ache within me that has no physical cause, which has not been lessened by the dreadfulness of what lay outside my door. The flies that could no longer take wing covered everything, their repulsive droning so insistent that the troops were terrified to leave the barracks, and one man was driven almost mad by his fright. I am sure the smithy, who is a man of action, saved as many of our horses and mules as he could by clearing their breathing passages; but three horses and two mules were beyond saving and died what must have been an agonizing death. The grazing detail managed to return before the flies descended in the millions, but the wood detail had no time to do so before this curse was upon them; they managed to free the mules from their traces and huddle under the wagon, and they wrapped their shirts around their faces so they might breathe, though they say the flies were so thick at times they feared for their lives even with this protection. They found the mules and the horses in a circle, their noses to the center and almost to the ground, and not an animal perished. The mules were unruly thereafter and it took some time to put them back in the harnesses and then drive them through the coal-black landscape that almost immediately began to shimmer with the white dust that is being carried by ceaseless winds, now much diminished. Of the fate of the hunting detail, and of the scavenging detail sent to ride the old emigrant trail, I cannot but despair. And now cannot but wait.

I have never seen so dismal a sight as this forsaken land and the pitiful state of ourselves within it.

In this disaster, I am ashamed to admit, I almost completely lost sight of my role as commander. If this outpost were a ship wrecked upon high seas, I would have abandoned it and left its sailors to flounder, to drown. I have been stunned by the realization.

I had the misfortune of having to strike one of the troops. They are hard pressed to keep their wits about them, have succumbed to a stuporous hysteria that leaves them wallowing in superstition and increasingly resistant to duty. I would fear them to be mutinous if I did not find them so dispirited. They do not know that I have written to my superiors, asking what it is we are doing here. After suffering what I can only describe as a dreadful assault of nature, which can only be construed as the worst of signs by even a sane mind, and having been relegated to this forsaken place for far too long, the soldiers are surely asking themselves the same question.

In the turmoil before the pestilence descended, and in the turmoil thereafter, I—unforgivable, this—forgot Abigail Buwell, the redeemed captive who has remained with us and is with child. It was only when she appeared, wandering about stunned and disoriented, trailed by the horse that is her protector, that I realized she was left to fend for herself: of all of us within the outpost she was the only one without shelter. That she survived perhaps indicates that she has seen such travesty before, or worse, for she has long been in this wilderness with the savages; but her condition was palpably worsened by the experience, and upon contemplating this I am amazed that she did not birth from the shock alone. She has crawled into a corner hay rack, however, and the horse that accompanies her everywhere allows no one near that end of the stable now. I quite fear for her sanity, and, more and more, for my own.

Ah, Lavinia, a man of my age needs a hearth and a home. As you know.

Dr. Matthews, it is certain, will leave with his wife as soon as she is able to travel, and perhaps they will not even wait that long. I will then be bereft of the only companionship I have here, and it is no comfort to think I will be alone but for my books, some cognac, and a young lieutenant—how I long for Hastings' safe return— whose sense of duty must surely be strained, and the packets of your letters I hold so dear. To hear your voice, feel your hand upon my brow—oh, these wishful desires are unimaginable. To sleep peacefully, to awake beloved, this too is beyond even my wildest dreams. I am certainly falling apart, without news from you, without word of how our dear son is. I fear I have begun to suffer private hallucinations in this void. And I fear I am not even half the man, not to mention the soldier, I once was.

Ah, I am a sniveling, self-pitying wreck. Pay me no mind. By the grace of heaven, surely one day the mails will arrive, and perchance a scented letter written in your lovely hand, or a package from beyond. Until then, my dearest wife, until the post is reestablished and I can send you this letter, I remain your loving husband. And from thence forward, forevermore.

He drops his pen, looks at the page before him. Having always prided himself on the neatness of his hand, the straightness of the lines, the lack of ink drops and smudges, Cutter is annoyed to see that his script is not as perfect as it once was, and he wonders whether his wife will notice. No matter, he tells himself, and blows out the flame that illuminates the room. He sits for a long while without moving, though his joints ache, and tries to imagine the sound of his wife's voice, the shape of her face, the smell of her hair. Unable to conjure anything, he finally rises and feels his way to his bed, lies upon it, stares at the darkness. He is disturbed by the silence of the night, by the boy he again glimpsed leaning against the stockade, by the conversation he has had with Matthews in which they, for the first time, disagreed. For when Cutter told the doctor that he, Cutter, now had to ride out alone in search of the scavenging party, Matthews had objected. Send anyone else, he said.

I can send no one. For I can trust no one to return. Sending anyone else would be pure folly; he'd simply head for the hills.

Maybe not the hills, the doctor responded ruefully.

Well, then, anywhere but here.

There's no one to leave in charge, Robert. If you leave, the rest would be mounted and gone by the time you turn your back.

There's Cole, Cutter said. I could leave him in charge.

Matthews looked at him in astonishment. He weighed his words before speaking, then spoke plainly.

They'd never stand for it.

They wouldn't have a choice. He's a soldier, after all. A man and a soldier.

He's a smithy in their eyes. And less a man because of his color.

A war was fought that decided such things.

There are many who wouldn't agree.

The major glanced sharply at the doctor then. I'm not among them, Robert, he said. But if you asked the troops here what the war meant, they would say it was fought to hold a nation together. That's not the same as making them serve under a man such as Cole.

The nation stood for, stands for, certain things. And soldiers don't get to choose their commanders.

They're not very good soldiers, Matthews reminded Cutter gently. From what I can surmise, most of them are not even very good men.

That's a harsh judgment, one I am not willing to make.

Then assign someone else to ride out.

Cutter, feeling cornered, again stubbornly insisted he would indeed hand over temporary command to Cole.

You'll be turning the universe on its head, Matthews warned. And the troops won't stand for it.

You're wrong, Thomas. The troops left to me have been sorely tried by the worst of circumstances. They haven't seen decent food or clothing for far too long; they haven't been paid. But they're all I have, and I have to assume they would remain beholden to a sense of duty, stay loyal to their oath, serve any commander I appoint.

You know as well as I do, the doctor replied, that the men who are still here haven't the courage of their convictions, or they're misfits, or both. You know as well as I do, he continued, waving off the major's protest, that most of them are serving because they don't fit anywhere; they're drunkards, or they've abandoned their families, or they haven't any other vocation. Most of them are indolent, insubordinate, and would like nothing more than to vent their resentment in bloodshed. You've had to discipline most of them for flagrant infractions at one time or another—brawls, dereliction of duty, drunkenness, insolence. Today you had to strike one of them.

Cutter did not want to be reminded of this. He did not want to think of the incident, nor recall his shock at not recognizing the unruly and badly shaken soldier— Elias Carter—who looked hardly older than a boy and who baldly refused, in front of other troops, to hitch a team to pull the dead horses from where they lay, already bloating and stiffening. Without thinking, and infuriated, Cutter struck out. The force of the blow knocked Carter sideways.

No matter what else they might be, Cutter finally said to Matthews, they are soldiers. And being soldiers, they must believe in—if nothing else—honor and duty.

Robert, you've taken leave of your senses. There is nothing honorable about these men, and as for duty, they feel they've more than done it.

Good night, Thomas, the major responded. But Matthews would not let him go. Wait, he said, and poured them both a measure of whisky. After the second glass—ah, the major had thought, how lovely to hold a glass instead of a tin cup—and in the silence that softened the edges between them, Matthews announced that he wished to leave the outpost. I am afraid, he said, that Susan cannot suffer here much longer.

I'm afraid none of us can.

But her life depends on being treated. As you know what she means to me, you can imagine my frustration at not being able to do anything for her, not as her husband, not as a doctor.

Do what you must, Thomas.

I'll need your leave.

Cutter rose then, drained his glass, handed it to the doctor. You have it, he said, not wanting to say the words, not knowing whether Matthews would ever know how much his company meant. And not knowing whether their opposing views had anything to do with Matthews' request.

Cutter stares at the darkness in the room, longing for sleep. It will not come, no matter how hard he tries to empty himself of every thought, to will his mind into blankness.

Unbeknownst to him, Abigail Buwell's water has broken; she feels the wetness on her inner thighs, the warmth and then the cold of it upon her doeskin skirts, and shudders with the contractions she tries desperately to slow, to stop, writhing, biting her bottom lip until she tastes her own blood. When the child's head finally presses into her pelvis and pushes into the world, Abigail Buwell pushes it back with her hands, sucks her breath in with all her might, tries to pull the infant's unwilling body back into her own.

She battles the birth silently, pressing her thighs

together, gasping at the spasms, the pain. She hears nothing but the breathing of the horse below her, the songs of death she has learned to chant by heart, the wind. She would rather be eaten alive than let this infant be born, she would rather have her skin flayed from her and her body left to be devoured by animals until her bones were stripped clean than allow this hapless creature that is now clawing and kicking and slinking its way into existence, pushing out through the canal, come headlong into a world to which it does not belong. She places her hands on the crown of its head and tries once again to suck it back into her. There is warmth and wetness in the struggle.

It is born just after dawn. There is nothing more she can do to stop it, and though she cuts the umbilical cord with the knife she used on her hair, her scalp, she does not blow into the infant's mouth nor clear its nostrils. The afterbirth slides out of her, an excrescent, bloody mess, as the infant first wails. When she finally sees her second-born in the dawn's half-light, in the drift of dustblow carried by the now gentler winds, Abigail Buwell moans in despair and takes it from between her knees and cradles it, undoes the robe about her breast and gives it suck. Its eyes are rheumy with dust, their sightless orbs black as flies.

She will give it no name.

It will not live.

Ten

With the passing of the moon cycle that wreaked its pestilential havoc, the light shed by pinprick stars in the midnight skies hued bluish and the nights were colder. The indifferent and canopied universe above the outpost became even more immense, and more distant, with the moon's disappearance, and the troops within the stockade felt much diminished by the expanse above them. Sentries shuddered on night duty, chills not unlike cold fingers played upon their spines and raised the hackles on the backs of their necks, they thought strangers danced on their graves. They grew ever more morose and superstitious, imagined sounds that left them disturbed for hours on end, feared their own unrelenting isolation, hated the decrepitude of their existence, felt themselves starving. Their threadbare clothes and uniforms, even after being washed in the boiler cauldron by Maria, retained the stench of their unwashed bodies, their armpit and crotch sweat, the acrid odor of the coal fires they bucketed in their quarters and of woodsmoke that rose nightly from the pits over which they cooked. The little bacon left to them was rancid, the hardtack moldy, the suet wormed, and the beans weevily. Their teeth loosened in their heads. They could not for the world fathom what had become of the boys they once were.

The major had not ridden out in search of the scavenging party, nor had it returned. The winds died, and sand mottled with dead flies was swept out of the stables, the barracks, the empty chicken coop, the doctor's quarters, Maria's leanto, the major's rooms, from everywhere but the former dwelling of the quartermaster, where none entered. The wheelbarrows were dumped beyond the outpost gates and their contents heaped onto the equine graves now mounded with the swept and carted fly-infested sands. The mounds spooked the sentries at night as they stared endlessly out at the rolling pitch of the indefinable horizon, and they could not say whether their minds played tricks or the mounds changed shape, taking on unearthly forms. The grazing detail was brought close by the outpost, the horses—pawing at wild grass nubs and finding little else to eat—grew thin; the wood detail was canceled. The troops lounged and slept and cooked vile meals, dug nits out of their hair, crushed lice between their fingers, played cards in silence for slivers of wood, scratched themselves so repeatedly they drew blood. From time to time the few who could read were summoned by others to do so aloud, but the magazine articles and dime novels made them sick with remembrance of the world that lay far beyond them. The readers were hushed soon after they began or lost their audience, the men about them rising one by one and perambulating senselessly, their deep-socketed eyes unfocused.

The sutler's place was closed and seemed unlikely to open ever again, and Ezekiel Pace remained cloistered but for his visits to the washerwoman. He glared at the men and spit whenever asked, when passing them by, if he could extend more credit and unlock his place, retorting that they had long ago bankrupted him. He took to carrying a pistol and sleeping with it, and the troops sensed that he was afraid, which fueled both their resentment of him—for their despicable meals being prepared from his rotting stores—and their delusions of what goods he might be secreting from them. Rumors abounded: barrels of corned tongue and salted beef, sacks of unspoiled flour, cured hams, a root cellar full of carrots and onions and potatoes, soap, candles. Some thought of breaking into his store, others of killing the man outright. The men stopped going to Maria even to have her wash their clothes, and she no longer flirted with them or asked them for money or favors; they had neither to give. They despised her liaison with the sutler, and they kept their distance and went about in filthy rags. The major did nothing about the company the washerwoman kept, nor about the troops' demoralized condition—and the soldiers hated him the more.

The hunting party had not returned. Neither had Bean, and the troops openly told one another they would have done the same, ridden out, taken their chances, headed east until the horse or rider or both gave out, never come back. They peered over the stockade and thought to themselves that no one would ever return. More of them deserted, taking the best horses, and those left behind swore the savages and the devil could have this worthless spot on earth; they knew no emigrants would ever pass this way again and feared that their own fate was simply to become vulture feed and buzzard pickings. They wandered about the confines of the outpost with great unease, their indolence reinforced by their decline and anxiety, and in their resentment they became explosive, dangerous, illogical. They wordlessly glared at Abigail Buwell and the sickly infant she dragged about with her, and to a man—except Cole, whom they shunned—were convinced that her return from captivity had everything to do with all that had befallen them.

As she first suckles the infant, wiping the dust from its dark, sightless eyes, something tears apart inside of her. The sensation is physical, exhausting, dazing. Abigail Buwell feels herself cleaving like a slow-splitting tree, its trunk holing, its bark gnarling about an unaccountable emptiness; she feels herself becoming a shell around a petrified wound. When the infant ceases to feed, it does not cry, does not close its eyes, does not gurgle or move its limbs. It simply lies in her arms and breathes.

The horse paws once below her and raises its head, tilts upward a curious eye. She lays the naked infant on the raspy straw and it does not protest, then she knifescrapes her robe free of the afterbirth as best she can and cuts away a piece of her skirt and gathers into it the bloody mess and folds the corners of the doeskin and pushes it away from her, then takes the infant up again. If she were among the savages, there would be a ritual cleansing, an herb-scented fire, women preparing bowls of steaming, leeched acorns mixed with suet and pemmican, as when her first child was born. She banishes the remembrance of that other birth, of the birthing place, makes it drain from her, wills it to disappear into the emptiness within her. She closes her eyes, listens to the rustle of the animal below her, the movements of the black man who busies himself near the roan, finds solace in the strokes of Cole's hammer, the whoosh of his bellows, the scalding hiss of redhot metal being thrust into water; and she drifts upon these sounds and upon the songs he sings quietly to himself, to the blue roan, to her, until she is aggrieved by an outrageous hunger and rights herself, the babe unprotesting. When she descends the hay rack, she holds the infant in one arm, the folded doeskin in the other hand, and the horse pricks its ears and puts its nose to the newborn's belly and blows gently upon it, then follows her past Cole, who straightens and simply nods in the direction of the tin plate. She glides past him and puts the doeskin down and eats with one filthy hand what is there, then takes up the parcel again and steps out into the light, the horse at her heels.

It is thus she begins what the men will consider a haunting of the outpost.

The brindle cur—which everyone, including the major, thought dead—appears from nowhere. It tags along beside her, sniffing at the doeskin, at her skirts, and then sits with its head lowered in curiosity, drooling and licking its jowls, as Abigail Buwell digs with her knife and her bare hands a hole in a far corner beyond the corral and buries the doeskin. When she has covered it with the loosened earth, she then places stones on it, making a mournful, cooing sound the while. What she has interred is that which kept the child alive within her, and it is both holy and a torment to her. For what this placenta once nurtured, she knows, the world will not long sustain. Beside her, for an instant, stand the infant's father and brother. Both touch her face, where the red circle on her cheek has begun to fade, and then they are gone.

The major suffers a melancholy he cannot fathom and from which he cannot surface. He pours over the strangest and most incomprehensible of the dead quartermaster's scribblings, feels unable to leave his rooms, forces himself to do so. Outside his quarters, he witnesses the stupor of the troops, winces inwardly at Matthews' packing, turns away from the sight of Abigail Buwell wandering the grounds with the skeletal infant in her arms. He is stricken at seeing—even in broad daylight now—the boy who appears and disappears before his eyes. Cutter tells himself that he has become morbid, that he is surrounded by a morbidity he must escape. To avoid sequestering himself in his quarters and yet evade the troops, the sight of Matthews readying for departure, the redeemed captive and the apparition that haunts him, Cutter begins to spend part of each day exercising the chestnut gelding he has had for seven years, riding the outer walls of the outpost endlessly and solitary but for the sentries who stare down at him from their stations and the closeby grazing detail whose troops at times lift their eyes to watch him, then look away. Try as he may, Cutter seems incapable of recognizing a man among them or of remembering their names, and so he does not look at them as he puts the gelding through its paces, repeatedly circling the stockade, studying the sheer emptiness of the landscape that stretches away from him in all directions.

He always wonders, circling the outpost, whether he will ever again see the world from which he came. The barren vista makes him long for forests of pine and spruce and maple and birch, for mountains echoing with birdcry, for cascading streams and silent ponds, for meadows bordered with mossy stone walls and ringed with chestnuts and oaks; and he longs for farmhouses and barns, homesteads and hamlets, for graveyards—yes, even those—where headstones demarcate the final resting places of the dead, where urns are potted with fountain grass; he longs, in short, for any sight that will break the grip of this dreary infinity that daily unnerves and oppresses him. With its hostile space, its somber colors of gray and brown and mottled chalk, its horizons betraying no convexity and lying perfectly level, the earth appears so awesome, so flat that—were he not a logical man—Cutter would fear that Hastings and the hunting detail, the scavenging detail, Bean, and all deserters had simply disappeared into it, had actually fallen off its edge.

The appearance of savages would be a relief to him. But on this day, as on all others, there is nothing. Cutter scans the horizon one last time before giving the chestnut its head, and the horse stretches its neck, drops its nose, plods the length of the outpost wall, carries him within the gates. He sees Cole walk toward him. And then the boy materializes, grabs the gelding's bridle. Whether Cutter spooks the horse or whether the chestnut sees the apparition hardly matters, for at that instant the gelding rears and throws Cutter, whose boot catches in a stirrup. He is dragged by the panicked horse before Cole manages to catch at the reins and pull the creature to a halt. Cutter disentangles his foot and, shaken, remains in the dust.

Can't say I know what happened just then, Cole tells him, just as Cutter is about to demand: *Did you see it? Did you?*

Looks like the horse just spooked, sir, Cole adds. He reaches a hand down and Cutter grips it, is pulled to his feet. Brushing the dirt from his unwashed clothes, the major shakes his head and thinks: It's time I tell Matthews about the boy.

You might stop by the doctor's, Cole suggests before he begins to lead the still-skittish chestnut away. He was looking to speak with you.

Matthews had only wanted to tell Cutter that they were packed, but that his wife has taken a turn for the worse and could go nowhere at the moment. I can only pray, the doctor says, holding Cutter's wrist over a porcelain bowl and watching the major's blood drip into it, that she'll rally.

Cutter insisted upon being bled, but he cannot bring himself to tell Matthews about the boy, who is now everywhere—walking the corral's top rails with his arms outspread like wings, turning cartwheels among the troops, rolling barrel hoops beneath the sentries' noses, perching on top of the walls, leap-frogging over the cur, invading the corners of Cutter's rooms, appearing and disappearing—and maliciously, this day, grabbing the chestnut's bridle.

Matthews bleeds the major every day for four days, though he does so reluctantly. The doctor has no leeches, so each time he punctures a vein and holds the major's wrist just so, lets the blood flow, applies pressure around the puncture until it closes. That's it, Matthews says this last time.

I'm not sure what's ailing me has been purged.

I'm not sure what's ailing you, Matthews tells him, is a matter for purging.

It's the prescriptive for melancholy.

There are better things.

Such as.

Such as, Matthews sighs, taking command of the situation here. Cutter meets his eyes evenly, then shakes his head almost imperceptibly. No, Thomas, I've relinquished that.

You're not allowed that privilege. Lives depend on you.

There's nothing I can do.

There is, the doctor says gently. The men are purposeless, the wood supply is dwindling, they need to work the coal seams. Without wood they can't cook, and without coal they'll freeze to death when the season worsens.

We'll all die from starvation before then.

Lt. Hastings will return, Robert.

I doubt it.

If you doubt it, you've got to make other arrangements. I assume you don't want to be held accountable for the deaths of your men.

I've been accountable for so many deaths, for which I honestly believe I'm now suffering a terrible debilitation that is twisting my mind, that I can't imagine a handful more would make any difference.

It might make all the difference in the world.

The major says nothing. After a long moment Matthews rises from the chair, drags it over to the wall, raises a hand in farewell, goes toward the door. When he opens it, Cutter's voice arrests him. Thomas, he asks, do you ever see things that are not there?

Matthews turns about and looks at him curiously. Never.

The trouble is, Cutter tells him thoughtfully, neither do I.

Lavinia, I can now only think that Bean, that Lt. Hastings, that the scavenging detail will never return. Indeed, I am beginning to doubt that anything exists beyond this place except within the recesses of my false memory. My troops ride off into the distance and, no matter in which direction, are never heard from again; they are swallowed by the vastness of the landscape and vanish without a trace. I can't say that I recognize any of the remaining soldiers. Matthews will leave—and this brings me great sorrow—tomorrow, or the day after, or the day after that. The supply wagons will never come. I hide in my quarters, throw my waste from the doorway into the stench beyond the steps, want no food and little water, touch the walls with my hands when I move about as if terrified of losing myself to whatever vortex surrounds this place and sucks everything into thin air. If I had the courage of my conscience I would abandon this outpost, and instead I seem to cling to it. Never in the midst of battle was I ever so immobilized, so powerless as now: for in battle I understood life and death. Now there is only this terror, my own, which I cannot control.

The apparition—yes, an apparition—of a boy, the same which has haunted me outside my quarters for so long, has now moved within, and I have no way of escaping. There are nights when this thing falls upon me in my sleep, puts its head on my chest or runs its small hands over my face, and other nights when I awake to find it enshadowed in some corner. I have heard it breathing, I have smelled its child's breath, the sweetly sickening scent of its flesh. Think not that I suffer mere nightmares, my dear, for though what I describe has the quality of a hateful dream it is not made of such stuff: the child also appears at random to me in the light of day, I can sometimes sense its presence and when I turn there it is and then is gone, this small and ferocious and unspent spirit that appears to none other, who haunts no one else, of that I have no doubt. What I do doubt is my sanity, for I think I have been singled out by a vision created by my own disturbed mind.

I made Matthews bleed me, to no avail. I think often of our poor Henry, for whom, even in his worst moments— when trussed to a bed or bound to a chair, when being purged—I never felt the slightest twinge of sympathy; for I found his derangements, quite truthfully, incomprehensible. Now I fear that I know their source: for surely *there is some long hidden fault within my character, one he inherited and suffered from all his life. I am hardly comforted by this, though you might find it a relief to know that what we always thought a mysterious and aberrant affliction surely springs from my loins, and that neither he nor your family is at fault. I pray, as you can imagine, that Henry is well. I have no news, of course, of him: would that he were with you, that he might not suffer so. And would that I were with you, for the same reason.*

If only you could send me a sign, a word. If only Lt. Hastings and his troops, or the scavenging detail, or Bean would return. If only Matthews would not leave; if only the supply wagons would arrive; if only I could face my superiors and resign this command. If only—

Eleven

Major Robert Cutter looks up to find Abigail Buwell standing framed in the doorway, the naked infant lying limply in one crooked arm. His pen is still in his hand.

Come in, he says.

What hair remains on her shorn head is filthy. The once perfect red circle on her cheek is now not more than a smear beneath the grime. Her hands and forearms are caked with dirt. Her garments are foul. The infant does not move. And she does not step forward, comes no closer than where she stands.

The smell of his own waste wafts in from outside. Cutter pushes back his chair as if to rise, then remembers his breeches are undone, unbuttoned, and so he eases back down and reaches for his suspenders and pulls them over his shoulders instead. He feels the emptiness in his stomach and then an extraordinary pang of hunger, as though he had just awoken from a comatose starvation, rubs a hand over his face, feels his breath catch in his chest, brushes the hand holding the pen through the air as if to clear a cobweb. It is a gesture of apology, and of despair, but if Abigail Buwell understands this, she gives no indication of such.

I'm sorry, he says then. I've neglected…I've been very remiss.

There is a slight sideways movement of her head. He cannot be sure of her expression, backlit as she is. The infant does not move, does not cry. He wonders if it is dead. Wonders if she will speak.

She says nothing.

He finally looks down at the letter before him, then sets down the pen, gathers the loose pages, puts them beneath the ledgers and logbook on the corner of his writing table, clears his throat. Your child should be seen by the doctor, is all he manages to say.

She stands very still, as though weighing his words. And then she is gone. He can hear the plod of the roan as it follows her.

Cutter does not look himself in the mirror when he gets up from the chair, retucks his shirt as best he can with the suspenders over his shoulders, buttons his breeches, pulls his boots over his holed socks. Then he puts on his frayed jacket but pays no mind to fastening its buttons, and when he leaves the room he is momentarily amazed at how weak his legs are, how like air he feels, how blurred his vision is. He squints against the waning light and breathes shallowly the cold air, walks with an uneven gait past the men crouching before the firepits, as unheeded as a ghost among them. They are as unshaven as he, their threadbare clothes are as filthy as his, and they too could be ghosts, for they are much like shadows of their former selves, thinning on their heels, raising their heads to reveal bony faces and hollow eyes before dropping their gazes again.

Only Cole salutes him, standing by his unlit forge, a man the color of night darkening in the evening shadows. Cutter returns the salute, draws himself a bit straighter, winces at the pain in his knee, hesitates. You'll find her with the horses, Cole says, and Cutter continues on around the stables, sees the much diminished herd, almost walks into the washerwoman. Roberto, she says, startled, casting a look over her shoulder toward the leanto and then says, in a louder voice, Major. Cutter looks beyond Maria, to where the sutler is disappearing into a blanketed doorway.

Cutter brushes past her and at the boiler cauldron pauses and kicks dirt onto the cold ashes beneath it. Maria is suddenly beside him, tugging at his sleeve, but he pulls his arm away and stoops and puts a hand to the ashes, rubs a bit between his fingers, then straightens and looks at her. The men are in a terrible way, he says. She shrugs, tosses her head of black hair.

They don't come for washing, she tells him. They can't pay.

You don't work for money right now.

Her mouth opens, closes. Her eyes slant sideways to the leanto, back again.

Tomorrow morning you go get their clothes.

Maybe they got nothing to wear if I do.

I don't care.

And your clothes, Roberto. Will you give me them, she leans toward him, her voice dropping to a whisper, so I could wash them first, before the others? You could come, you know, and sit inside, for I could wash you too.

Maybe this time you would like it.

I'm sure I'd find it crowded.

Oh, him, she says dismissively. He's nothing to me.

That's good, for tomorrow he'll have nothing to give you.

Cutter regrets this the moment he says it, then thinks: Let her tell him this. Let him panic. Let Pace fear that, tomorrow, everything left in his store will be requisitioned, taken, distributed.

The washerwoman studies Cutter, furrowing her brow, then pouts. You talk nonsense, she complains. Feel free to repeat what I say, comes his response as he looks away, singles out the blue roan beyond the corralled horses.

She's crazy, the washerwoman says. When Cutter walks away from Maria, she runs to her leanto and goes inside. The roan raises its head and flattens its ears, but Cutter does not go near it, for Abigail Buwell is not sitting by the horse but inside the corral, with her back against a fence pole. He stoops and steps through the crosspoles and walks toward her as the roan begins to prance and snort beyond the corral railing. She rocks the infant in her arms and does not look up at him until he bends over her and puts a hand on her wrist. Come with me, he says, and she gets to her feet effortlessly and allows him to lead her among the horses that swish their tails, crook their necks, swing their hindquarters around. Her horse trots to where they exit the corral, and as Cutter trusts the roan not to hurt her, he puts her through the crossrails first. She raises a hand to the horse and it stops in its tracks, jerking its head back, comes no closer, does not follow them. When they pass by the troops, the men look up, openmouthed, and stare. She stinks worse than we do, one of them says. Others rise and spit on the ground, then hunker down before their fires, their messes, as before.

Cutter knocks at the doctor's door and Matthews opens it. The major catches a glimpse of the doctor's sleeping wife, her head at an awkward angle, the skin on her thin face stretched taut, the slit of her mouth slightly open. Matthews stares over Cutter's shoulder at Abigail Buwell and is appalled when the woman turns away, dangling the infant from one hand like a useless rag doll. Take her to your quarters, I'll come immediately, Matthews says, half-closing his door, and Cutter rushes after her, catches at the infant, places it firmly in her arms, guides her. The doctor follows so quickly that the three push into the major's rooms almost as one, Matthews blocking the door until one lamp is lit, then another. Cutter drags a chair toward Abigail Buwell, but she sidles to a wall and slides down against it, sits on the floor. Matthews crouches before her and puts his hands beneath the infant, raises it up, then places it again in her arms. It weighs no more than a handful of dry leaves. She does not look at Matthews as he bends to examine the infant, nor when he straightens, aghast at her suffocating smell. He takes a deep breath and holds it, then drops to his knees, places an ear against the infant's chest, exhales, breathes through his mouth and holds his breath.

The infant doesn't move. Its flesh is cool against his ear, but beneath the coolness Matthews can feel a surging heat. The faint heartbeat he hears is too rapid, too erratic, and masked by the fluid in the infant's lungs.

He raises his head and sees that under where the umbilical cord was knotted and pushed inward is a splotchy, suppurating welt. He speaks to Abigail Buwell then, asking questions that go unanswered and, he surmises, unheard. She turns her head away and he snaps his fingers near her ear and finally manages to get her to gaze at his hand, but then she turns her head from him again. She does not notice, never mind protest, when Matthews opens her robe, revealing her leaking breasts, the chapped nipples, the thin pinkish fluid that leaks from them, then closes her robes and lays his hands upon the infant. The major looks away then, the image of her breasts now within him.

Is the babe dead, he asks without inflection when Matthews finally rises.

Not yet, Matthews answers, gazing down at Abigail Buwell, then stooping to feel her brow. She does not recoil at his touch; indeed, it is as if she does not feel his hand. When he straightens again he looks at Cutter and opens his palms in a gesture of futility.

She needs to be bathed, this filthy thing she wears discarded. She needs to eat, to stop sleeping in horse dung. The infant—and now Matthews' voice trails off: he does not want to say the obvious. I can't say, he continues after clearing his throat, which seems suddenly parched. I can't say what will become of her either.

She is to be redeemed.

The bitterness in the major's voice astounds Matthews.

That's not what I meant, Robert. But, as a matter of fact, this place was to serve as her transition back to civilization, and she's been left to fend for herself. As have—and here the doctor pauses, thinking better of what he is about to say but then saying it anyway—the rest of us.

Cutter absently studies the closed ledger before him. I'll do what I can for her, he finally tells Matthews. Though I fear it will be little.

It would be something.

She does not resist when he tries awkwardly to wash her face, her hands and wrists, with a wet bandana. At first his attempts serve little purpose but to smear the dirt, but Cutter patiently wipes Abigail Buwell's face again, removing layers of caked grime, rinses and wrings the piece of cloth. He separates her long fingers, traces their outlines, strokes the length of her neck once more. A rivulet of mud streams down her throat, streaks below her clavicle. The pulse of blood in a vein arrests him, and Cutter stares a long time at it, then begins again. He daubs at her without a practiced hand, thinks enviously of how simply, how intimately, a cat cleans its young, realizes how inept he is. At no time does Abigail Buwell look at him, not even when he turns his attention to the infant and passes the cold, wet cloth over its bluish skin. He thinks to wrap the babe in something, but he has nothing save a blanket soiled with the sweat of his unwashed body.

He brings the blanket, and a piece of hardtack, but she pushes the blanket away and turns her head from him, clenching her jaw. He leaves the hardtack beside her. She closes her eyes, resting her head against the wall, and does not open them to watch him undress, standing away from her in the inner room, unhitching his suspenders, removing his shirt, his boots, his pants, all but the stained piece of long underwear that conceals his thin thighs, sagging buttocks, hollowing chest. His flesh itches and he resists the urge to scratch himself raw, instead turns and lies on his blanketless bed and tries to imagine her breathing, the rise and fall of her breasts. An intense exhaustion floods through him, as palpable as the cold. He finds it impossible to turn over his outstretched hands; though he struggles with this stasis, not unlike some sudden paralysis, he feels himself yielding to it, for Abigail Buwell's presence, he somehow trusts, will keep the boy at bay. When Cutter finally sleeps, he succumbs to the slumber of the dead.

Abigail Buwell awakes in the night to a soft neigh, listens to the horse move about beyond the walls, leans forward and crosses her legs under her, rearranges her skirts and lays the infant in the recess she creates. She does not know where she is for a moment, then remembers the man with brass buttons and the other one, the doctor, and the feel of cold water upon her skin. Her eyes grow accustomed to the dark within the major's quarters until she can make out the shape of the writing table and the open doorway to the other room, from whence comes the sound of male breathing, deep and harsh. The blanket is pooled in a heap beside her, and she reaches out a hand unthinkingly, feels the texture of rough wool, then pulls her hand back as if from hot coals—too late, for memory washes over her with the touch of it. She was clad in such material once, she can see herself as a child, feel the tug as hands pull a woolen dress over her head, smell the fibers that rub against her face, her skin. She does not want to remember, but she is powerless to stem the images, the sensations that flood through her: the snow in the streets, the feel of hand-knit stockings as coarse as the dress, the sound of women's voices still heavy and soft with sleep.

She looks down at the infant in her lap and runs her hands over its incredibly cold-hot thin body. It does not cry, but she remembers crying as the dress is pulled over her head, at the coarseness of the stockings on her legs, as she listened to the cadence of the women's voices. Her mother's hands are freezing to the touch, and her face is very near, her mouth unpainted, with dark smudges around her eyes. You'll have your own pony, her mother says. Your very own. Stop snuffling now, or he won't want you. And then you'll never get to have your own pony.

She doesn't want to leave this place, she doesn't want to leave her mother. This house, if it is a house—for it has many rooms, and many women live there—is better than the shack with newspapered walls; it is warmer, for there are many stoves, and it has a huge kitchen where she plays with the women who spill out of doorways and into the corridors just after dawn, their flimsy, fantastical cobalt and red robes flung around them and tied at their waists with long pieces of cord. Their breaths are sleep-sour, morning-smelling. They laugh as they warm themselves before the massive woodstove in the kitchen, the strong scent of coffee

boiling and tea steeping and bread toasting upon the
stovetop familiar. They chuck her under the chin with
warmed hands, tickle her, tease her hair into curls with
their fingers, fuss over her, light cheroots and blow
smoke rings and make her sip from their bitter dregs and
give her burnt crusts thick with butter. The men don't
come until the evening, and sometimes they take her
upon their laps. The one who slapped her at the circus,
the one who used to stay with them in the shack from
time to time and did things to her mother, never comes.

She stops crying. Her mother takes a satchel in one
hand and pulls her along with the other. In the long
corridor some of the women stand in their doorways and
watch wordlessly and blow her kisses. The kitchen is
still cold. It is her mother who starts the fire that day,
but before the milk is heated the man arrives, dressed in
black but for a white starched collar. The snow is
melting on his shoulders, on his hat. She buries her
head in her mother's robe when she sees him, clings to
her. Go sit at the table, her mother says, go sit with your
father. And unclenching the child's hands from her robe,
her mother pushes her into a chair. The women do not
come, and she sits, fidgeting, fighting the tears that well
up inside of her, stares at the steaming milk when it is
finally placed before her. A handkerchief of coins clinks
onto the table.

For god's sake, her mother says, then pockets the
bundle. Her hand works deep in her robe, fingering the
money.

You don't have to count it, is all he says.

No. Well. Her fingers stop; she sighs, turns her
back, busies herself with the stove. Go ahead, then, her

mother tells him, take her.

The man rises as the child places both hands around the steaming bowl of milk. He picks up the satchel and plucks the child from her chair, the bowl clattering to the floor, the hot liquid spilling. You'll have your own pony, her mother calls out, but the child is wailing, her voice filling the house and then the street, where shuttered windows open here and there at her cries and the snow falls thick and silent and the man lifts her onto a wagon seat and holds her there with one hand as he clambers up and pushes at her to make room and then takes up the reins, the dray's head jerking and its rump rising. They trot into the whiteness, and the house and the street and then the town disappears. The river they cross, over an uncovered wooden bridge, is choked with floes.

Abigail Buwell will remember that her mother told her the year and season of her birth, but she will never know the exact date. She will never be told the name of the town she was taken from, but she knows it was on a river. She will not remember, if she ever knew, her mother's name. She will be called her given name, Abigail, by the man in black and by his sullen, childless wife. She will learn to memorize scripture and to read and write and count, and she will be taught to pray, to spin wool, to weave, to sew, to cook, to pluck chickens and to dress slaughtered pigs and cattle, to churn butter and clean hen roosts, and to dread, above all, his visitations upon her in the depths of the barn.

She will not have her own pony.

She will not be given his, their, name. She will not go to school. She will be told repeatedly, when alone with his dour, mean wife, that she is the devil's own child. When he dies of influenza, in what the child counts as her fourteenth year, his widow will shortly thereafter give her to a man selling remedies from a horsedrawn cart. She will watch the coins drop upon the table and then take up the small satchel she arrived with seven years previously and, with those things in it left her by her mother—a child's handmirror, a comb, two hair ribbons, and an empty cameo locket, her only possessions in the world but for the clothes she is wearing—walk out of the house before him, without looking back.

Abigail Buwell reaches out and touches the wool blanket once again. This time she does not withdraw her hand, but feels its roughness and swallows hard, struggles to put her thoughts in order. She blows into the sightless eyes of her infant and then passes her free hand over them, charming death to come. This is no world, she finds herself whispering to the motionless babe, to be born into. No world at all.

Twelve

Report to Cmdr First Army
Re: Conditions at Outpost 2881

This dispatch is being delivered by Doctor Thomas Matthews, heaven willing, to whom I have given leave in the hope that he may save his dear wife's life. Susan Matthews has been failing for many months, and her health is so precarious that it is clear she will perish unless the good doctor can safely rejoin her, and himself, to civilization. You might consider my decision to release the doctor from his duties here to be highly irregular, but I have taken into consideration that he can no longer, given the present circumstances, minister to the troops with little at hand but his wisdom. There are no medical supplies left to us. It is true that Matthews is a qualified surgeon, but those things that now ail us can hardly be addressed by his scalpel, unless mercy killings have become the province of science.

In short, the isolation we have suffered and suffer yet is now a matter of life and death. With no supply wagons having reached us, we who remain here face certain starvation. Be advised that our numbers are few. A scavenging detail of ten, sent along the old emigrant trail, is long overdue and has not returned. A hunting detail of twenty-four under Lt. John Hastings is likewise long overdue: I fear both details have vanished. One man, charged with delivering a mail pouch to the garrison beyond Fort H, has not returned. Our numbers have been further reduced by 10 deserters, who took with them 23 branded horses some days after we were beset by a plague of flies, of which Matthews will report to you in person. The desertions are now a blessing in disguise, as there are fewer mouths to feed.

Accompanying the doctor, for his and his wife's safety and, in my estimation, to spare their lives, are another six troops. Therefore, we remain here, including myself, 16, plus the sutler, one washerwoman, and the redeemed captive Abigail Buwell. As to her situation, I can only describe it as deplorable. The woman gave birth to a sickly infant shortly after her redemption, and the babe has since died. The shock of her—unwanted—return and the loss of her infant have sadly affected her; and as conditions here have hardly afforded a modicum of normality to ease her transition to civilization, she has made no visible progress toward embracing her past way of life. She remains disoriented, speechless, and inconsolable; her adoption of the savages' ways seems to have left her completely transformed and incapable of functioning within civilized society. Whether she would survive, even under the best circumstances—none of which exist here—is, to my mind, questionable.

I can hardly pretend to any longer command a viable

military unit. Indeed, I daily question whether it is in the interests of the nation for us to continue here, in dire straits, in the name of securing a frontier that God knows we cannot secure and is so inhospitable, in any event, that it was forsaken by settlers and has long been avoided by emigrants wishing to push westward.

Please advise.

I realize that my tone is improper, but Dr. Matthews will surely describe in detail our present situation and my helplessness. I deplore the fact that the mission with which I was charged has become, for reasons beyond my control, impossible to fulfill, though I will hold my ground and continue to await orders, though I've little enough hope that any will ever come. Please rest assured that I intend to resign my commission and retire from further service as soon as humanly possible. Until that time, I remain, yrs truly, Major Robert Cutter

She does not lift her head from her arms when the scratching from his pen stops. He looks at her bent into herself, knees raised, back against the wall, sitting on the floor, far distant, lost to him, and thinks of those things he cannot write, things he has not written to his superiors. That the sutler is in chains, confined to the old chicken coop, his store looted, his skin jaundicing. That he himself has taken to latching the door of his quarters at night, locking in Abigail Buwell, for he believes her presence keeps the boy away. That she did not allow the dead infant to be taken from her but climbed atop the stable roof and left it to carrion birds, which no long swoop and settle, for the creatures are now uninterested in the small, mummifying body devoid of eyes and nose and tongue and entrails, its lungs and liver and stomach and intestines and spleen and kidneys days ago squabbled over, ripped away, gobbled by the squawking vultures. That she ascends to the stable roof whenever she leaves Cutter's rooms and sits for hours beside the infant's remains, singing in a strange tongue an unmelodic lament that sets the nerves of the troops on edge. That the stench of death is unbearable, that the infant's skin has blackened and split, dried and hardened: not even insects crawl upon it now that fluids no longer spill from its bowels and the hollowed cavity of its stomach. That, after her daily rites of mourning, Abigail Buwell has taken to riding the roan, lying her back upon its back or drooping her arms about its neck and dropping her head onto its mane as it wanders at will. That the troops despise her, believe that her redemption has something to do with the curse that has befallen them. That they look at the major sideways, throw glances of disgust at him as he trails after her. That his ship is foundering, its crew all but mutinous. That he suffers an ache in his chest whenever she turns to gaze at him from the back of the horse. That he sleeps deeply and dreamlessly now that he has taken to confining her within his rooms, that he wakes oddly refreshed as he did before the war, before the death of his brother, before he witnessed destruction on a scale he once thought unimaginable. That his beard is rough and his hands unwashed and his clothes stinking and his teeth loosening he no longer finds bothersome. That he has stopped fastening his brass buttons and attaching his collar and wiping his boots, and that he demands nothing of the sort from his troops. That he has lost all hope.

She raises her head at the knock on the door. Matthews comes in without waiting for a response, and she rises and glides past him, disappears into the light beyond Cutter's quarters. The major folds the report and seals it with wax, gets up from behind the writing table, hands it to the doctor. Well, Thomas, he says, swallowing the lump that has suddenly risen in his throat and clearing it with a cough, I leave it to you to give an oral report of all that has happened here, on our situation. I'm afraid I've painted a bleak picture.

You could do little else.

Cutter nods curtly, extends his hand. When the doctor takes it, he is shaken by the diminished, forlorn figure the major cuts, wonders if by the time he reaches civilization anyone here will be left alive.

Robert, Matthews pleads, come with us. Mount everyone, leave the outpost behind. There's not a man here who won't say that you did so in order to save their lives. There's not a man here who won't be grateful.

You know I can't do that.

Matthews knows and does not know. He hesitates, wanting to argue his point, but instead of speaking just shakes his head, clasps Cutter's hand the harder, releases it. And then it is over, and the two men walk out into the day. Six mounts are tacked, the soldiers beside them holding their reins. The wagon on which Susan Matthews lies has barrels of water and supplies lashed to its sides. The two horses in harness stand patiently, and two other horses tied to the rear of the wagon rest against each other's flanks. The remaining troops mill about, clearly unsettled, cursing their fate; the major chose from among them the strongest men, those whose skin did not hang from their cheekbones, those whose hands did not tremble badly, those he thought might survive, without deserting, the journey. The piece of canvas that serves as a shelter, poled above the wagon sides, sags. The air is cold and unmistakably tainted with the smell of death, of unwashed bodies, rotting breath.

The sutler is crying out from the coop to be released, to be allowed to leave with the doctor. From atop the stable roof, Abigail Buwell chants her atonal song. Susan Matthews is shivering under the blankets that cover her, her eyes eating into her face; piled about her are chairs and chests and cookware and more bedding. Cole busies himself with the harnesses, then checks the meager provisions carried by the motley entourage. It's time, Cutter says, but the men do not so much as swing into their saddles as climb slowly, with great effort, onto them. Matthews pulls himself onto the buckboard and takes the reins as the gates are swung open, and then salutes the major smartly. Without a word, Cutter salutes in return.

By the time the gates are closed, several troops have already dragged their belongings into the doctor's quarters, raising their voices and their fists to one another, threatening one another before the door. A boot is flung and hits someone in his temple, a gun is drawn and fired into the air, the men separate from one another and the disgruntled draw away snarling, carrying their bedding back to the barracks, back into the sutler's emptied store, as the two men who have won the doctor's rooms for themselves stand in the doorway, arms crossed, openmouthed, and dully watch the others retreat. Abigail Buwell climbs down from the stable roof and wanders about, the horse following her doglike. The men hiss at her, spit, raise their hands as though to slap at her, but they keep their distance, wary of the roan. The sutler howls, enraged. The major watches as Abigail Buwell passes, reaches the gate, runs her hands along the crosspole like one who is blind. The horse cribs at it, gnashing its teeth.

That creature would eat its way through for her if it could, Cole says.

It is exactly what Cutter was thinking.

Dr. Thomas Matthews will testify at the court-martial of Major Robert Cutter that he cannot explain why, in the report he carried, the major did not mention that the sutler was at that time in chains, that his store had been looted. Matthews knows from the tenor of the questioning that the court is not taking kindly to the arrest and detention of a civilian and the seizure of his property, and he surmises that Cutter could not readily admit in his memorandum to having imprisoned the man and allowed his troops to take what goods there were—mostly whisky, which Matthews knows could hardly have kept anyone alive but which certainly made their sufferings more bearable. He does not mention the liquor, however, nor that the troops behaved in true soldierly fashion after finding it, remaining in various states of drunkenness for as long as the supply lasted. He opines that the major certainly had every intention of restoring the sutler to freedom, that he believes the major imprisoned him for his own safety, that Cutter would see to it that Ezekiel Pace be fairly paid, in supplies or money, when the outpost was finally relieved. Matthews' opinions, incorrect though he knows them to be, are disallowed as evidence. What is allowed by the court is Matthews' recollection of events, which he states clearly: the sutler had refused to distribute what goods that remained because of the impossibility of payment. The doctor also testified that he felt the major had no recourse but to requisition the supplies the sutler had, as the conditions at the outpost were grievous, and that the sutler put up such resistance that nothing less than putting him in chains—both to empty his store and keep him safe—seemed necessary at the time. The court-martial reminded Matthews that it was not interested in what he felt, but in the actuality of the circumstances.

The actuality of the circumstances, he responded with gravity, was that men were beginning to starve.

The blame for that actuality, the doctor knew, was being laid squarely upon Cutter's shoulders. The sutler glares at the doctor throughout his testimony. Later, when Ezekiel Pace takes the stand, he will state that he had eventually been reimbursed for the goods that were pilfered, as well as for the liquor, the quantities of which raise eyebrows all around. But he charges that not only had he been unjustly imprisoned—having broken no sutlering laws, as he puts it—by someone with no authority to do so, but, worse, that he was denied his freedom as a civilian when it would have been possible to leave the outpost with Matthews and the accompanying troops. He will testify that his unjust detention was tantamount to torture, and that it irrevocably destroyed his health.

When asked the reason Major Robert Cutter had denied Pace's request to leave the outpost, the sutler said he could only explain this as punishment for having openly criticized the major's initial negligence of, and later growing obsession with, the redeemed captive Abigail Buwell.

Thomas Matthews was as startled by this as was the major, and the accusation gave him an unpleasant, uncomfortable feeling. Matthews had never heard the sutler say anything concerning Cutter and Abigail Buwell, and the doctor had no opinion as to what the relationship between Cutter and the redeemed captive might have been or became. Matthews was not called upon again to testify. And he sat sadly through the remainder of his day in court, unable to do more than nod in Cutter's direction and finger the black armband he wore in memory of his beloved wife.

The men settle into groups of twos and threes and curse their misfortune at being left behind, help themselves to the sutler's whisky, and watch Abigail Buwell wander the outpost, climb to the stable roof, descend it to lie on the back of the horse they both fear and despise. The drink dulls their garrulousness with one another, and they sit morose in the cold, on porches and on the few logs they have dragged about to serve as benches. Someone drunk enough pours more whisky into a filthy tin cup and rounds the far corner of the stable and returns with the washerwoman. Some of the troops clear a place for her on a log and she drinks with them, sitting shoulder to shoulder, hunched against the bite of the cold. Now and then a man gets up and goes over to the latrines, now and then a man throws firewood into a pit, now and then they glance over at the major's quarters, where the bonethin cur lies curled before his door, its ribs showing through its dusty coat. The liquor numbs the troops, their wrists and tongues loosen, they momentarily forget their contempt for the sutler, and after a time they let Maria bring a cupful of brew, then another, to Ezekiel Pace. After the third cup the sutler begins to sing sad barroom songs, in a surprisingly melodious voice, and the men study their filthy hands, the dirt under their nails, grow more despondent, drink more. Only Cole is excluded from their circle, and Abigail Buwell.

A lone vulture soars overhead, swoops over the stable roof, hangs low in the air on an uplifting draft, drifts away. That thing, what's left of it, ought to be buried, someone says. Makes me sick to know it's rotting up there. A few men nod, clenching their jaws, thinking on it. They settle their eyes on the stable roof, look away. Someone spits. They fill their cups, listen to the sutler, watch the vulture return. This time it descends, lands on the roof, hops over to the infant's body and cocks its scaly head to better peer at the remains. That's it, someone says, and a few of the men get to their feet and stand unsteadily. Maria rises as well, but someone places a hand on her shoulder and pushes her back down. She teeters on the edge of the log, rights herself, laughs.

Cole watches them come. They walk past him as

though he doesn't exist, but when he looks toward the major's quarters one of them stops in his tracks and snarls: This ain't none of his business.

That baby ain't none of yours, Cole tells him.

Yours neither.

Two men have already gained the roof. One is Elias Carter. At the sight of the half-devoured infant whose small body has turned a leathery greenish black, his stomach turns. As he retches, the other man, older by far, experimentally toes a limb with so little delicacy that it flops and twists unnaturally at the knee. He studies what he has done and contemplates that the body will fall apart if he tries to pick it up. We need something to put it in, he calls down to the men below. Carter straightens over his vomit, cleans the corners of his mouth with the back of his hand.

It is the washerwoman's shawl they throw up to him. They leave her sitting where she is and ignore the insults she screams at them.

Cutter opens his door and takes it all in: the troops milling about in front of the stable, the two men on the roof, Abigail Buwell astride the horse. Cutter watches one of the men lay the shawl over what is left of the infant, scoop up the remains, make a bundle, carry it satchel-like to the roof's edge, give a whoop and drop it onto the ground below. It thuds on impact, and the drunken men form a circle about it. Maria sways where she sits, screams curses at them learned from soldiers, from coarse men, from the sutler. Ezekiel Pace sings drunkenly at the top of his lungs. Cole walks out from under the stable's shadows, and Abigail Buwell rides her horse slowly over to the outpost's gates.

The men move toward Abigail Buwell, with Elias Carter in the lead. It is a slovenly, imbalanced procession bearing flesh and bones in an old shawl. Cutter steps away from his quarters to intercept them, and as he approaches the gates the blue roan snorts, tosses its head nervously, lays its ears back. The men pause, swaying on their feet, out of reach of the roan, unsure how to get around it and open the gates. Shoot the goddamn horse, someone says. Cutter pushes his way between the men and Abigail Buwell, and Carter steps forward, comes close enough so Cutter can smell the whisky, the vomit, on his breath. He holds the bundle before him and shifts his weight from foot to foot. There is something disconnected in his eyes that reminds the major of a rabid dog. This is the soldier he struck, Cutter realizes then.

Get her to move off, Carter says, slurring his words.

The major blinks.

Remember your rank, Cutter warns. Someone guffaws. Cutter looks at the men behind Carter, takes in their bloodshot eyes, their unsteady stances, their grizzled beards, the gaunt lines that cut deeply into their cheeks, the dark circles under their eyes, their matted hair, their mismatched, filthy outfits, and he is appalled and deeply shaken and unexpectedly frightened, for they seem to him hardly human. And he thinks: This is it, this is how it will end.

The men begin to mutter. Carter's head jerks violently several times; the tic is so severe that it leaves a trace of froth in the corners of his mouth. We're getting rid of this, we're opening these gates and taking it out of here, he says. Move her off.

Put it back on the roof. That's an order.

Carter toes a line in the dust with a boot whose sole is split, turns and looks at the men behind and on either side of him. Goddamn, someone grumbles.

An order, Cutter repeats. Everyone else, disperse.

No one goes for his throat, no one shoots the horse, and then his waiting is over, the explosive moment of mutiny Major Robert Cutter dreads is defused. The liquor that goaded the men on now weakens their resolve, and they slowly drift away, singly and in pairs, to drink more, fall into stupors, pass out where they will, awake hungrier than they awoke this day, become angrier, become weaker. C'mon Carter, someone says, but Carter shrugs the man off without looking at him and stands where he is until he is the only one left.

It ain't right, Carter says, dropping the bundle into the dust at his feet. Cutter hears the horse snap its teeth just behind his shoulder, hears the sutler singing at the top of his lungs: *And she pulled her petticoat to her knee, I saw all that I could see, and the drinks were on the house, on the house, on the house, boys, the drinks were on the house.* You ain't right neither, Carter tells him.

The major feels, suddenly, exhausted. His legs tremble, his palms sweat. He is glad that his breeches hang off him, hide the tremors; he clenches his fists, stands stockstill for a moment, then throws a punch that lands squarely on Carter's cheekbone and knocks the man backward. Carter catches himself from falling, rights himself, takes several unsteady steps, turns on his heel, staggers away. Abigail Buwell slips off the horse's back, brushes past Cutter, scoops the bundle into her arms, and walks toward the stable. The roan skirts

Cutter and follows her, swishing its tail. When Abigail Buwell passes Cole, the man touches a finger to his forehead as though touching the brim of a hat.

At the major's trial, Elias Carter will testify that he was struck several times, fully in the face, on two occasions by his commanding officer. He will say he in no way refused to follow orders, but questioned such, and that he was greatly humiliated by the unwarranted blows, especially in consideration of the poor conditions that prevailed at the outpost, the blame for which he laid squarely on the major's shoulders. Men need to be led, he will testify, by officers they respect. That's what soldiering is. I had no respect for Major Robert Cutter because he led us down the path of demoralization; he could not even beat respect into me. I would also like to point out that I held fast to military discipline by not knocking him down, or worse.

Thirteen

Maria's shawl will be found the next morning, tied to a corral crosspole and flapping in the wind, spooking the horses to huddle in the far corner. The washerwoman will retrieve it with a stick and burn it. The infant's body, which Abigail Buwell had returned to its place on the stable roof, will be gone. It will never be found, weighted with a stone and sunk as it is into the putrid and liquefying muck of a latrine trench. The troops will be uneasy at its disappearance, they who wanted to rid the outpost of it, and not one of them will step forward to brag loudly or to whisper guiltily: It's done, I took care of it. This leaves them oddly shaken, suspicious not of one another but of forces they cannot name, not because they remain half-drunk—which they do—but because profound desperation has a way of making human beings cling to the irrational. The men's superstitious natures unhinge them, and eventually everything becomes a portent: the hawk that plummets from the sky, dropping dead before the quartermaster's place; the way grains of sand settle in their tin cups; the shapes of clouds that skipper across the sky. To all they give meaning, and they awake in the dead of night beside the fires to see their mothers' faces in the glow of coals, they stop flipping cards for fear of turning up with the joker, they no longer look at their palms if the lines on them end far above the wristbone. When they gaze upon remote stars they no longer recognize the clusters, constellations they could once distinguish; the heavens' once decipherable symmetry now seems pure chaos; and in their worst imaginings they conjure in the night sky's patterns an end to its edges. They believe that demons drawn in the corners of old maps actually lurk beyond a finite world, that the outpost sits in the center of the universe, that farther than what their eyes can see there exists a nothingness inhabited by monsters. They read their futures by examining the bloody rivulets that foul their feces, by the sores that break out and suppurate on their ankles, by the gnarled roots of the teeth that drop out of their mouths. To ward off the evil of such signs they tie colored strings around their fingers, keep odd-shaped stones in their pockets to protect them, hang rusting nails tied in crosses or their own teeth about their necks. No one can say what is real or, more exactly, what is unreal, and in the lethargy and drunkenness that define them they stop remembering who they had been, and fail to imagine what they can again become.

And so on the morning that Abigail Buwell discovers that the body of her infant no longer exists, the men tell one another: She disappeared it. Or, worse: She fed upon it. She sits that day in silence upon the stable roof next to where her infant is no longer, so that they cannot forget her, cannot push her from their minds. They watch and run their fingernails along their shirtseams and crush the lice they find, they pick at the scabs on their scalps, they drink heavily. When at day's end, in the eerie descent of dusk, Abigail Buwell begins to wail, the unearthly sounds that tear from her throat raise their hackles, make the mules kick at their stalls, silence the sutler's cries for food. Maria wanders the grounds with her hands over her ears.

Abigail Buwell wails into the darkness, long into the night, the unsettled horse below her pawing and turning endlessly. As her voice rends the air, she beats her face with her fists, tears at her hair, scratches her cheeks, bites her hands. She wails until she is hoarse, and then she weeps, and then she rants.

Cutter treads every square foot within the outpost, looking for a disturbance of the earth, for a shallow grave, for the infant's bones. He finds nothing. He questions every man, and every man, to the last, denies he had anything to do with it. Not even Cole, who the major knows to be prescient, sheds any light upon the mystery.

Though he is the only man who can.

When in the middle of the night Abigail Buwell finally loses her voice and, exhausted, can no longer mourn aloud the travesty that befell the unnamed and disappeared infant whose spirit will now never be released to the skies—for her beliefs are those of a savage, a body must be placed above the earth and allowed to lie face upward until wild birds and the elements have reduced it to nothingness—she sits in the cold, under the remote and lifeless stars, stunned by the lucidity that has begun to course through her mind and by the resignation that drowns her soul. Below her the lathered roan quiets and cools, the fires die out, the men sleep their drunken sleep. The sutler raises his voice once, calling out forlornly for Maria, then begins to sob from within the chicken coop; but for this, there is no sound in the universe. When Abigail Buwell finally rises she can barely discern the shapes of the sentries who no longer keep watch sleeping with their backs against the stockade, and beyond the top of the wall the darkness stretching to the immensity of the even darker place that must, she knows, be a horizon. She stands alone, unconscious of being silhouetted against the night sky, and listens to her breathing, feels the pulse of blood within her rise to her throat, hears her heart. She is nothing but this, the sum total of a body that is not yet dead, surrounded by death. The infant she willed unborn was born and in death vanished; she could not guide its spirit to the other world; there is no brush of a hand on her cheek where the circle once was. She tenses and waits, but they do not come, neither the man who fathered her children nor the child she left behind; there is not the faintest hint of them, they who have been with her until today, until tonight.

There is only the boy, sitting quietly on the roof's edge with his back turned, dangling his legs: but he has no truck with her, he exists for the man who fears him. She gazes at him and blinks: now there is nothing. And because she knows that those beings that haunt the earth are never dead—the dead do not return, only the living can assume other forms, become otherworldly manifestations—she is deeply and with great clarity aware that the man who drew the circle upon her face and the child who once clung to her robes no longer inhabit the universe of the living.

She wants to die. The void within her is vast. She breathes and pulsates and is yet alive. When she finally climbs down from the roof, she stands for a long time by the blue roan, all that is left to her but the robes she wears, and she runs a hand along its wet neck, buries her fingers in its mane, lets go. She does not lead the horse to the corral and bed herself there as she once had wished, among the horses, to listen to them move about, feel the reel of the earth beneath her back, watch the turn of the receding heavens in this moon of distant stars. Instead, she goes to the major's quarters, moving through the darkness like a somnambulant, the horse plodding behind. Before she opens the door she catches in the corner of her eye a fleeting impression of the boy, skipping.

Major Robert Cutter has a blanket about his shoulders. His drawn face is ghoulish from the light cast by the lamp before him, grooving it, reflecting red in his eyes, illuminating the bones of his forehead and cheeks, the nostrils of his long nose, the skin below his chin. He pauses from his writing, holds the pen in midair, watches her close the door behind her and sit where she chooses, on the floor, her back against the wall. She raises her knees but does not place her arms about them, does not lower her head onto them. Instead, Abigail Buwell looks at him.

I am making a list of good and evil, he says. She turns her head from him, but he doesn't notice she has looked away, or he does not care, or he assumes she does not understand.

I find it difficult to think clearly these days, Cutter continues, except with a pen in hand. Not that it's possible to make sense of what appears to be perfectly senseless. I'm not a man of faith, after all: the mysteries of life always provided far more questions than answers, but unanswerable questions are intolerable if one is given to logic.

He looks at her pensively. Who would have thought I would find myself in the middle of nowhere, clinging to what little sanity I have, plagued by the inexplicable, and making such a list? he asks. She rests the back of her head on the wall then, looks directly at him once again. Surprise flits across Cutter's face, is gone; he blinks several times, as if uncertain of what he sees. I confess, he tells Abigail Buwell, that when you were first brought here, I thought I heard you speak. Now I don't know whether you did. I don't know whether you understand anything at all. I had a daughter who would be about your age, had she lived. Just this moment, I thought you were her.

He is suddenly horrified to think that he has imagined undressing in Abigail Buwell's presence, revealing his caved chest and protruding ribs, his milkwhite abdomen, his bony hips, his flaccid sex, lank thighs, puckered scars, the nubs of his knees, his thin calves, bloodless ankles, gnarled toes. He has fallen asleep, at times, thinking of touching her, not his wife, not the washerwoman; he has imagined performing slow, flat-footed pirouettes naked before her, shivering in the lamplight, turning round and round to some unhurried and measured rhythm born of awkward primordial dance perhaps signifying nothing, certainly less of a mating ritual than an expression of the pure impotence he has long felt. Cutter slept well after such fantasies. Especially because he kept her within his quarters at night, at first holding a dying infant on her lap and then alone; and it was when she held nothing that he longed to strip before her, shed all inhibition, disregard the contempt with which he holds his aging, forget his sense of utter futility, his rank, the boundaries of behavior. He cringes now at the desire, aghast that he allowed himself such fantasies because Abigail Buwell's passivity, her otherness, her captivity here—for was she not a captive, within his charge, and defenseless?—struck an anarchic chord within him, released his mind, allowed him to imagine a lewdness he had never allowed himself with any woman. His heart pounding, his breath short, the pain in his chest delightful, the stirrings within him as magical as recovered youth.

Cutter meets her gaze, follows the flickering light that plays upon her cheek, her throat, her clavicle. He wants to weep for his dead daughter, his dead children. He passes his hands over his eyes and groans.

I'm afraid, he says, I have made a terrible mistake.

Abigail Buwell is never to know what he means by this remark. She will remember it, and the timbre of his voice as he spoke these words to her, for the rest of her days. What he says now will come to her again—not often, but in the least expected moments: at dawn when she awakes on a hard wooden floor in the asylum, at the moment she is thrust into one of many curative ice baths that cure her of nothing, at times when she is bound into a straightjacket, once in a dream.

At this moment, Abigail Buwell merely surmises that the major has confused her with his dead daughter, and she feels nothing at all, as if she is disembodied: for his memory and his confusion do not belong to her. Later, she will come to think of his pronouncement as a perfectly lucid if grievous epiphany, a dire judgment upon his entire life. She will pity Major Robert Cutter long after she is taken away from him. By then, she will know that for her, as for him, it has all been a terrible mistake.

She spends her days disconsolate, the horse she loves her only tie to a past otherwise lost to her, wandering the confines of the outpost. The men no longer hiss or glare or spit at her, nor brush the air with their hands as though to rid it of her smell, for their senses are closing down, their eyesight dimming, their hearing fading, their minds numbing as much from the liquor that is the mainstay of their sustenance as from their hunger, which has diminished as their stomachs have shrunk, their flesh wasted. She passes from time to time more closely to them or sits the walkway above them, where none bother any longer to climb, and listens to them, not rediscovering words—for she remembers her first language—so much as allowing these to displace the tongue she will never again speak. At other times she crouches near Maria's quarters, content to watch the washerwoman sweep her earthen floors, sprinkle them with water, trod upon them with her bare feet despite the deep, still cold that has settled over all. On two occasions, slowly and with as much strength as she could muster, Maria dragged wood to the pit beneath the boiler cauldron and fired it, once to boil the dirt from the blankets she hangs in her doors, once to launder her clothes, but at neither time did she so much as speak to or acknowledge Abigail Buwell, for she had not forgiven her the loss of her shawl and, besides, she considered the redeemed captive a savage. She tolerates the woman's presence so long as she keeps herself and the horse, of which Maria is terrified, at a distance.

Only Cole can approach the blue roan. Abigail Buwell has heard him speak to it, seen him palm his hand outward and wait for the creature to put its nose into it, watched him stroke the horse about the eyes, touch its neck, mane, withers. He says no words to her. His separateness, his isolation from the men, from the washerwoman, his silence with her, his way with her horse, his color, reinforce her belief that he is the embodiment of another's soul, and he becomes for her hallowed and unquestionable. She rejects nothing he gives to her, not the encrusted beans from his cooking pan, not the pieces of moldy hardtack; she accepts food from him as though it were an offering from the netherworld, though how he comes by it is hardly as mysterious as the fact that he and only he seems not to suffer the ravages of the others. For though he has become gaunt, the smithy has not stopped mending his clothes, has not stopped shaving or washing. He goes about his diminished business, bellows his fire, checks the horses and mules for lameness, repairs pails, water buckets, pots, pans, bits, stirrup irons.

Cole always acknowledges Abigail Buwell with a silent nod. He watches as her face heals from the scratches and the bruises fade from the bites on her hands; he notes that her scalp has healed, that her hair is growing in, that there is a clarity in her eyes, an expressiveness to her face. She will never know that he does not speak to her because of his color, her sex, her color. Nor does she ever learn that he buried her infant as best he could, carrying the shame of it to his grave so as to save Major Robert Cutter from certain mutiny. Thereby saving, he knows until the day he dies, his own life. Which surely would have been taken in any confrontation between the major and the troops.

Fourteen

The court-martial will examine Major Robert Cutter's papers, paying great attention to copies of his reports to the commander of the First Army, his entries in the dead quartermaster's ledgers, the unkept daily log, and the occasional copy of his unsent letters to his wife. Its members will be distressed and displeased by the absence of all orders and directives received by Cutter, but they will be more deeply troubled by one particular page they find in the ledger, bearing the title *A List of Good and Evil*. They will argue among themselves the import of this page, and in the end they will agree that it must weigh heavily in their determination of Major Robert Cutter's state of mind during the outpost's time of crisis; consequently, it affects their verdict. Even those unsympathetic to the man, those unforgiving of his behavior, cannot but in the end admit that any fair judgment as to his fate must take into account his deteriorating mental state.

The ledgers and all other documents pertaining to Major Robert Cutter's command at the outpost will be sealed after his court-martial for, per court order, fifty years. They will be destroyed in storage, by a fire twelve years after his trial.

Good: reads his first entry. *It is known that the earth is round and that it revolves around the sun. Evil: Knowledge can mean absolutely nothing. Here there is not a curve to the horizon in any direction, we can feel no turning under our feet even though the sun comes, goes, the night comes, goes. I cannot but suspect, like the ancients, that many have fallen off the face of the earth.*

Good: I am a man. Evil: I am less the man I ever thought I was.

Good: I am alive. Evil: I no longer know the difference between life and death. Life is a matter of presence, and death a matter of absence. But I am absent from the rest of the world, all of us here are absent from the rest of the world: Are we not dead?

Good: I am not alone. Evil: I hide from those with me here, for in their company I am more isolated than if I were the last man on the face of the earth. Evil: I am alone.

Good: I am an officer who has served his country in war and peace. Evil: The war stole from me those I loved, and there is no meaning to peace.

Good: I love my wife. Evil: I cannot remember the sound of her voice.

Good: I command a frontier outpost. Evil: I command a frontier outpost.

Good: reads his last entry, before—and this the court-martial will never know—his interruption by Abigail Buwell, *Our lives will eventually be judged by the higher Being who created us. Evil: Neither His temperament, nor His judgment—given what it is He managed to create—should be trusted.*

Fifteen

It is Cole who suggests that they slaughter the mules. He finds the major leaning on the corral fence, chin resting on his forearms in the posture of a boy looking at an idyllic summer scene. The blanket has dropped from his shoulders, lies pooled behind him in the dirt. Cutter is thinking not of an idyll but of having been reduced to eating horseflesh when Cole speaks up.

Cole tells him that they should kill two mules, the weakest and the most ornery of those remaining. That they have no choice. That after a few days of solid food the men might begin to recover their strength. That in a week's time they might be strong enough to ride. That the horses and mules left would last the troops a trek of several weeks, some to be used as pack animals and others for riding and the rest for killing and eating along the way. If departure is the major's intention.

Cutter has never eaten mule or horse before. He doesn't respond to Cole. He tries to remember what he has read of the vagaries of starvation, the strangeness of the human appetite. He recalls tales of a colony that starved from want of flesh though there was an abundance of seafood at hand: as meat-eaters unaccustomed to living by the sea, they disregarded the mussels to be culled from the shallows, the clams to be dug, the crabs walking about, the tunny fish schooling just beyond the shallows; they turned their backs on the bay, the straits, and resigned themselves to starvation after their animals sickened and died, after their seeds rotted in the saline earth, rather than reap the seashore's harvest, rather than continue in miserable isolation. He has read of sailors unable to swim, but so loath to eat fish that they would risk their lives, risk drowning, to go ashore and gather turtles, reptiles, birds' nests. He has heard of emigrants stuck in winter snows, cannibalizing one another rather than eat their dogs. Cutter works his mouth and studies the horses in the corral: he is not hungry, he has forgotten what hunger is. The troops won't eat these animals, he thinks.

The men don't have any choice, Cole says. There's nothing else.

The major leans back, drops his forehead onto his arms, peers down at his broken boots. He has no strength to kill and skin and butcher a rabbit or a chicken, least of all a mule. He reflects that he wouldn't have enough strength even to cook such a thing.

Have the washerwoman fire her cauldron, Cole says.

Abigail Buwell and the washerwoman are the only two who see Cole shoot the mules. He does so separately, thoughtful to bring the first alone, with blinders and a halter on, behind the stables, near to Maria's quarters. He keeps as much distance as he can from the corral, talks to the animal, strokes it. The mule's ears are back, the creature listens intently as if trying to understand. Cole feels profound regret: this is the oldest mule, one now debilitated by age, one that Cole has with great consistency given the least tasking work—as a saddle animal on the grazing detail, which demanded little of this most sensible creature—until the mule began, on occasion, to buckle under even the lightest rider's weight. When he shoots it, Cole does so standing beside it. The one bullet piercing its brain drops the animal onto its knees, Cole's hand yet on its neck. And then it keels over.

The second mule, though blindfolded with a rag, is more problematic, for it can smell death. The men always complained the creature was ill-tempered and dishonest, and Cole knows both to be true, whether from former abuse or from a constantly sore back or whether from character, he cannot say. But now the animal is frightened, sensing the other mule nearby with blood pooling blackly about its head. The blindfolded mule bucks and dances until Cole manages to grab and twist one of its ears, and not until the mule's head is almost underneath him does the creature begin to calm, paying more attention to Cole's visor-like grip than to its own fear. And at that point he shoots it, the gun so close to the mule's head that there is a smell of scorched flesh, and the mule drops cleanly, as if a thread that had been attached from it to the heavens were severed.

The washerwoman comes with a knife. Cole has his own. He does not look at Abigail Buwell, nor at the roan, nor at the other horses that mill about nervously at the far end of the corral. When he finally looks up from the flaying, Abigail Buwell and her horse are no longer there.

Much later the men straggle toward the smell of boiling flesh. They stand openmouthed and drool, weave on their legs, stare at the hide and severed head and hooves and tail and legs, the enormous pile of bloodied, bluish guts, the bloodsoaked ground, before making a wide circle around these. They watch Cole manage to pulley the one partially butchered mule, hook it, hang it. They watch the washerwoman stoke the fire. They wander away, return with their tins and spoons and forks, hunker down, wait, raise their noses and sniff the air like bird dogs. By the time the meat is ready to serve, some of them have even had the presence of mind to scrape their plates clean, rub them with sand, wipe their spoons and forks and knives on their ratty shirtfronts.

There is no salt in the thin broth, but no one complains. The troops drop onto the ground as soon as they fill their plates, they burn their mouths with the first bite or the first spoonful of steaming liquid, but they do not care. They eat too quickly, as though they will never eat again, without looking at one another. They barely chew the meat and they slurp down the broth, let it spill onto their chins, their shirts, then get up silently and fill their plates again. They eye the second mule's carcass, now dangling in the cold. Their stomachs swell, they feel as though their insides are crawling with blowflies, but they refill their plates again and eat until they think they will burst. When they can consume no more, some of them crawl back to their places and others stagger throughout the outpost as though drunk. Later they vomit and roll about the ground, groaning in pain as the gases in their intestines churn and their bodies suffer the shock of having to digest what cannot be digested.

The sutler is saved from such agony, for Maria brings him only a small amount of broth, as much as she herself has consumed. She tells Ezekiel Pace to drink it slowly, listens to him whimper and slurp. From where she sits, she can see the major's door is closed, and she knows from the horse standing before it that Abigail Buwell is within. Is it good? she asks the sutler. He responds with more slurping sounds, lip smackings, a belch, and then she rises and returns to the cauldron. A few of the troops have crawled back, sit cross-legged around it, and with their fingers bring small pieces of meat or bones they suck for the marrow to their mouths. Maria does not look at their round, ghoulish eyes as she walks past them and fills a tin bowl, then leaves them behind and makes her way to Cutter's quarters.

She has never been inside, but she does not knock. She pushes the door open with a foot and shoulders her way in. The lamp glows on the writing table, the major sitting behind it; Abigail Buwell is on the floor, her back against a wall. The washerwoman ignores her, walks boldly forward, puts the tin on the table and her hands on her hips.

You should knock before entering.

I have only two hands.

One will do. To knock.

She bites her lip, hesitates. Roberto—

Don't call me that.

You should let him out now. The men have food,

their bellies are swollen, it's not his fault there was nothing left.

For a moment Cutter is nonplussed. The odor of the meat seems rank to him, and he pushes the plate as far away as he can. Pace is none of your concern, he says.

I ask you a favor. That's all. Once you asked favors from me.

Something akin to anger flashes through his eyes and then is gone. A tint of color rises beneath the graying pallor of his face. Abigail Buwell rises and walks out the open door. He listens to the roan plod after her. The washerwoman does not move.

Cutter pushes his chair back then, places both palms on the table, examines the backs of his hands as though he has never noticed them before.

You were paid, Cutter finally says. There were never any favors. Pace is a thief and a liar. He stays where he is until I decide otherwise.

She folds her arms. Maybe you decide otherwise fast.

I don't think so.

I think so. Or I will tell the men how you are, not even a man. You take your clothes off and poof, nothing. You want just to touch, to look. Maybe I will make them laugh, maybe I will tell them you do the same with that crazy woman. Maybe they will tell your wife.

Maria knows she has gone too far, and she takes a step back as he rises. His knuckles press white against the table, and for a moment she holds her breath, afraid that he will come around it. He does not, but there is something in his face, a set to his mouth she has never seen before.

Pack up, Maria. This outpost has no need for you anymore.

She looks about her, frightened, then back at him. Her voice cracks when she speaks, and her words are barely audible. But their clothes, she says. I'm their washerwoman.

You leave tomorrow, Cutter says harshly. The men have no clothes left to wash.

Sixteen

Two days after the washerwoman disappears into the horizon, melting into nothingness with a mule Cole helped to provision, the major begins to read to Abigail Buwell. He peruses the texts of official dispatches, citing passages to her before destroying them, but one—ordering, in no veiled terms, the definitive suppression of the savages—he reads aloud to her in its entirety, then rereads it silently before he burns it, the paper curling black and the ashes falling into the washbasin.

He also reads to her the accounting of the outpost's supplies, he reads to her copies of reports he has sent to his superiors; he reads aloud the names and ranks of men the quartermaster once recorded, he reads the lunatic entries in the quartermaster's ledgers and shows her the sketches; he reads passages from his unsent letters to his wife. But he never opens the packets of old letters from Lavinia, never reads his wife's words to Abigail Buwell; nor does he read to her from his only living son's few letters. These he destroys.

Whether she understands anything, Cutter cannot say. He does not know that she often wants to cover her ears with her hands to stop the words, that she feels their onslaught at times as a violation. Her skin absorbs them, they flow through her body, they lodge deep within her. In the night she hardly sleeps for the shape, the taste of them; they cluster and break free within her, float and sink in her soul, bubble and burst in her mind. They absorb her, exhaust her, prick her memory; and she does not want to remember. She listens because she can do nothing else, and sometimes she is moved by the beauty of the words, and at other times she is stirred simply by the sound of them—the words pomegranate and delicacy, for instance, remind her of cascading water—and even when she wants to glean no meaning from what Major Robert Cutter reads, even when she wants his voice to be nothing other than a voice, she cannot help but take in the words, feel them reclaim her. She says nothing at all, eats sparely of the broth and meat, wants not to live, and wishes she could strangle this language he speaks, silence it, keep it from stealing back into her in the dead of night.

The savages divined meaning from bird chatter, eagle screams, owl hoots, raccoon cries, fox yips, deer and mountain goat bleats, dog whines, grouse chirps, horse neighs; they believed that the bear and otter and buffalo spoke the world into existence when they first encountered one another. The savages taught their children that the first words enunciated by humans were sung, echoing the languages of birds and beasts; Abigail Buwell too learned these songs. They said that even after the most clever of men had devised ways to speak only to his ilk, the animals laughed, for they too knew mankind's language; and their laughter made mountain winds sough and rivers sing and streams burble and trees whisper and canyons echo, the sounds soft and harsh and guttural and whistling and haunting.

She listens to the man whose brass buttons go unpolished and feels bitter sorrow, for she knows she will never again hear the language of animals, of the savages.

Ah, Cutter exclaims, the blanket hanging about his shoulders, I have found it. Listen. This is Clarence's nightmare:

> *Methoughts that I had broken from the Tower,*
> *And was embark'd to cross to Burgundy*
> *And, in my company, my brother Gloucester;*
> *Who from my cabin tempted me to walk*
> *Upon the hatches...*
> *Methought that Gloucester stumbled; and, in falling,*
> *Struck me, that thought to stay him, overboard,*
> *Into the tumbling billows of the main.*
> *Lord, Lord! methought, what pain it was to drown!*
> *What dreadful noise of waters in mine ears!*
> *What ugly sights of death within mine eyes!*
> *Methought I saw a thousand fearful wrecks;*
> *Ten thousand men that fishes gnaw'd upon;*
> *Wedges of gold, great anchors, heaps of pearls,*
> *Inestimable stones, unvalued jewels,*
> *All scatter'd in the bottom of the sea:*
> *Some lay in dead men's skulls; and, in those holes*
> *Where eyes did once inhabit, there were crept*
> *As 'twere in scorn of eyes, reflecting gems,*
> *Which woo'd the slimy bottom of the deep,*
> *And mock'd the dead bones that lay scatter'd by.*

Melanie Wallace

Abigail Buwell watches him read, his brow furrowed, his face deeply creased by the flickering lamplight. When Cutter stops he does not look at her, but retraces the lines with a finger, his face a play of shadows. When he finally looks up, he sighs. I have had similar dreams, he says thoughtfully. Not of being locked into a tower, waiting to be murdered; not even of drowning; but of being pushed overboard from a ship. No, he corrects himself, now looking at her, the most horrible of the nightmares, of my own imaginings even during the day, is that this—this place—is a ship. A world unto itself, floating in an immense and empty and still sea. The men full of mutiny, but too weak to act. My existence always precarious as the ship's commander who cannot affect the wind, cannot feed the crew who blame and curse me for their fate. In a recurring nightmare, I become the only man left alive on the ship, and I'm afraid. Not of dying, not of drowning, but of the dead who lie strewn about the decks, for I don't trust them to remain dead. I don't trust those who have thrown themselves overboard and drowned to remain under the sea. I walk the ship's decks and behind me I feel someone stir, or see a hand break the surface of the water, or see a movement in the galley. Every time I look about, their bodies have changed positions, postures. I never understand why I am alive. I never understand why they don't remain dead. I don't understand why there is no land, why the sea is still, why I am so marooned.

There is never any conclusion to the dream, he continues. Perhaps no nightmares, no fears, are ever concluded. Perhaps nothing is ever concluded.

All things end, she almost says. Almost says: All

things end. That is all.

He watches her. She turns her gaze away.

Well, Cutter muses, perhaps Shakespeare is not to your liking. Let me think. And he rises and goes to the bookcase, the blanket trailing on the dirt floor, stands bent and peering at the titles. Here, he finally says, his back to her, here is a story based on the truth, but not truly told. A saga of a man marooned: *Crusoe*.

She catches her breath. He walks back to his chair and seats himself, opens the book before him. No! she wants to cry out, but she swallows the word, and he does not notice that she pulls back into herself, tries to make herself small, tries to push herself into the planking of the wall.

Abigail Buwell knows *Robinson Crusoe* well, for she used to read it aloud to the traveling medicine man. She does not want to remember him, or that part of her life; she does not want to remember at all. *I was born in the year 1632, in the city of York, of a good family,* the major begins. And she sees herself as she was, a thin girl perched on a wagon seat in the heavy heat of a summer's night, reading by lamplight to a man lying on his side below her, chewing a blade of grass. She read without understanding all the words, but she did not falter nor stop. If she read until he fell asleep, she had learned, she would not be beaten.

He was a charlatan and a mean fool, and his name was Hiram Worth, or so he said. Put some Worth into your lives, he'd tell the womenfolk on farmsteads— wives, grandmothers, daughters, aunts, sisters-in-law—

I've got cures for whatever ails you. Or your menfolk, he'd laugh, winking, making the women turn their faces away and giggle into their hands. Lookee this girl here, he'd say, my very own daughter, why you wouldn't know it but she was born half-cripple, yessirree, and no doctor could mend her, which is why I took to studying folkways, and I traveled far and wide and learned 'bout potions and 'lixirs, rubbing oils and salves, and discovered many a thing. Cured her myself, I did, look at her walk straight as an arrow, with the laying on of hands and Bible reading and a secret remedy I'll take to my grave, so help me I will, and when she finally stood up one day and said, Oh father I'm cured, I promised the Lord I'd do nothing but good the rest of my days, wander the earth mendicant and just about penniless, dispensing what I could at prices anyone can afford. What ails you, lady?—Abbie, get up for the women here, let 'em see you, go on and raise up that skirt, show those straight legs you got despite those deformity scars—something ails everyone, don't I know it. Go on now.

And she would get down from the wagon and walk, raise her skirt almost to her knees. There were always gasps at the sight of her puckered calves—he'd scarred her expertly by blistering her with horse liniment and rubbing the sores with dirt and ground glass, pieces of which she could feel like grains of sand if she ran her fingers lightly along her skin—and then headshaking, wonderment. On cue, she would lower her skirts and politely ask for a cup of water, which was never denied, and which sometimes gained him entrance to their houses.

If the farmstead had a lone woman whose man was

working elsewhere or gone or buried, Hiram Worth sometimes gave a signal after she finished sipping her water, touching a finger to his nose, for her to slip away. She'd excuse herself then, saying she would look after the horses, put on their nosebags, pick their hooves. And then she'd watch for a sign of the husband, or father, or brother, and take to whistling if man or boy showed.

Hiram Worth sold opium in whisky, whisky by itself, snake oils, mercury, vinegars, powders, calomel, rum, corn liquor, salts from what he claimed was the Dead Sea, crushed shells, trinkets to ward off evil, ribbons, grease laced with pepper, ointments used to blister animals, dried tubers shaped like sexual organs, herb roots, peculiar jars, incense, teas, laxatives, emetics, poison, chocolate, dried berries, sugar pills, glass eyeballs, cat gut, rennet. He had the dried hands of stillborns with six fingers wrapped in waxen paper, horsetail hairs tied by the dozen with blue thread, rare feathers, colored stones, and the knowledge as to which to use and where to place these to conceive or to abort, to thwart pregnancies, to prevent twins. He spoke with authority on neuralgia and gout, guessed at people's illnesses, read their eyes and fears. He had an easy and loose way about him, a face that somehow invited trust, good teeth, and a rough-edged charm that allowed him to speak familiarly with women, got them to let him touch them when demonstrating a salve's efficacy, rubbing it into their palms or onto their wrists, their ankles, their feet, their temples. He massaged them tenderly, whispered to them, showed them false credentials and bogus degrees and a daughter who was no more his daughter than anyone else's and who was crippled in ways that would never heal. He told them of miraculous cures and plied them with laudanum, the effect of which made them happier, duller, more malleable. They bought his goods, and every so often they accepted his advances and did him sexual favors, which he liked to think he did them. Whenever they turned their backs, he shamelessly stole a bit of their money from wherever he could find it.

Hiram Worth never covered the same route twice. When they stopped in a town, they took one room as father and daughter. He did not work the towns, for he was leery of constables and judges, but in them stabled his horses and wagon, locked his goods within chests, gambled, whored, and drank. His two rules were never to mix drinking with games of chance or with women, for one could lose one's shirt with either, and to stay one step ahead of whoever might be looking for him.

In every town they stayed, Abigail Buwell looked for her mother. She wandered through alleyways, dance halls, saloons. She visited brothels. Sometimes the brothels had large kitchens and long hallways, and sometimes she heard the sweet laughter of tired women. She spoke to madams and whores and scrutinized their faces, no longer knowing what her mother looked like, barely recalling anything about her but the shape of her red mouth and her scent. No town seemed familiar, and those with rivers were all alike; she did not know her own last name, or her mother's, nor did she know the name of the town she had been taken from. She did not know how far she might be from where she had begun, and no one ever recalled knowing a man called Abraham Hume, which was the name of the man who had kept her for seven years. She did not know what would happen if she found her mother, and but for searching she did not know what else to do.

There was little to do, except wait for the bad times. They came often and with terrible consequence, for Hiram Worth had a violent streak in him, something the women he preyed upon occasionally divined. He beat her near-senseless the first night he took her from the Hume farm, bruising her where none could see, punching her hard enough to knock the breath out of her, leaving her ribs and back and stomach discolored with bruises, her thighs welted. He would tie her hands behind her back, make her stand up straight, strike her repeatedly until she dropped to her knees, then kick her in the small of her back until she curled into a fetal position. In the beginning she thought she would die, and then she realized, despondently, she would not, for Hiram Worth was methodical and precise; and he instilled in her a profound passivity and utter compliance, extraordinary hatred, fathomless fear. She did not try to run away, for there was nowhere to go. In her nightmares she freed herself and would then turn a street corner, or break out from a forest, or wander along a winding dirt road, and he would suddenly be there, waiting, crawling toward her on his hands and knees, with snakes in his mouth and lunacy in his eyes; try as she might, she could not outrun or escape him, and her cries would wake them both.

Her intelligence and sense of self-preservation led her to divine Hiram Worth's moods and anticipate his rages. She became adept at not angering him; she learned never to look him in the eye and to do immediately anything he told her, never to question him, and to take his abuse as silently as possible. She never understood the pattern of the beatings, nor did she ever respond to his tenderness in the intervals between, when he would dress her hair with ribbons and pinch her cheeks, fuss over her, fluff her skirts, seat her beside him on the wagon rather than making her ride in the back, the pain of every sore rib and bruise jolting her as the wagon rocked through their journeying. Beside him she would watch the landscape roll endlessly on, pray for farmsteads to appear where he might appease his rage in some other manner, hold her breath at crossroads that he might turn the horses in the direction of a town.

Towns were her salvation. In them she was left to crawl into herself and heal as best she could, visit brothels, lounge about cheap hotel rooms, read. He had books in the wagon; every self-respecting doctor, Hiram Worth said, carried books. He could barely read beyond the labels he had made for the products that bore his name and a phony patent number and a false address, along with fantastical titles and one-line claims, but Abigail Buwell read everything he had—Elizabethan tracts and a few plays, pamphlets on the uses of medicinal herbs, mail-order catalogs, *Great Expectations, The Scarlet Letter, The Adventures of Huckleberry Finn, Robinson Crusoe*. She never touched the Bible; her memories of those episodes in the barn, rather than fading with time and distance and Hiram Worth's beatings, instead festered, rubbed her mind raw, and the Scriptures only worsened the wounds, made pus leak, left her with the taste of raw sex in her mouth. If the books she read over and again led into worlds she could hardly imagine—leaving a boy who had staged his own death to float freely down the river with a slave, a good woman to be branded an adulterer and another to recluse herself within a dead house, a shipwrecked man to contemplate the vagaries of fate and divine will before being rescued—they removed her from the world in which she had been cast, one in which she was utterly alone, isolated by her fate from the rest of humanity, living an aberrant life over which she had no control.

She read aloud when on the road because she realized that only reading could keep Hiram Worth at bay. He listened, sprawled below her on the ground, while she sat the wagon seat and turned the pages beneath the lamplight spooling from a pole until her voice lulled him to sleep. In between the times he beat her, he taught her to ride the gentle saddle horse he kept tethered to the back of the wagon and to drive the wagon team. He also taught her to shave him, to cut his hair, to block his hat, to act the part of a loving daughter, and to be silent whenever confronted by lawmen and highwaymen. He showed her how to rub mercury into the pox that broke out on his skin, and not to fear him when he frothed at the mouth while taking the cure. He dragged her all over the universe with his chicanery, until she marveled and despaired at its magnitude. Until the day a farmwoman to whom Hiram Worth could not sell a thing sternly pointed to a well at the girl's request for water and, looking at the gray streaking Hiram Worth's hair, asked suspiciously why his daughter wasn't married. Don't seem to be no life for a young woman, she remarked, hands on her hips, her flint-colored eyes narrowing. If you took such pains to cure her crippledness, seems you might be kindly enough to find her a husband.

That night he beat her until her ribs cracked. The next morning she could not bear the jolting of the wagon, and so she walked ahead of it on the dusty, endless road, with a thin shawl tied tightly about her middle and with her arms wrapped about her.

Here and there they passed lone farmsteads, stands of pine and oak, crossed streams. She walked in the direction in which the sun would set and wondered where it ended, wherever in the world it might sink beneath the curve of the earth. From time to time Hiram Worth called out to her to stop, but she ignored him: he could beat her to death if he wanted, but she would continue and not turn to acknowledge him. For some reason, he did not insist. When the sun lay low they came to a crossroads and she read the signs and chose the direction in which she thought a town might lie, and she walked until she thought she would drop but continued on, Hiram Worth driving behind her. Long after dusk they came to several farms, and then houses began to line the road, and finally an ill-lit main street materialized, with clapboard shanties and mean, timbered houses, an inn and two gaming saloons. She climbed the steps to the inn, asked for two rooms, drank a glass of water, and waited for Hiram Worth to stable the horses. When he joined her he said nothing nor remarked on the price of the rooms, but paid for them both and watched her enter one, heard her slide the bolt behind her. In the room, she lit the oil lamp and sat the edge of the bed, thinking: I would rather be dead, I would rather be dead than live like this. When she finally stretched out on the mattress, she lay on her back and raised her knees to lessen the pain; and when she finally slept, she remained aware of the ache in her bones.

She asked the innkeeper before breakfast the next morning if there were a constable in the town. He raised his eyebrows and told her there was only a judge, some twenty miles distant. Hiram Worth, with dark circles under his eyes from a night of drinking, watched her wordlessly from the table where he sat as she left. He caught up to her at the edge of town, where a caravan of wagons was being hitched, the emigrants readying themselves for another day's trek westward. Thin men and women and listless children attended their chores, harnessing oxen and mules and horses, filling and covering water barrels, cleaning and storing cooking utensils, dampening fires. She wandered among the wagons holding onto her sides, her hair unkempt, and when they started from the town she simply trailed along behind. Worth took no time to ready his wagon and catch up to her. You can't walk forever, he said when he drew alongside her. She stopped dead in her tracks and stared him down, making him look up and at the wagons receding before them. He coughed in their dust, cleared his throat. C'mon, he said. We'll follow a ways.

She climbed up and sat beside him and wrapped the shawl tightly around her middle, braced herself when the road rutted or heaved. By nightfall, long after they'd set camp, Hiram Worth was working the emigrants for all they had, but cautiously, throwing no glances or winks at the women and regarding the men with respect. He told them of the sicknesses they'd encounter along the way, unspecific agues, lung fever, malaria, kidney and liver derangements, the bloody flux, dysentery, intestinal inertia, sudden baldness, Asiatic cholera, measles, whooping cough. He listed the ailments and talked of cures, even of preventatives: opium, salves, castor oil, quinine, laudanum, tincture of camphor, peppermint essence, sweet tallow (which he concocted from brandy, sugar and mutton fat), whisky, clove oil, rum. The men listened uneasily, the women worriedly checked their medicine stores, the children hovered wide-eyed. Worth did not speak of curing his daughter of being crippled, having noticed that several men cast glances in her direction; nor did she acknowledge him as she dumped his bedding onto the ground and settled herself into the wagon for the night.

As long as they were among others, she knew, there would be no beatings.

They ate sparsely and traveled together in silence. She chose to walk much of the time, and after several days managed to ride the saddle horse without wincing, and took to positioning herself in front of Hiram Worth so she wouldn't have to look at the wagon. She read at night as he sat about the campfires, his vials and powders and potions on hand, talking his talk. Men dug into their pockets, womenfolk packed his cures and amerioratives among those they had; headaches disappeared, sore eyes were soothed, toothaches numbed. Late at night Hiram Worth drank whisky with the unmarried men, speaking confidentially to them, selling them potions they would need before and after brothel visits, on their wedding nights, in their marriage beds. He warned them against loose women, described the pox he knew so intimately, dispensed vials of mercury, praised chastity as the highest virtue among what he called the fairer sex.

Nodding in the direction of his alleged daughter, reading silently to herself and unwitting of what had come into his head, he would say: Now there's a girl as true as they come. Not a word of argument from her in my entire life, reminds me of her loving mother, she does. Takes care of me morning, noon, and night. Has a way with horses, too. Don't know what I'd do without her. But the time has to come, I'd say, the time will come. I know I'll have to part with her, that I do. It'll be a sad day, and the Lord knows I'll exact a price. But it will come.

Eugene Buwell pays attention to what Hiram Worth says. Unbeknownst to his brother James, with whom he is traveling, he asks for her hand ten days after meeting Hiram Worth. He wants the saddle horse as well. He doesn't know her ribs are sore, nor that she is not the daughter of Hiram Worth. Worth drives a hard bargain, claiming he'd misspoken; he says sadly that he cannot think of parting with her after all. Eugene Buwell toes the dirt and then squats on his haunches, trying to figure the man's price. Women are scarce where he is going, mail-order brides a risk. His brother will not like the idea. But he senses Hiram Worth is not on the level, he likes the quietness of the girl, and he thinks that if his offer is more than fair, Eugene Buwell will have himself a wife. He calculates the value of the horse, looks up at the traveling medicine man, names what he is willing to pay.

Hiram Worth asks if there is a preacher among them. Beyond them, she sits with her head bent over a book.

"...and it may not be amiss for all people who shall meet with my story, to make this just observation from it,

viz., how frequently, in the course of our lives, the evil which in itself we seek most to shun, and which, when we are fallen into it, is the most dreadful to us, is oftentimes the very means or door of our deliverance, by which alone we can be raised from the afflictions we are fallen into."
She raises her eyes from the passage. Hiram Worth is tugging at her skirt, telling her to rise at dawn and wash herself head to toe, wash her hair, be sure to put on her other gingham dress, the one he likes better. She stares at him, trying to understand the import of what he is saying, and the pit of her stomach churns. This is it, she thinks, he has decided to turn back, to strike out on his own again; the emigrants have bought from him all they can afford, there's no profit to accompanying them farther. He climbs into the seat and takes the book from her hand, tosses it into the back of the wagon, hops down and repeats what he has told her. She wordlessly retrieves the book, opens it, finds the passage she has just read, reads it again.

You'll need a good night's sleep, Hiram Worth remarks. You might think on getting it.

He leaves her alone. The next morning she rises before dawn, washes herself, her hair, dresses herself in her other gingham dress, prepares herself solemnly like one about to be led to the gallows. Hiram Worth hitches his team to the wagon, readies all for departure, and then signals to her.

This is when I say I'm not going with him, she tells herself. This is when he murders me, or lets me be.

He fetches the saddle horse and brings it, hands her the halter lead. Your groom bought you one fine horse, he grins.

She looks at him as though he has lost his mind, and he laughs, leans close to her. We're parting ways, Abbie. And with that he takes her by the wrist and leads her leading the horse toward the group of people who have gathered by the wagons they have readied. Teams are hitched in place, the campfires dampened, the light in the sky gray, the sun obscured by a leaden cast of rippled clouds that remind her of the underside of a fish. People part ways, the women and children and men are wordless as they pass, solemnly close in behind them. In the center of the circle they form stands a young man with a dark beard and darker eyes, and before him a man holding a Bible.

Hiram Worth gives her free hand to the man with the beard. Eugene Buwell, he says, I hereby deliver my daughter Abbie to you, for your safe keeping.

The service is short. The saddle horse nudges her repeatedly. The preacher reads a passage she does not hear, for she is not listening. He pronounces them married, and there are handshakes and congratulations offered. She knows no one's name, nor does she ask, for it hardly matters. She knows only that she is being shifted once again from one man to another, and that her life might or might not be the worse for it. She avoids looking at the man who is now her husband.

Hiram Worth kisses her upon both cheeks and leaves only to return with the satchel she has carried with her since her mother first gave her away. In it are two hair ribbons, a comb, the cameo, a child's handmirror. Don't forget to write your loving father when you have settled, Hiram Worth says to her, shaking Eugene Buwell's hand. I hardly know how I'll manage without you, my dear.

Speechless, Abigail Buwell watches him go. Her knuckles are white, for she is clutching the satchel and the horse's lead, and her cheeks are pale. Eugene Buwell looks at his boots. Well, he mumbles shyly to the ground, we've got to get moving.

He waits for her to say something. When she finally turns her face to him, he is aghast at her expression.

I don't know who you are, she finally says, her voice barely audible.

He turns his body so that he stands in front of her, as if shielding her from the others who have already gone. Beyond them all is quiet commotion, people checking harnesses, the coverings atop side barrels, the hitches of the horses that will follow the wagons. He doesn't know why he says what he next says, for it is not what he means to say, it is not what is on his mind, but he says: I won't hurt you. Which makes her study him for a long moment, with a seriousness that unnerves him, with such gravity that he has to turn his eyes from hers.

I will hold you to that, she tells him.

He turns away. She follows, holding the satchel and leading the horse, as Hiram Worth slaps the reins over the rumps of his team and sets off at a trot.

If Defoe understood nothing else, the major says, putting down *Crusoe,* he understood how every miserable condition can be made worse.

Abigail Buwell stirs. She thinks to tell him that she cannot bear what *Crusoe* evokes in her, says nothing. She believes no condition can be more miserable than the one she now suffers, having been returned to a world she wants only to forget.

She is wrong. For the next day, as though her memory is nothing if not precipitous, James Buwell will arrive.

Seventeen

My dearest Lavinia, you cannot imagine what has become of us here, where wolves that never show so much as a shadow of themselves howl distant in the night, this landscape teeming with nothingness impossibly echoing their cries: how this can be, as there are no canyons, no mountains to catch such or any sounds and roll them back in diminishing swells, I cannot say, and it unnerves me so that I begin to think that the heavens are solid, that it is the distant and dark ceiling above us that repels the howling and remits it back to earth. Yes, I have been reduced to such mad notions, and we to a condition none of us could ever have imagined, for all our strength is spent in gobbling the flesh of mules and sucking on their bones and retching, with not a man among us who isn't haunted by memories of a time when we were not like this. We live without greeting or comradeship, we are unwashed, our clothes hang in shreds; we wear blankets over our shoulders or hung ghoulishly from our heads; the troops fight over scraps, contest one another for pieces of thread, *lie about the fires they somehow manage to keep burning. The season is mean cold, the washerwoman has been dismissed and is—thankfully—gone. The outpost's gate has remained open to the world for days. There are no longer sentries, no longer any duties but the unspoken ones of survival, and even in the slaughtering and skinning and gutting of the mules, the cooking of their flesh, the men now manage only weakly and with great disorder and exhaustion, and to my dismay no one grows stronger, as if our very constitutions recoil at consuming these companionable creatures upon which we once depended for our livelihood. Not a few troops have begun to insist that we have violated the laws of nature by eating our beasts of burden, and one man has descended into quiet lunacy, refusing to do more than drink a broth made of bark and rotten leather. Even Cole, the stalwart smithy, has weakened substantially, and he was the strongest among us.*

It tires me to write. I fear this letter is nothing more than a record of horror as to how we go to our end. Abigail Buwell has withdrawn into sleep on my floor, her back to the wall. She seems barely to breathe. And, irony of ironies, she has not been redeemed, for redemption means having been returned to civilization and we are not even a modicum of such. I took great pains to read aloud to her, when I had the strength, for companionship and in the hope that her native tongue would return, for I knew not what else to do nor could I imagine that she saw her redemption as anything but another captivity, more fatal than the other, one that rent her from a life we cannot envisage but which may have suited her satisfactorily; here she has suffered, and life continues under ruinous circumstances. She wears savage garb yet and is as unclean as the rest of us, she shares the same horrid repast of mule broth and bone and flesh as the rest of us, and until two days ago she simply suffered her confinement here like the rest of us, pitiably. And then, her brother in law arrived.

It was a shock to all to hear a voice calling in the distance.

He was like a creature from another world. Dusty and grimed from his journey, but uncompromised in his faculties, riding a good horse and leading a thin mare, his saddlebags loaded with foodstuffs for the return journey, his rifle oiled, his leggings untorn, his boots without holes, his hat and duster intact, his saddle rolls tied, he seemed to us the epitome of what we were not. He rode in and dismounted and watered his horses and not one man rose, and he hardly looked at the troops for he cared not for anything but the taking of Abigail Buwell, who came across the quadrant and did not acknowledge him, her horse as always at her heels, and upon approaching me as I stood watching from my doorway, said: Keep me from him. Then brushed past me and entered my quarters.

And so, Lavinia, I had not imagined her first words after all.

Her horse stood between the man and me, guarding the doorway. It is a creature of great sensitivity, with which—and here I assure you, I know this though I doubt I understand anything else in this world but my undying love for you—the redeemed captive communes, for it knows her every wish, her every mood. Surely James Buwell knew he would have been trampled to death by it had he approached, which he did not. And so I had to walk over to him with as much dignity and remembrance of my *command as I could muster. The troops lie about muttering, saying, finally, good riddance, send her off; for they believe her presence is somehow the fount of their misfortunes; as you know, my dearest, in the worst of times humanity succumbs to superstition and fallacies. Buwell took something wrapped in newspaper from a saddlebag, tossed it at my feet, and told me to have the woman readied for her journey. I took the bundle and brought it to my quarters, but when I gave Abigail Buwell the package she put it on my writing table, where I sit now. I am not yours to give to him, she said, and he is nothing to me. His brother was my husband, that is all, and he is long dead.*

He pauses, unsure of how to continue, unsure of his hand which has begun to tremble. The pain in his shoulder and his aching knee shred his concentration. A shadow passes before the door and Cutter freezes as Abigail Buwell stirs in her sleep on the floor, and then the boy is gone. Fragments of what he wants to write flit through his mind, but he loses their thread, everything becomes the sum total of two words: honor, the one, duty, the other. There was a time Cutter could ruminate upon the profundity of both ideals, he once believed honor to be a gentleman's guiding principle, he waged war believing in duty, and now he is unable to imagine anything that could be justified by either, for he is distraught by his sense of having committed a heinous act. He thinks, I should simply write what I must inevitably confess, that I have murdered a man in cold blood. Instead, he begins to cry. He weeps silently though his chest is heaving, with his head bent, the tears dripping down his nose, spattering on the letter, wetting the backs of his hands. The oil in the lamp is almost gone, the flame lessens, and he sits in shame and cries bitterly until the light dies, and he continues to weep long after being cast into darkness.

Much later Abigail Buwell hears him move about the room, fumble with the lamp to refill it, strike a match. A diaphanous blue wells within her eyelids and she tightens her eyes against the glow, throws a forearm over her face, listens to Cutter shuffle back to his writing table. The words before him are blotched, but he takes up his pen again, measures a space between what he has written and what he is about to write, continues.

Never have I considered myself a murderer, not even during the war, though the gravity of sending men to their deaths always weighed heavily upon me, as did killing those we fought against. The military has always survived by mathematics: strategy is nothing without a calculated assessment of numbers, every battle plan is writ with an expected sacrifice of life, every breaking point dependent upon casualty figures that will determine rout or victory, but I can tell you that neither in the deliberation of strategy nor in the heat of battle did the concept of murder ever cross my mind. Waste, yes, wanton destruction, certainly, even tragedy: these are the terms I have used, these are the mainstays of battle, someone must win, someone must lose when sides representing irreconcilable differences declare war over matters greater than us all. But differences between men are dissimilar from those of nations, even of tribes: and these differences, I always believed, should be settled by peaceful means. No matter of honor, let alone property, demands resolution by anything but reasoned argument; I always abhorred dueling of any sort, not only that of so-called gentlemen, choosing weapons and pacing off at dawn, but also that of today, when drunken men take to one another with knives, rocks, and broken bottles. But, Lavinia, what could I do, faced with the certainty that this man had come for a woman who was not, in her eyes, his to take? Faced with demoralized, starving troops who wanted her gone from here, who would not have raised a hand to protect her even if I had so ordered? Not that any of this crossed my mind in so many words, and that is the pity of it: I barely thought at all. There was his horse, and there was his gun.

It is the only time in her life that Abigail Buwell refuses to be remanded to yet another human being. When she says what she does to Major Robert Cutter, to this gaunt man whose rasping voice has begun to sound like the clacking of reeds roughed by winter winds, she has no idea of what will happen. She is waiting for death, she knows it is just a matter of time, and she does not want James Buwell to steal her from it, she does not want to die within his grasp, subjected to the vagaries of a mean, estranged psyche and perverse sexual demands. Of inestimable sorrow, she can bear no more.

Major Robert Cutter does not know what he is about to do. Everything happens as though in a dream: there is James Buwell watching him approach, there is the sound of muttering from the troops beyond, there is the shine of the worn saddle on Buwell's horse and the shape of the mare's ewed neck. Cutter sees himself place a hand on the saddlehorn, watches himself look off in the direction of the open gates, hears himself say to James Buwell: You haven't asked about her child.

Buwell spits. I ain't rightly interested, he replies.

They stand in the cold, in silence. The mare nudges the hind of Buwell's mount and Buwell hisses, shoos her.

Well, Buwell finally says, it looks like I'm just gonna have to go get Abbie. And then he stares down at the hand that catches his sleeve, incredulous, and when he raises his eyes he sees a man who resembles nothing if not a lunatic scarecrow. He pulls his arm from Cutter's grasp and Cutter watches the blow come, sees the horses shy sideways as one, knows he is on his knees because he is no taller than their legs, tastes blood and spits out a piece of an impossibly yellow tooth.

Cutter does not remember getting to his feet. By the time he takes aim, Buwell is halfway to his quarters. That bitch, James Buwell is thinking, envisioning Abigail Buwell bedding this rickety, aged officer, that bitch, whore of a medicine-show huckster, my brother's whore, the savages' whore, whore born of a whore.

It is his last thought, his last conscious grasp of the universe. For the bullet that hits James Buwell severs his spinal cord, folds him backward even as he flips airborne, his head hitting the ground before his feet do, and by that time—long before the major lets the rifle slip from his hands—he is dead. Cutter will always remember the fierce beauty of blood and bone exploding, and the astonishingly perfect rag doll arc of the man's body in midair, defying gravity, in James Buwell's last solitary act between life and death.

Two days later, Lt. John Hastings, the hunting detail, and Reed Gabriel, accompanied or rather led by Colonel Harold Chapman and his relief column, ride in through the outpost's open gates. Their horses throw back their heads and flatten their ears as the troops and their officers pick their way among the human debris, the hollow-eyed and blanketed men gawking at them, grabbing at the bones strewn about, ferreting pieces of mule meat under their clothing. The stench of over-boiled meat and rotting broth, of unwashed bodies, of overflowing latrines, of the decomposing flesh of the dead man yet in the throes of rigor mortis, is overpowering; even Colonel Chapman pulls a bandana over his mouth and nose as the irate vultures squawk and rise heavily, wings flapping, from James Buwell's bloated corpse. Abigail Buwell rounds the stable corner as Chapman calls out to his troops, and they fall in behind him, awaiting orders to dismount, which they do in unison as they look in her direction, see her dressed in her filthy animal robes, wonder at her shorn, grimy hair, the blue roan that follows her. She meets their stares not with equanimity but with horror, for scalps and ears and scrotum sacs hang from their necks, their saddles, from the manes of their horses. When she recognizes the scalps of her firstborn child and of the man who was the father of her two children, Abigail Buwell drops to her knees. Both Hastings and Colonel Chapman mistake this for a sign that she welcomes their presence, a gesture of pure thanksgiving.

On her knees Abigail Buwell fights to breathe, wants not to breathe. She knew they were dead when they stopped appearing to her, but this, this finality, cruelly unhinges her. When she finally manages to stand, her legs tremble. She forces herself to walk shakily toward the troops who, untacking their mounts, allow her to pass among them as though she were an embodiment of some specter from the killing fields they'd left behind, until she reaches one of the soldiers and rips two scalps from him. The man grabs at them but she steps back, raising the scalps to her face, and lets out an unearthly cry as she covers her eyes and nose and mouth with them, breathes into them as though she would give them life by so doing, feels the reel of the earth beneath her, drops once again to her knees and bends over, inhales the smell of death, crumples the softness of their hair, feels the dry and incredibly small pieces of skin cut from their heads, wails the louder. The debilitated, half-starved troops lying about try to rise, push themselves onto their elbows and knees, crawl about in their waste. From inside the chicken coop come inhuman cries that raise the colonel's hackles. An unbelievably emaciated brindle cur appears from nowhere and staggers across the quadrant, its ribs rubbing through the open sores of its skin.

Major Robert Cutter stands in his doorway, the blanket around his shoulders, and struggles with the buttons on his jacket. His thin hair wisps long in the light, his beard is matted; and he is so gaunt, his eyes so sunken, his face so lined that Hastings hardly recognizes the skeletal figure who finally stops fussing with his ungainly appearance and gives wide berth to the stinking corpse as he hobbles toward the dismounted troops. Cutter's jacket remains unbuttoned. His hand shakes as he salutes or perhaps simply shades his brow from the dull glare of the cold sun. His mouth works soundlessly. When he finally drops his hand from his forehead, he covers his mouth with it in a gesture of pure anguish.

He sees all that Colonel Harold Chapman surveys. In the middle of a stride, Cutter stops and turns full circle, takes in every face, sees the half-dead and the dead, the boy near the gate, the collapsing roofs, the rickety stables. He hears Ezekiel Pace's screams and Abigail Buwell's wails, sees the spindly dog, the blue roan, the unbelievable filth, the open gates. Beyond the gates he sees the dust raised by the approach of the supply wagons. This rivets him to the spot, for he cannot believe his eyes, finds it impossible to look elsewhere. He ignores Hastings, the colonel, Reed Gabriel, the troops, and stands stockstill, openmouthed, at the sight of the washerwoman riding a mule at the head of the procession. Beside her, a young man—wearing an improbable green hat and a dandy's jacket despite the cold—whoops and hollers from the back of his horse and then breaks rank and canters toward the gates, tearing the hat from his head with one hand and pulling the horse up short upon entering, making it rear and prance in its own tracks. Father! Father! he cries.

Major Robert Cutter makes a sound akin to a goat's bleat and bursts into sobs.

Abigail Buwell does not stop wailing.

Good lord almighty, Reed Gabriel says.

Colonel Harold Chapman grimly and immediately relieves Major Robert Cutter of his command. He does not tell Cutter that the simple process of replacement will become instead a matter of inquiry, but Chapman makes it very clear that what he sees he construes to be the result of outrageous incompetence, wanton negligence, grave dereliction of duty, possible criminality. A man given to harsh and quickfire judgment, Chapman has never counted patience among his assets, and within the space of several hours troops have been detailed in a dozen directions and given as many tasks: the supply wagons are unloaded, munitions and uniforms and food dispensed, horses corralled and fed; by twilight a common mess for the troops has been erected, barracks and quarters swept, leantos cleared, tents poled, the grounds cleaned of bones and refuse, new latrine trenches dug, bonfires built for burning refuse, James Buwell buried. At Maria's hysterical insistence, and with Colonel Chapman's concurrence, the chicken coop is opened. The scarcely human figure within crawls out on his hands and knees, the sutler as soiled as the rags on his back and more jaundiced than seems possible. His reek forces even the hardened colonel to take a step back.

Even now, as Colonel Chapman confronts Cutter in the major's quarters, Cutter's troops are being stripped naked and made to wash, the remnants of their lice-infested clothes burned, and Abigail Buwell's horse hobbled and tethered—not by the troops, who had no luck in roping and subduing it—but by Cole, who hopes to protect it from being destroyed. He cannot protect Abigail Buwell, however, who now sits naked within Maria's quarters, clutching two scalps, as her bloody, stinking robes curl in the flames of a bonfire before which Ezekiel Pace lies, dazed.

Reed Gabriel will attend Major Robert Cutter's court-martial. He will be openly critical of it, and of Colonel Harold Chapman, and of a military system that left the outpost isolated and without supplies for far too long. Reed Gabriel will write that what occurred at the outpost was an unfortunate, and highly avoidable, catastrophe. He will write that had Lt. John Hastings and the quite successful hunting detail not been intercepted by Chapman and ordered on a chase to decimate the savages, and the supply wagons not been ordered by Chapman to wait until such operations were concluded, conditions at Outpost 2881 would never have so deteriorated.

But Reed Gabriel will not be called upon to testify. He will come to believe, wrongly, that Major Robert Cutter had never received any orders for the final elimination of the savages. And he will never understand why Abigail Buwell, who will end her life incarcerated in an institution for lunatics, will refuse to share with him and the world the story of her captivity. He will visit Abigail Buwell repeatedly during her stay at Clearwater Asylum; he will believe—until her death—that upon the next visit, or the next, she will come to recognize his feelings. Like a human in a zoo, waiting for that secret signal from an ape that acknowledges *we are one, we are of the same ilk*, Reed Gabriel will steadfastly believe that, one day, Abigail Buwell would turn her sage-green eyes to meet his, smile, and say: Yes, it's time to talk.

The only thing Abigail Buwell will ever say to Reed Gabriel, several months before her death, will be encompassed in one sad and lucid sentence. He will take to his death her words, the words he never wrote, as well as his memories of the weeks he spent riding with Lt. John Hastings and the hunting detail and of their interception by Colonel Harold Chapman. He will suffer terrible dreams his entire life, nightmares shaped by what he witnessed when Chapman's troops slaughtered the savages they encountered. The visions that pass before his eyes as he draws his last breath will be of savages mowed down, used for target practice, hunted to the last being as if for sport, their bodies afterward defiled, eviscerated, scalped. For as long as he lives, moaning winds will always remind him of the savages' wails, the pitiful cries of dying men, women, and children; muddy rivulets created by rainstorms will remind him how their blood flowed and mixed with the blood of their massacred ponies and horses. He will often try to imagine what Abigail Buwell suffered when Colonel Chapman's troops rode into the outpost sporting the ears, fingers, scrotum sacs, and scalps of the slaughtered; he will fail to do so.

As an old man, Reed Gabriel will sit by a window in a parlor, look onto the city street below, and watch with drooping eyelids and bad vision the ebb and flow of humanity. He will wish he'd never lost the packet of scribblings he received from the lunatic asylum upon the death of Abigail Buwell, in her handwriting. Of these, he will especially remember two lines she wrote on a small piece of paper: *It is not a pity that we die / but that we die in all the wrong places.*

Abigail Buwell comes to Cutter's quarters in the dead of night, wanting to tear off the woolen clothes in which she has been dressed, the smell of them redolent of tallow, the weave of the fibers harsh upon her skin. The troops sleep but for the sentries pacing the stockade; the hobbled, tethered roan can no longer follow her. She comes to his room in the dead of night because she longs for the sound of Cutter's voice, the scratch of his pen, their slow dying which has now been interrupted. She comes to his quarters because she knows not what else to do.

She is shocked by his appearance. He is clean. His hair is short and combed; his beard is gone; he wears a new uniform, albeit one far too large for his thin frame; his collar is white, his jacket is buttoned, and the buttons shine. The sergeant who tidied the rooms and removed the old bedding, the blanket, and the major's filthy clothes is snoring, asleep on a cot in Cutter's inner room. The washbasin and pitcher gleam, the oil lamps and inkwell are full, the writing table waxed. The ledgers and logbook are gone. Only Cutter's letters remain on the writing table.

Cutter and a young man holding a flask watch her enter. She stands just within the open door, hesitant. Ah, the white savage, the young man exclaims, jumping up from his seat and clapping his hands. *Parlez-vous français?*

Henry, the major says sharply.

But Father, I'm a master at languages! French, Italian, Chinese, Arabic! Let her but say a word in any tongue, and I'll immediately begin speaking it. Come in, come in, he says delightedly, please come in!

She turns to leave, but Lt. John Hastings is suddenly

behind her. She does not want to brush past him, does not want to touch him, and so she steps into the room. The lieutenant looks sheepish, ducks his long frame through the door, stands just inside, salutes his former commander. No need! Henry cries. There's no need for ceremony here!

Hastings cannot help but look abashed. Sorry, Major, he says to Cutter. I know it's late.

No matter, John.

I just wanted you to know that a mail courier will be dispatched in the morning. Perhaps you hadn't been told…. In case you've something to send your wife.

His wife! Henry hoots. What, a letter for my mother? Why, she'd never read it, Lieutenant. She'd never even receive it. Unless—Henry pauses, tips the flask to his mouth, sips prettily, swallows, and with great mirth continues—unless the cemetery in which she's lain these many years employs gardeners to read at the gravesites.

Hastings feels the blood rise in his face at the sight of Cutter's anguished expression. Abigail Buwell moves toward a wall and, with her back against it, slides into a sitting position.

I take it, Major Robert Cutter says with as much dignity as he can muster, that you will arrange a comfortable place for my son to sleep, Lieutenant.

Of course, Hastings replies.

The sergeant in my quarters is drunk; even his snores stink. Our mad son Henry sleeps somewhere outside these rooms; I imagine him in repose as when he was small,

curled catlike, his hands tucked in fists and pulled close to
him. The night is long. I shot a man in the back, Lavinia,
and he is dead. Abigail Buwell sleeps on my floor. Relief
troops and supply wagons and a new commander, as well
as Henry, have arrived. If I understand nothing else it is
that I have finally been relieved of my duties here, though
the joy I anticipated I am no longer capable of feeling, for
our—my—condition upon their arrival was unspeakable.
My superior has intimated such, I am disgraced, and the
humiliation and helplessness I feel, my inability to put into
words the events and circumstances of our gradual and
perhaps unavoidable decline, the troublesome fate that
will befall Abigail Buwell, Henry's worrisome antics, the
disarray of the outpost's records, all weigh heavily upon me.
If only you were here to stroke my brow.

We are redeemed, curiously: we will not starve, we will
regain our strength, order will reign, the troops have a new
commander, they will be paid, I have been recalled, some
of us are to return to civilization. But redemption? Now I
wonder at the meaning of the word. Delivered from sure
death we are, but not from that which will rub salt into our
wounded memories: what redemption is this, in which
there is no delight? Is this what Abigail Buwell, taken from
a life among the savages, wonders? Who can say?

Not I. My only happiness, thinly felt, for it comes so
late, is the thought that I will soon join you. Tell me, my
dearest, where: name the place, the time, let me come to
you in the way I dream I may, so that you might comfort
me and I might stay by your side, for at this age—and I
have surely aged miserably—as I've written before, there's
naught but companionship to be desired, born of the love
we have so long shared, a closeness I swear I will never

again abdicate, come what may. My thoughts, dear, dear Lavinia, are only of you. I kiss your likeness before me, the packets of letters tied with ribbons I keep, and pray your forgiveness for all I have done and will now do, faced as I am with certain dishonor. Until such time as we are joined, my love, I remain, your faithful husband.

Are you writing to a dead woman? Abigail Buwell asks.

He did not realize she was awake, nor does she move from where she lies against the wall. Are you? she whispers.

In the lamplight Cutter nods slowly, in unbearable sadness. The sound of her voice thudding in his heart.

They are gone from us, she says then, after a long silence. We cannot let them go, but they are gone.

Perhaps they come back.

She rises into a sitting position, hating the rub of cloth against her skin. Never, she says.

He thinks of his brother, of their unfulfilled pact: the one who died first never returned, left any sign, spoke through dreams. With Lavinia there had been no time, no accord. Cutter never anticipated she would die first, she was nowhere near the battle lines, never saw the clash of armies, the wasted lives; she nursed their children and accompanied three of them to their graves; she had always waited for him; he'd believed she would always be there, waiting. There was a time he could no more imagine life without her than he could envisage her rotting in the earth. She died far from him and was buried without his presence: it was as though she had simply left, taken a journey from which she would one day return.

I have seen the afterdead, he tells her. I've been touched by them. They have lain upon me, I've been haunted. I see a boy no one else sees.

His mouth opens, closes.

The boy is from this world, not the other, she says after a long time. He is undead.

He looks at her, enshadowed against the wall. He cannot read her eyes, see their clarity.

How do you know?

She shrugs, almost imperceptibly. She can still feel the softness of their hair in her hands, the thinness of the scalps where their skin was attached. The dead are dead, she says. Only the living can come to us.

And the boy?

He is gone now.

He watches Abigail Buwell bring her hands to her face then, rest her elbows on her knees. She does not want to say: Your son is here. So she says nothing at all.

Eighteen

This will never become her story, for Abigail Buwell will not tell it. In the morning when she goes to the hobbled horse, she feels herself to be oblique, transparent, for she has chosen to irrevocably withdraw from the edge of the terrifying world to which she has been returned. She had the choice to speak or not to speak, and she stepped back from it, retreated once again into herself, and anchored what is left—her resolve—to silence. Gently confronted by Colonel Chapman, a man not given to gentleness, in the presence of Major Robert Cutter, Lt. Hastings and Reed Gabriel, she considered for a brief moment—one that seemed to last an eternity—answering the one simple question that would have compromised her forever: *Do you understand what I am saying?*

The major turned his eyes from her. He stared at the floor beneath his feet as scales tipped, as words hung in the balance before she swallowed them, which she did as the colonel turned to Cutter and demanded, *Well, Major, does she?* Cutter felt a constriction in his chest and was afraid to look at her, for he was about to betray her—he didn't know what else to do—and then she rose from the floor on which she had slept for the last time and removed herself from the room as though the men did not exist. She left behind her silence. Cutter knew then that if he said yes, he would lose her forever—she who would be lost to him anyway—and he cleared his throat and said: No. The colonel requisitioned Cutter's quarters then, and relegated Cutter to the dead quartermaster's rooms, where he sorted his books, pen tips and inkwell and letters, and put them in an empty chest and awaited his departure, without knowing what would become of her.

Reed Gabriel never believed that Abigail Buwell was aphasic. He did not believe that this would never become her story, because he did not understand that Abigail Buwell knew nothing would be learned from it, nothing would be changed by it. She sits by the blue roan and thinks: I could have said this, that I was born, truly born, under a sky of shooting stars, beside a herd of grazing horses wearing moonlight on their coats. That the air smelled of water and juniper, and that I was born like this, whole. That I lived only for some four years: this was the span of my true life. That I knew the taste of a man's skin and the wonder of desire, gave birth, knew laughter and the names of all things. There is not a moment I cannot recall in those fifty-odd moons, there were no holes in my existence, no warp to time. She thinks: I could have said that only in one captivity did I become free, in one captivity did I live freely, and was loved and loved in return. I slept among horses if I wished, I crushed pine needles beneath my bare feet and smelled their wonder, I sewed with sinew, I ate raw flesh, I watched women bathe naked in play and men break trails in snow as deep as their thighs, I walked dry riverbeds and slept on mountain crests and broke down wickups and ran my tongue over saltlicks that tasted of fawn and bear and goat saliva; I sang when the hunt was good, I thrust my arms into the birth canals of mares whose foals were breached, I listened to underground rivers flow and felt the earth turn. I could have said: Before I was redeemed I was joyful, in my four years of life I felt the fullness of muted ecstasy with every dawn, every sunset, every rainfall, every snowfall, for I was unhurt then and I spoke true and longed for nothing. Nothing. I could have said: The nightmares are of the world before my birth and after my death, and these were never dreamed.

She sits by the blue roan and knows that the horse will not be allowed her much longer. That the scalps of the man who was the father of her children and of her child will be taken from her. That life will not be allowed her. She will not speak now, she decides, to Reed Gabriel, who comes toward her with bread in his hands, making signs, offering it to her in an awkward attempt to join her, to break through her code of silence. She will never speak to Colonel Chapman, to Cole, to Robert Cutter's mad son, nor, later, to anyone in the asylum. She will never tell her story because, if she does, she will in the end become the less for its telling. Too many pieces of her lie scattered, discarded in a town of snowbound streets, in a barn, in a snake-oil vendor's wagon, in a sodder's hut, in the scalps of some soldier's trove. For the rest of what Abigail Buwell will not consider to be her life, she will refuse to use a fork, she will repeatedly strip herself naked rather than tolerate the rub of cloth upon her skin, she will bite her hands and wrists, shear her head, wound her face by tearing at it with her nails until the circle once painted upon her cheek becomes a permanent scar.

Her story, she will sometimes reflect, is not unlike that of Crusoe's Friday, for she will always be regarded as a savage at the mercy of her saviors. But unlike Friday, she will often remind herself, she will refuse to don the garb or speak the language of those who redeemed her. Whatever kernel is left of her soul, she will guard preciously.

Colonel Harold Chapman had Abigail Buwell brought before him three times, always in the presence of Major Robert Cutter and Reed Gabriel, among others. All were silent during his questioning of her. During each session, she stared through the colonel as if fascinated by some spot on the wall behind him, refused to sit in a chair despite his attempts to persuade her to do so. She did not respond to any of his questions. The colonel concluded that Abigail Buwell was incapable of taking care of her person; her behavior and his prejudices convinced him that she had lost her knowledge of English and suffered such horrors among the savages as to become deranged. In the end, he decides to recommend—magnanimously, he thinks—that his superiors have Abigail Buwell fully examined by military medical staff and, should they concur with Chapman's assessment, remand her to the care of the nation and place her in an asylum. He assumes this to be the only hope for her to recover her civilized past. He does not understand that she wants nothing of the sort, and his interest in her will wane with his recommendation.

Colonel Chapman interviews Major Robert Cutter only once, and at length. He has seized—requisitioned, is the word he uses—from Cutter the dead quartermaster's ledgers and the major's logbook, with no entries in it except for copies of the major's dispatches and reports to headquarters and excerpts from his personal letters. He requests from Cutter all communiqués received. None exist, the major informs Chapman tersely. Chapman's adjutant is charged with taking depositions from the remainder of the major's troops, from the washerwoman and Ezekiel Pace, but Chapman chooses to interview Lt. Hastings himself. Only Cole is ignored, for the colonel has no use for black people; and though the man has taken to working his bellows once again, the colonel has seen to it that Cole's workspace is moved to beyond the old latrines. He orders his own smithy to make sure Cole does not tend any of his troops' mounts.

By the time the troops' pay arrives, the mail has been reestablished and Chapman has finished with his summary of the depositions and with his recommendation concerning Abigail Buwell. The half-starved men, including the sutler, have begun to put flesh on their bones and seem to have regained some of their strength, though two soldiers seem deranged and Elias Carter suffers random fits. Cutter, relieved of all duties, moves like a shadow about the outpost, dogged by his idiot son and by the bonethin brindle cur, and the man is given to sitting in the bleak winter light for hours, watching the repair of what Chapman thinks should never have fallen into such disrepair, observing the coming and going of wood and grazing details, the pacing of sentries, the constant parade drills. Abigail Buwell speaks to no one, nor has she sought out Cutter's company since his relocation to the dead quartermaster's rooms, which he shares with his son. Only Reed Gabriel is kind to the major; he cooks and shares his mess with Cutter and his son, and he is moved by Cutter's humiliation, confusion, and ineptitude with Henry, and by his loneliness and anxiety that worsen daily with the colonel's delay of his recall.

For Chapman is not content merely to send his findings and reports to headquarters; he then waits for a reply. When it finally arrives, the colonel summons Cutter and tells him that his recall will culminate in a formal inquiry and probable court-martial. The major's only recourse to dignity being his reticence, he says nothing. Chapman stares hard at Cutter, waiting for a response that does not come. There is not even a flicker of an eyelid, a turn to the mouth, a fleeting change of expression. And so Chapman informs Cutter that he will be placed under guard and accompanied to headquarters by Lt. Hastings, some troops, and a supply detail. He asks Cutter whether he wants to select an adjutant to see to his needs on the journey. When Cutter doesn't answer immediately, Colonel Chapman wonders if the man has understood anything he has been told.

Cole, the major says then.

You'll have to remind me who he is, Chapman frowns, annoyed that he does not recall the name.

The smithy.

The colonel's frown deepens, and he steels himself against registering the surprise he feels. I'm not sure he's your best choice, Chapman admonishes.

He's my choice nonetheless.

He's an enlisted man.

That shouldn't make a difference.

The colonel studies the man before him, measures his growing dislike of him. Cutter fights a sudden urge to walk out of the room.

So be it. And your son will undoubtedly accompany you.

Yes.

Abigail Buwell will also be sent back. If back is the correct term. I assume she is fit enough to travel.

She has nowhere to go.

Certain matters have been settled. Her welfare is not your concern. I simply need some confirmation that you think she is well enough to withstand the journey.

As well as any of us.

We'll make her as comfortable as possible in the wagon.

She won't be comfortable in it at all. Especially as you'll have to have her hogtied.

Chapman is affronted by Cutter's audacity. He feels his temper flare, works to control it. We've no mounts to spare, he rejoins tersely.

She has her own horse.

That horse belongs to the military now.

Cutter snorts. That horse will kill anyone who comes near it, except her. Except Cole. Abigail Buwell arrived here a civilian, mounted on that horse. It's hers.

As she is no longer my concern, as you say, she is yours. If you wish to do her no further harm, I suggest you give her her horse and let her travel on its back. As she should.

Not allowing her to travel in the manner of a savage seems to me to be in her best interest. And she'll hardly be able to ride in skirts.

I wouldn't assume that, Colonel, Robert Cutter says then. He rises abruptly, salutes sloppily. Besides, he remarks, after he has turned on his heel without being dismissed, there'll be hell to pay if you forcibly separate her from that roan.

His writing table and bookshelves and the chest holding his meager personal belongings, consisting of a likeness of his wife and packets of letters, books, a change of uniform, a mirror and shaving strop and razors, are put into the wagon with little fanfare. Cole and a quartermaster check the supplies, those already loaded and those waiting to be hoisted into the wagons. Troops tack horses and mules, check bridles and bits and stirrup leathers and girths, check the ties holding their sleeping rolls, take stock of their saddlebags. Abigail Buwell stays close to the blue roan, far from the troops, and tears at the preposterous outfit she has been forced to wear, a woolen dress over a petticoat over woolen trousers. Reed Gabriel watches her struggle to rid herself of the petticoat, thinks that she would tear the dress off if only she had a shirt—which she does not—and marvels when she finally manages to step out of the undergarment and away from the shoes she discards, then wraps the muffler she has been given about her waist and leaves the military-issue jacket she wears unbuttoned, as though she is impervious to the cold. The washerwoman retrieves the petticoat and shoes, curses at her, bundles them and walks over to give them to the quartermaster. He ignores her.

Reed Gabriel thinks Colonel Harold Chapman will not be pleased.

A fog has descended over the outpost; beyond the open gates lies a landscape of gray impenetrability, the earth and sky a leaden miasma. The troops, the mules, the horses, and Abigail Buwell are softened by this obscuring quality, and dawn's light does little to define the figures and animals moving about. Only Cole seems to have substance, for he is a continuation of his dark uniform. Everyone else has taken on the color of mother of pearl, each face appears ashen against an ashen backdrop. The blue roan is perfectly ghostly.

Cole has improvised a halter for the roan, with reins, and cinched a folded blanket onto its back to serve as a saddle. Abigail Buwell does not unfasten the cinch, discard the blanket, or tear the halter from the horse's head, though she needs none of these. She does not know where she will be taken, and it no longer matters to her: she regards the downward drift that has become her life as inescapable as quicksand. She feels neither exhilaration nor trepidation, but an overwhelming resignation. The spring and power of the horse beneath her, which once gave her great joy, will now carry her to greater sorrow. For when she finally reaches her destination, she knows, she will be parted from it forever.

She glances through the mist at the major, busy with the chestnut, checking its tack, fastening the girth, adjusting stirrups that need no adjusting, then gazing absently around him for the last time at this place of his undoing, which has become to him unrecognizable. Shingles have been cut and piled, roofs repaired, clapboard siding nailed, woodpiles replenished, new latrines dug, the stables and corral mucked, firepits covered with earth, tents erected, supplies stored, four messes established for enlisted men, and a common mess created for the officers; his former quarters have a new door, porches have been buttressed, the sutler's store converted to a barracks, coal from the seams beyond the outpost piled in several stalls, telegraph wire stored beneath the sentries' walkway. The men are fleshier, Abigail Buwell is without her robes. What happened here, under him, he can no longer reconstruct; and though Cutter will always believe he could no more have salvaged this ship than he could have commanded the wind, he knows only that he has been disgraced, that he will be forevermore a disgrace. Not one soldier of his remaining troops to be left behind so much as approaches him; they make themselves scarce, they will not salute his departure nor say a word to him, and as he raises his hand in farewell he halts the gesture. Only the washerwoman comes over to him, to spit at his feet, as the call to mount is given by Lt. Hastings. As he still respects the uniform he wears, Cutter will carry the humiliation of this leavetaking to his death.

Reed Gabriel swings onto the back of his horse and watches Cutter's peculiar son scramble onto his horse, raise his ridiculous green hat from his head and wave it in the air. Onward, Christian soldiers, Henry cries to no one in particular.

Colonel Harold Chapman is glad to see them leave. Among the papers he has forwarded to headquarters are his own deposition, those of the men who remained at the outpost until his arrival, and those of Lt. Hastings, Ezekiel Pace and the washerwoman. He has also sent the quartermaster's ledgers—its last entries, including Cutter's list of good and evil, Chapman considers a reflection not only of Cutter's deteriorated mental state but also of his insubordination—as well as the seriously neglected daily log. Separate from these is Chapman's recommendation that the formal inquiry focus on Cutter's culpability in allowing the situation at the outpost to degenerate, his inability to make decisions, his obvious and utter disregard of the rights of civilians—the sutler and washerwoman having been badly treated, and James Buwell murdered—as well as Cutter's admitted refusal to search for and punish deserters, his denial that he understood his mission, his ultimate abdication of command. Colonel Chapman adds a postscript to his recommendation that the inquiry be reminded it was apparent at war's end that Major Robert Cutter seemed to have sustained a mental collapse and was considered by some of his fellow officers to be unfit for continuing service. Chapman resists the temptation to add that the antics of the major's son point to some mental dysfunction that can only be ascribed to family bloodlines.

The officers conducting the formal inquiry will be baffled by many things, but primarily by Major Robert Cutter's reticence and inattentiveness. They will recommend his court-martial.

The ancient brindle cur tries its best to keep pace, but its spindly legs tire. The dog eventually hangs its head and swallows the sweatdrops on its tongue and falls so far behind that it can no longer see the rump of the blue roan or any rumps at all. Even when the cur breaks into a crablike trot, it fails to catch sight of them. Their scent is strong, but the dog is too old, too tired, too thin and too rickety for this journey; after a half day, exhaustion overcomes it and it sits back on skinny haunches and raises its muzzle and cries muted whimpers, then lies down, panting, and eventually curls into itself and sleeps. When it awakes, the cur snuffs about, back and forth along the lingering scent of their trail, as though undecided. The fog is unbothersome, the dog has for long seen all shapes through a milky haze, its sight an impaired sense; but now it stops in its tracks and peers in their direction, listens intently for what is far beyond its hearing, and then after some minutes plops down again, stretching its front paws straight before it, to wait for them.

The cur will not return to the outpost. Nor will it make the journey.

Reed Gabriel marvels at the impenetrability of the fog, at its beauty as the troops and wagons and woman ride into it. It does not lift, and Gabriel paces his horse so that he lags behind, watching the rumps of the chestnut and bays and mules and the magnificent blue roan swing, their tails lying quietly, the steam rising from their hindquarters, their riders phantasmal in a mist that becomes denser, more opaque. He has never seen anything quite so unearthly. From time to time a silhouetted, leafless tree appears, its moist branches etched darkly and their tips disappearing in the solidity of the seemingly endless and variegated murk that, marble-like, drapes its shades of gray—charcoal, ash, lead, graphite, slate, mercury, silver, granite—over the whole of the universe beyond. Infinity itself presses down upon that which is finite, over the troops and Lt. Hastings leaning from their saddles, peering at what must be a trail but who would know; and it seems to Gabriel that everything is suspended, floating, for the ground is barely visible beneath their mounts' hooves. By day's end they come upon the remnants of the old emigrant trail, and those things cast away that in broad daylight would look like nothing so much as pieces of rotting and rusting detritus take on ghostly and unrecognizable shapes in the fog. The horses roll their eyes and shy-step sideways, toss their heads nervously, spook, until the lieutenant finally signals a halt that is more heard than seen. The wagons creak to a stop, the clopping sounds are silenced, the men's breaths explode as their feet thud onto the ground in dismount. The lieutenant rides on and disappears, returns, moves them again, the troops leading their mounts closer to a stand of trees and to a shallow stream, where everyone drinks. Two by two, the horses are unsaddled and watered; the mules are unharnessed and untacked and also drink; and then the animals are strung along a tether line tied tightly to the trees. Only Abigail Buwell is left to herself, and she leaves the roan free. By the time the campfire is roaring and the mess is cooked, she has ripped her dress apart at the waist and pulled the skirt away, torn it into long strips so no one can ever force her to wear it again.

She is not moved by the fog's beauty, but she is not indifferent to it. They travel through a netherworld, one in which the spirits of the dead whose bodies were not raised toward the heavens, whose flesh was not picked clean by carrion birds, whose bones were not bleached by the sun and moonlight, reside; and she is leery of it, disturbed by it. When such a fog descended, the savages never strayed from their encampments and barely stirred from their wickups, which they closed hard against it. They would no more go into the fog than those who are not savages would willingly enter a tomb, a sarcophagus, a grave, to lay themselves down and breathe in mold and decay, share the dead's putrefaction. This fog holds the defiled dead—Abigail Buwell's infant, her other child, the man who fathered her children, his mother, sisters, father, aunts, cousins, uncles, the decimated band of savages whose scalps, scrotum sacs, ears and fingers became the trophies of soldiers—for their dishonored bodies lie yet upon the earth, have been bored into by maggots and beetles and ants, gnawed at by wolves and nocturnal creatures glad of the feast. What is left of their rotting flesh is seeping into the earth, condemning their unreleased spirits to evermore remain earthbound, enshrouded in fog. The dead are much with her, and she sits bitterly before the shredded skirt and with rancor contemplates this journey through a lost world to one long ago forsaken.

She hates the smell of the troops' food, their sweat, their clothes, their breath. The major's son comes toward her, stepping out of the fog, and delights in the shredded material, paws at the remnants of her skirt and takes the longest, widest piece, discards his hat and wraps the strip turbanlike about his head, then dances away. He is everywhere underfoot, annoying the troops, the cook, the lieutenant, embarrassing his father. Cole watches his antics and pities the major, who beside him seems exhausted, mournful. Henry imitates a dervish, whirls unstoppably and unstopped, his father staring dazedly at him, the deranged, repetitive circling making him slightly ill. Cole says, Turn away.

Look at me! Henry calls out, coming to a standstill with one hand on his turbaned head. Look! This is what I wore when I escaped! he cries excitedly. Remember, Father? Remember the time I was locked in a room in Auntie's house? Or so they thought! For at night I flew from there on a carpet, a turban on my head—yes, I did—to the land of the Hindus, he continues with a bow, where all men are magicians, where they charm snakes, put them into their nostrils and let them crawl out of their mouths, stuff them into their ears and pull them from their arses. The troops laugh, and there is derision in their laughter. Ha! Ha! you idiots, what do you know? Henry challenges. I went to the Hindu lands every night on a flying carpet, I learned their language like this—and he snaps his fingers, breaks into a staccato speech which no one understands, makes the soldiers guffaw, mesmerized now, for Henry has his audience in the palm of his hand. They close in about him, and Henry lunges at them, arms spread, and startles a few of the men who are elbowed by their fellows and laugh the harder.

A rug is all, Henry mock-pleads, raising his arms theatrically, a rug: my kingdom for a rug! The soldiers grin and shake their heads. A rug is all I need to fly away, to return to the Hindus, come, give me one, someone must have such a thing! But the cook rings for dinner, and men break up and take their plates and forks and head toward the food. Cutter goes to his son, takes the strip of skirt from Henry's head, walks over to where the cook is dishing out portions, tosses it onto the fire. Reed Gabriel looks up from his writing and watches as Cutter glances in the direction of his dejected son, wonders at whatever it was that went wrong. Knowing the answer is unknowable.

Abigail Buwell does not touch the food placed beside her, leaves the plate where it is, and disappears into the night with the roan. Lt. Hastings rises from where he squats before the fire and takes several strides in her direction before being stopped by a voice. John, the major calls to him, and Hastings halts in his tracks and turns and sees a few of the men and Henry palming steaming cups of coffee. Beyond the fire, Cutter sits with his back against a tree, his hand raised in a gesture of sanction.

Let her, Cutter says at Hastings' approach, there's no harm to it. Cole gets to his feet and moves off, leaving Hastings to stay or go, and the lieutenant drops to his haunches, sits beside the major, wishes suddenly he could offer the man a tumbler of cognac, that he could turn back time. He very much likes Cutter, feels with him an intimacy rare between men of differing ranks, and was always appreciative of those leisurely briefings, Cutter's offer of fine spirits, the way his quarters evoked a forgotten and now lost past. It's not harm that worries me, the lieutenant confides, settling his long legs into a comfortable position, it's disappearance.

Reed Gabriel turns onto his side, pulls a blanket over him, watches the two men, feels the cold damp of the earth beneath him, listens to their lowered voices.

She has nowhere to go, Cutter says.

She might go anyway.

She would have gone before this. The outpost's gates were open. You saw that for yourself.

Perhaps back there she wasn't reminded of—and he sweeps one arm at the fog, the beyond—this.

I'd guess she was reminded of nothing else.

The lieutenant looks sideways at the major, moves a bit to better read Cutter's expression, but all he sees are lines and shadows and unfathomable hollow eyes. On such a night as this, John, the major says unexpectedly, I imagine Hamlet walking the ramparts, speaking to his father's ghost.

The lieutenant nods. Beyond the encampment horses neigh and snort, and Hastings strains at the sounds, begins to rise. She won't leave, Lieutenant. At ease.

Hastings sits back down. Cutter is no longer anyone's commanding officer, and his *at ease* is more a plea than an order. Sorry, Hastings apologizes. I just can't imagine she wouldn't. I would, in her stead.

She's resigned to her fate, Cutter says tiredly. Thinks: As I am.

Resigned, sir? She has no idea of what her fate will be. Do you?

The lieutenant hesitates, unsure whether he is

about to overstep a boundary, unsure whether the major knows her destination, then decides he doesn't care, that it does not matter if it falls to him to say. To be put in an asylum. Most probably, Hastings amends.

Cutter groans, passes a hand over his face. We are such fools.

Perhaps it won't be so bad. Perhaps it will help her.

It will be a horrible end.

We can't know that. It's not a prison.

Why, then, 'tis none to you; for there is nothing either good or bad, but thinking makes it so: to me it is a prison. And to her.

Perhaps she'll learn to think it's not.

John, if the world exists at all for her, it probably exists as a prison.

You can't seriously believe that.

I've come seriously to believe that life might be nothing more than a prolonged captivity, or a series of such.

My senses would flee if I thought so.

From across the way a peal of laughter rings, oddly harsh. Henry stands with his head thrown back, gulping the air with a fish-mouthed motion. Suck in the stars, he cries, suck them in, even if you can't see them! And then you'll have sweet dreams!

I doubt that very much, the major says. And for a moment Hastings is not sure whether Cutter is responding to Henry or continuing the conversation. Before he makes up his mind, Cutter places a hand on his shoulder and gets to his feet. I doubt that, John.

Cole materializes from nowhere with a blanket in his hands.

Goodnight, Hastings says.

Sleep well, comes Cutter's rejoinder. And then he walks stiffly away, following on Cole's heels, skirting the campfire, his son, the troops, and is swallowed by the fog.

She hears them come, she knows their footsteps, she does not stir from where she lies on the ground. Cole speaks gently to the roan, leads Cutter around it as a spirit would guide a somnambulist and as carefully. He leads him to Abigail Buwell, and then Cutter does not so much sit as collapse. Cole places the blanket around his shoulders and then is gone.

Cutter lowers himself on his side, places his head upon her ankles, draws up his knees and puts his cold hands between them, feels bone press upon bone, and is awed by human folly and the sadness within him. He has no book, no passage, no letter in his hands, he has nothing to read aloud to her. His good shoulder is to the ground, there is a soreness where his heart is, and his bones settle and crack within his skin, which, he muses, is no thicker than the thinnest peel of birch bark, of parchment or the membrane of a bird's eye. He is not given to wonder at the thought, but to a shudder. He despises, mourns at this moment his own frailty.

Gone forever, he knows, is his body's joy. Never again will he feel the invincibility of youth, and his memories of such will become foreign to him. Even now he cannot conjure any remembrance of the pleasure once felt in the thrust and meld of their young, insatiable bodies, the heat of love, the burning within his loins, Lavinia's mewling, his own gasps. He wants to sob, he wants his tears to pour as libations upon Abigail Buwell's feet, upon her ankles, he wants to blubber and weep because his memories are like the husks of shelled wheat, emptied of fullness, shapes without substance. But the immediacy of the press of fog, of the darkness, and his awareness of every rib and joint and vertebra, his weak sinews, exhausted muscles, pronounced bones, thin skin, softening cartilage, flagging heartbeat, yellowing fingernails, loosened teeth, and ragged breathing allow him no tears. He is but a sack of blood and guts and shit and phlegm held together by some improbable sheath pulled taut over a ridiculous skeletal form, and there is no man within. He moans at the realization. The roan raises its head abruptly from its grazing, and Abigail Buwell's entire body spasms, jolts a lightning-quick response, as though she had misstepped into the void between wake and sleep.

And then, suddenly, Cutter realizes the cur is not with them.

That old dog just turned around and went back, will be Cole's first words to him in the gray thickness of dawn.

She knows this trail, Abigail Buwell could lead the men and the horses and the wagons along it even if her eyes had been gouged from her head, she can smell the tainted and fresh water sources, smell the shape of distant mountains, the plunge of faraway ravines, the contours of crests and dip of saddle passes. She could lead them by scent, she could lead them by sound. For a trail trodden by buffalo is flattened in a different way from one by mules or those by antelope herds or wild horses; and the trampled earth of each gives off a different sound. The trail they travel, this hardpacked, rutted road worn into the earth by plodding paupers and emigrants walking the continent's distance has its own melody, one she could follow just by listening. She knows they will pass those spots where she, Eugene Buwell, and his brother made camp, pass by trails that led far from this route, trails they mistakenly followed—and disappointedly double backed on—in the name of homesteading, hoping to discover a place that welcomed motionlessness and could relieve their unimaginable weariness. They feared the land was endless and endlessly inhospitable. They searched for a place where they might surrender to some instinctual need to nest, to dig in, to seek shelter beyond that afforded by their ill-used coats, their weather-beaten hats, the useless canvas stretched over their wagon that hardly shielded the sun, let in the rain, and was ripped by winds whose force no one had ever dreamed of or felt before. They sought out any refuge—a stand of trees, a bank of prairie, a roll of hill—where they might hew timber for walls or cut sod in blocks or burrow into the earth, say this is it, here we'll stay. Their judgment was sorely impaired and their souls smalled by the deprivations that seemed eternal.

But Abigail Buwell does not lead them; instead, she trails them, her legs and thinned hips free of the cumbersome skirt, the woolen pants scratching against her inner thighs and her seat where her body meets the roan. She ignores Reed Gabriel, who sometimes halts his mount and waits for her to pass, his quizzical eyes kind, and who always touches his hat and nods gravely to her and wants nothing more than for her to acknowledge him, break her code of silence. Which within her is no code at all, for she cannot keep the words from flowing through her, from gnawing at her; she cannot stop the agitation of them, nor stop the constant bubbling of memories. She carries the dead within her; she glimpses her mother's painted mouth, the infant she willed unborn sliding from her in a slime of bloody froth, Abraham Hume black-clad and ill-fitted in the planked coffin with a face as grim in final repose as it had been in life. She sees the massacred bodies of those whose names she will never again utter and whose words she will never again hear. She rides past countless graves of the unknown dead buried along the emigrant trail, the haphazard crosses tipping this way and that, leaning over depressions or lying where they fell, marking the ravages of cholera, dysentery, pneumonia, accidental shootings, intentional murders, smallpox, measles, lightning strikes, ague, marking the way through the fog. The troops mutter at the murk, swear at their nervous horses that spook at the spectral shapes of humpbacked animals curled in sleep, of crouching men, of monstrous dragons, which are only heaps of clothes, mounds of boots, rotting barrels or cast iron stoves, bales of fencing wire, the rib cages of long-dead milk cows, yokes and fragments of wagon hulls, kegs, wheels, rims, washtubs, trunks, mattresses, baking ovens, memorials all to some ill-fated passage. The men curse and saw at their horses' mouths and peer into the fog and shiver in the damp and curse the more.

Abigail Buwell rides with the reins loose on the

roan's withers. She does not speak the words that flow through her, she does not remark on the things she sees. When they come to a certain fork in the trail, however, she stills the horse and for a very long moment gazes in the direction of Eugene Buwell's homestead, where she lived as his wife who was not a wife. And then rides on.

The wagon train had come this far along the emigrant trail and too slowly, for the first of autumn was upon them. The sojourners were divided, and they argued as to whether to continue. Men with hard eyes insisted they should push stubbornly on, despite looking worriedly at their wasted animals and their wasted bodies and their wasted children and women. Others were persuaded. The Buwell brothers were not.

Following the wagon driven by one brother as the other herded their animals, Abigail Buwell had walked more than a month, leading the saddle horse whose coat had lost its luster and whose skin had tightened about its bones and whose flanks and chest and withers had been bitten sorely by bloodsucking insects. She had slept next to her husband's inert body for exactly two nights in the wagon, his brother bedded on the ground beneath them, and then slept beside him no more. If Eugene Buwell desired her, he had given no sign of this since the third night of their marriage, when he finally managed to overcome his mortifying shyness and had tentatively placed one hand on the side of her neck and brushed his lips below her ear. She was standing, pensive, before their campfire, watching the water in the coffee pot begin to boil. She had not heard him come up behind her, and his touch, his tenderness, startled her. When she turned to him tears rose to her eyes: no one had been so gentle with her since her early childhood, when women who laughed had held her on their laps in a large kitchen.

You miss your father, Eugene Buwell ventured, unsure what her tears meant and embarrassed by the presence of his brother, who had remarked crudely to Eugene that day: You ain't done it yet. I been listening good and from what I hear I could be bunking beneath the dead for as much excitement as is going on.

She shakes her head and says something that gets caught in her throat. The coffee boils and hisses as it spills onto the coals, and she takes up her skirt and with it grabs the handle, puts the pot on a flat rock, ladles cold water into it to settle the grounds. When she straightens, she takes another deep breath and says to Eugene Buwell: He wasn't my father. He was someone who bought me, and I'd been bought before.

James Buwell saunters over, pours himself a cup of coffee, one for his brother, and flashes Eugene a well-well, eyebrows-raised look as he hands it to him. Eugene Buwell studies the steaming liquid, swirls it in the tin cup. We better sit down, he says.

She sits across from him so she can see Eugene Buwell's face. It is a good face, a lean face; the shape of his mouth is fuller than his beard reveals. She likes his dark eyes—there is something melancholic in them, something kind—and his thick brows, which are furrowed much of the time, give him a thoughtful countenance, though she knows nothing of what he thinks. For she knows nothing about him at all, except that he has treated her fairly for three whole days and two nights, helped her to stoke the fire, carry water, care for the animals, that he has asked nothing of her and said little. At those times when he caught her eye, a smile played at the corners of his mouth. She has found herself looking down at her body while walking, knowing that bruises still discolor her ribs, examining the thinness of her wrists, hiding her broken fingernails in clenched hands; she has been self-conscious, felt her step to be off kilter, her movements awkward, her being inadequate. A shyness has flooded over her with the cessation of abuse, with Eugene Buwell's lack of demands upon her, with his glances. It has struck her that this man, her husband, might be a good man, and that notion terrifies her. Abigail Buwell has never known a good man, but she knows without having ever met one that no good man should be deceived. Which he has already been.

She takes a deep breath again and repeats: Hiram Worth was not my father. And she tells him what she has never told anyone: that she knows she was born in a town with a river, that she remembers a newspaper-walled shack, then a brothel, and the color of her mother's mouth; that she doesn't know her mother's name or her own last name; that she remembers a kitchen and corridors with many doors, and kind women with a bruised look to their eyes. She tells him that a man by the name of Abraham Hume took her from her mother and brought her to his childless farm and there, for the years she stayed, made her perform acts such as are seen in barnyards and do things never seen in barnyards while his childless wife cloistered herself in the house, remaining to the end a silent accomplice. She told Eugene Buwell that at the age of fourteen, by her own counting—for she was taught to read and write, and she knows her numbers—she was given or, rather, sold by Hume's widow to Hiram Worth, who often beat her senseless, from time to time put ribbons in her hair, and always paraded her about as his daughter, which suited his scams. She told him of the towns she had seen and the brothels she had visited in the hope of finding her mother, in the hope of finding someone who would remember her, and of the farmsteads Hiram Worth had in part conned and in part robbed, of the women he had satiated or cowed, of the remedies he had concocted, of the lies he and she had lived.

Abigail Buwell will not have this marriage be a lie.

When she finishes speaking, she sits in the dim glow of the waning fire, her back to the darkness, her soul filled with anguish, her eyes downcast. She does not look at Eugene Buwell now, for she has watched his face cloud, seen him bite his lower lip, noted the whitening of his knuckles. She waits for him to speak, but Eugene Buwell says nothing. And so she says the only thing left to say: You can turn me away.

She's the daughter of a whore, she's been degraded by one man and abused by another: this is all Eugene Buwell can think. That, and: I've married her. Eugene Buwell wants to cry or kill someone, or both; within him there is hurt and fury, but he does nothing, for there is nothing to do. When she finally looks at him, she swallows hard. He finds her long neck beautiful, tears his eyes from it.

By your reckoning, he remarks pensively, you're seventeen.

It is not what she expects him to say, and for a moment she is confused. She nods, and when he hears no answer he looks at her questioningly. Yes, she says.

He studies her for what seems an eternity, then purses his lips, frowns. I would no more send a woman by herself back along this trail than a child, he pronounces slowly. If you choose to continue on with the others, you're free to do so.

And if I choose to stay.

He rises and looks down at her and does not know what to say, what to do, opens his hands in a gesture of pure helplessness. You might not choose wisely.

And then he turns away from her, turns his back on those things she has said that will keep him from being her husband. James Buwell, lounging on the other side of the fire, watches him go.

The brothers stand together, their heads bent, voices low, as the rest of the wagon train readies for departure. Abigail Buwell does what she has done each morning for a month since being married: makes breakfast; washes the pots, pans, plates, cutlery; waters the animals; damps the fire. Now she stands apart with the saddle horse, letting it graze, watching the brothers. When they finally break apart, Eugene Buwell strides over to the lead wagon, speaks with the family whose children are climbing into it as dawn streaks crimson on the horizon behind them. Then he turns and comes toward her, head down; and when he reaches her, he does not look her in the eye. She stoops and gathers the horse's tether. He reaches out a hand and palms the horse's shoulder, gazes somewhere over its back.

Look, he tells her, we won't go on with the rest.
They've agreed to take you with them.

She swallows hard, the world swimming before her.
The horse turns its head and rubs its nose on her hip,
and she feels the universe roaring about her and a
shriveling within. In a constricted voice, she says: But
they are nothing to me.

He looks sharply at her and is pained to see her
pallor, her dejected mouth, the tears in her eyes, and
then he looks away and shifts his weight, hears his name
called, raises his arm and waves the wagons off before
he is even aware of his gesture. The first team lunges
forward at the crack of a whip and the wagons creak and
heave and then roll, and people yell and whistle at their
animals, the oldest children leading horses or herding
cows, the caged hens making a racket, the dogs barking.
When he turns back to her, she does not move except to
lower her eyes.

I can't promise you a thing, he says bitterly, and
instantly regrets his tone, his words, but he cannot hide
the truth. Oh God, he thinks then, let her speak, let her
say something. But she only drops her head as if in
shame, until his brother calls out and she looks up
sharply in James Buwell's direction. Before Eugene
Buwell knows it, she presses the horse's tether into his
hand and walks rapidly away. He watches her go, her
body too thin, her head bent, her hands clutching the
skirt that falls from her girl's hips, marching away from
the wagon train and in the direction of the rising sun. Its
rose-hued and yellow rays bend around her. Eugene
Buwell calls to her, and she walks faster, does not stop.

After a moment, he swings onto the saddle horse's back, nudges it with his heels. When he catches up to her, he cuts her off. She tries to go around the horse, once, twice, but he blocks her way both times.

I don't want the horse, she says.

I'm not stopping you to give you the horse.

I've made my choice. Leave me be.

You can go with the others, but you can't go back alone. I've said this once, now again. You'll simply perish, and this my conscience will not abide.

Be easy, she says then, raising her terrible eyes to him, for I believe I perished long ago.

Take the tether, he tells her, slipping from the horse's back, for he cannot bear what he sees in her eyes. Time is wasting. And when she neither responds nor moves nor allows him to hand her the horse, he says, despite himself: Come. Matters can be settled later.

You know differently, she replies ruefully. As do I.

His brother yells again, and he looks beyond her to see James Buwell striding impatiently in their direction. Panic rattles him, for he wants his brother to be no part of this. During the night the two bedded far beyond the wagon, and James Buwell had ended their argument cruelly. A whore's whelp, James said derisively, you managed to find yourself a whore's whelp, so why not keep her? We could share her. She's done worse, and winter's coming on. Eugene had thrown an elbow into his brother's stomach, then listened to him expel his breath painfully before rolling away, taking the blanket with him. She'll leave with the others in the morning, Eugene Buwell said.

He was wrong. And he cannot, will not, let her walk

away alone.

Let's go, Eugene Buwell says sternly, wary of his brother's approach. It's time, James Buwell says, stopping some paces from them and looking from one to the other, a stupid grin on his face. Eugene Buwell gives her the horse to lead, and she takes the tether. When she passes them and heads toward the wagon, she does not see the playful punch James Buwell throws at his brother. But she has already seen the leer in James Buwell's eyes.

The major has noted the days, and when he sees Abigail Buwell halt her horse at the fork in the trail and gaze in the direction of her past, he calculates they have ridden a whole day longer than he imagined the Buwells' homestead turnoff to be, their pace slowed by the denseness of the fog. She has not spoken a word along this journey, at each day's end removed herself from their midst, stayed close by the horses, given wide berth to the troops, slept upon the hard, cold ground with Cutter's head upon her ankles. She has eaten little and tended the blue roan; but her constancy is such that Lt. Hastings no longer frets when she drifts away from their campsite or apart at their halts to let the horse graze.

Reed Gabriel is never far from her on the trail. He has taken to speaking to her, insistently but always gently. He finds something in her eyes, in her way of seeing through him and her way of looking, that convinces him Abigail Buwell has no more forgotten the only language they share than he has. But he can find no common ground to bridge whatever abyss lies between them, between her and the world; though the Lord knows, he remarks to himself, he tries. No matter what stories he tells her, no matter his banter, no matter his thoughtful pronouncements, no matter the sweet songs he sometimes sings, Abigail Buwell seldom tolerates his closeness for long, but turns or quickens her horse with the imperceptible pressure of her calf or knee or seat, rides before him or lags behind. When dismounted, Gabriel sometimes approaches her only to watch her walk away elsewhere. She seldom meets his eyes, and he has never once been able to come close to her from behind without her moving off, regardless of the lightness of his tread, his cautious silence. He has watched—with what, he wonders, envy? curiosity? desire?—Cutter remove himself each evening from the campfire, disappear into the darkness beyond it on stiff legs and with a painful gait, in her direction; and one morning, at the first intimation of dawn, he found them, saw for himself Cutter sleeping at her feet, and almost yelped when Cole unexpectedly came up behind Gabriel and touched him on his elbow. The major deserves some respect as yet, Cole said to him, and Gabriel felt the color rise to his face even as he pulled his arm away and walked off, feeling he had made a fool of himself.

No more a fool than Cutter's mad son, certainly, Gabriel consoles himself. For Henry, with his silly hat and ridiculous clothes, has tired the troops with his antics, with his impersonations of those who people his mind—charwomen and itinerant tinsmiths and errant knights and John the Baptist, conquistadors, alligator wrestlers, buffalo hunters, French counts, coolie laborers, distressed damsels, blanket peddlers, hump-backs and harlequins, Turkish courtesans. Henry's constant babble has become intolerable, his clever and tireless imitations irritating. The tongues in which he performs, his romping to and fro, his hide-and-seek play no longer make him the butt of laughter but of contempt. The same troops who once egged him on now break ranks to avoid him; they curse him, mutter at him under their breath, and in the evenings find themselves so weary of him that he is ostracized by their turned backs and closed congregation and sullen withdrawal. Their resentment at times pushes him over some precipice, where he falls into utter torpor, refuses to speak even when spoken to, sits before the fire as froth rimes the corners of his mouth and drool drips down his chin, his eyes blank as the night, until his silence rivets them once more, for they cannot find the buffoon in their midst. And then they cajole him until he comes to life, until they tire of him again.

Reed Gabriel has no idea what Henry is doing with them, or why he made the journey with Colonel Chapman's troops, or what truck he might have with his father, for the major says little to his son. Whatever ties bind them are of no usual sort; there is no affection between them, they hardly ever share a mess, though the young man sometimes trails the major like a moron on an escorted jaunt, whimpering to himself, or rolling his eyes, or lolling his head, his tongue long and loose and playing about his mouth, his chin, the tip of his nose. In his moments of rare lucidity, Henry rankles the major with reminiscences: he mentions his dead siblings, his mother, his aunt, plies Cutter with questions—Will we farm or will we ranch? Can we raise blood horses? What about longhorns? Have you money, Father? for I've almost none—that Cutter does not answer, for he doesn't see the point anymore. His son cannot understand that Cutter's professional life is over, that, at the very least, he will be stripped of rank and pension. What money he had, except the back pay he now pockets—which will surely not be enough to cover the cost of Henry's doctors and the asylum, if that is where he must go—is gone, was invested badly or lent to Lavinia's sister, who can repay nothing, or thrown at his hapless son's education and at his physicians, or poured into the upkeep of a worthless family homestead that long ago went to seed around his brother's gravesite, or simply wasted, as money always is.

If Reed Gabriel cannot imagine what Henry is doing with them, Cutter cannot fathom what he will do with his son when they finally reach their destination. He will not be able to give his only living offspring a decent life. He himself has no future. Abigail Buwell rides past, he feels the familiar blow to his chest, realizes: This is what we share, what she and I have in common: we have no future.

Reed Gabriel waits until Cole has gone to tend the horses before offering the major a drink from the flask he takes from the bottom of a saddlebag. Cutter seems pleased; he accepts the flask and drinks and holds the liquor in his mouth, tasting it until tears come to his eyes, then swallows and feels the heat rush into his gut before handing back the flask. The fog about them, impossibly thick, seems to seep upward from the earth itself. Abigail Buwell crosses their line of vision trailed by the roan, disappears. Eight days, Gabriel remarks, watching her, watching nothing, of just being able to see our hands in front of our faces. He drinks and gives the flask to Cutter again.

Appreciate it.

They sit almost shoulder to shoulder as they pass the flask back and forth, watching the men come and go in the thickening night, dragging wood, making the fire, readying the mess. I've been meaning to ask you, Gabriel says after a while, about Abigail Buwell.

There's nothing I could tell you.

Mostly I'm interested in what you think.

I'm not much given to thought these days, Cutter says, astonished at the ease with which the lie is spoken. It falls between them like a gauntlet, and Gabriel lets it be. The major is grateful Gabriel does not persist, and for the first time admits to himself that the journalist has some sensitivity, and certainly a reticence Cutter finds amiable. Cutter muses that the man must be good at cards and with women and maybe even with words, for he uses them sparingly. They drink in silence and Gabriel lets the major have his way, doesn't press him further; things that want telling get told, someone once said to him, it's just that sometimes you have to wait. So he lets the liquor take its effect, minds not at all Cutter's disinclination to speak, and is mildly surprised when the major says, Sorry to be evasive.

It's understandable.

Cutter wonders if it is. Then says, with honesty: It's just that it won't matter what I think. Not in the end.

Gabriel holds the flask in midair, waits.

What will matter in the end is what she thinks.

Of?

Of what she's been through. Of what the savages meant to her—of everything, I suspect. Of what she thinks of us, this, civilization.

She's one of us.

Not by choice, it seems. And if she is, I can't begin to imagine what that means to her.

What does it mean to you?

At this point in my life, he finally replies, I'd say that it means being part of some inexplicable abomination.

She will tell Robert Cutter only one thing of her life with Eugene Buwell, and this only long after they pass Fort H, long after they escape the fog, long after they parallel the endless railroad tracks that stretch to the continent's beginning and witness mile upon mile of sunbleached buffalo bones stacked higher than any train's height, where the slaughtered beasts were hauled and skinned for their hides and humps and nothing more and left to rot by the millions. She will speak of the man she married only long after they pass by the first farmlands and the towns that began and ended on the one street that led through them, where hard-looking men peered at them from beneath their hats and worn women shaded their foreheads with their hands to better see the faces of the troops and the clownish figure cut by the major's son and the supply wagons and the black man in uniform and the rail-thin woman with shorn hair riding in breeches astride a blue horse. She will speak of Eugene Buwell only long after they reach their destination—a large town sprawled between two rivers, where they are billeted within a fort on a bluff— and long after she is taken from that fort and escorted to the asylum by Lt. Hastings, who is accompanied by Cutter, Reed Gabriel, Cole, the major's mad son, and a handful of troops; and long after her confinement therein. She will tell Robert Cutter what she does because he remarks, upon one of his many visits to her, how forlorn she seemed when she stopped the roan at a certain place along the emigrant trail and gazed for a long moment in a direction that led away from it. She will tell Robert Cutter what she does because he asks her if she was sorry to have lost Eugene Buwell. To which she will say only: I came to have a quiet liking for him.

The Buwells struck southward the day they left the wagon train, through an inhospitable landscape the likes of which she had never seen in her travels with Hiram Worth. She had, she thought, seen everything: beech and oak forests, lush rolling hills in which farmsteads nestled, fields yielding wheat and barley, tobacco and cotton; they had driven upon levee roads banked above endless swamps, roads upon which snakes as thick as her arms dozed in the sweltering afternoon heat; she had seen sycamores smothered by moss, smelled a delta's decay of ooze and muck. They had traveled through flatlands of corn and sunflower, skirted mountains of granite and slate and others dense with juniper and hemlock; they trespassed mean mining communities strung along mountain valley bottoms, followed railroads long in disuse. They had sometimes been snowbound;

she had seen floods and forded streams, and once—where a bridge had washed away—they had been ferried across a swollen river. But they always traveled roads or what passed as roads, sometimes badly rutted trails wide enough to allow only the passage of one wagon; and no matter how remote the homesteads or how great the distances between towns, Hiram Worth had the sense to push them along routes that had water sources, the occasional decrepit inn, and the infrequent but inevitable signposts. Which he would study at length, as though making a momentous decision, before turning the wagon toward somewhere he had not been.

But the Buwell brothers traveled by the sun and their sense of south. When the trail finally vanished, they found and followed the wash of a river sunk beneath its bed. She led the saddle horse behind them and watched the wagon sway and thump over the uneven going, over clumps of thorn and scrub, boulders and anthills, the cows before it lowing and distressed by the heat and the flies, the oxen growing stubborn enough to roll their placid eyes and thirsty enough that their tongues hung from their mouths. They pushed on, hoping the scrubland around them would give way to something better; in the indeterminable distance they glimpsed hues of color they mistook for verdant growth, distant knolls in shadow they mistook for trees. The scrub eventually began to give way to prairie grass, thick and tough and certainly hell on the wheelspokes of any wagon, and they pushed on in the dry riverbed. Eventually they reached a shallow waterhole full of silt and so covered with insects that they had to lay a good piece of cloth over it and weigh this down with stones, so that it sank and filtered the water before they allowed themselves and their animals to drink. That night they made no fire, and she bedded herself alone in the wagon and the brothers slept outside, and the next day they pushed on again, the animals sorely reluctant, following the riverbed. Toward that day's end they saw, somewhere within the expansive dusk lying upon the flat earth, a thin trail of white smoke rising into the sky. Before nightfall they reached a point where the river began to surface, the water a trickle and farther on a paltry flow, and they looked about at the grazing and the thick prairie grasses and at how the land was beginning to heave and cleft, having been raked glacially eons before, and they came upon a clay bank and stands of sparse-leafed trees and breathed a sigh of relief that they had come far enough.

The next day the brothers left her with the cows and oxen, the saddle and pack horses, and set out on their mounts to try to find the source of the smoke they'd seen. When they returned late the following day, the horses much used, she could see in their faces brutal disappointment. But they had in tow a small flatbed cart with two solid wheels, on which lay a sod cutter they had borrowed from their nearest and only neighbors, the Smiths, whose place had been difficult to find. The smoke they had seen came from a cave dug into a hillock, and though the front of the cave had been extended with sod walls, its roof looked exactly like the prairie that had yielded it. Long after the brothers had watered and tethered their horses and eaten, drained the coffee pot, and she had settled herself into the wagon, Eugene Buwell knocked on its frame and opened the flap and said to her, This is the place. For the life of her, she could not muster a response, and he was gone before she thought to have said in return, Well, that's good.

The brothers set about cutting sod and downing several trees a considerable distance away and digging into the curve of a rise where they determined the house would best be protected from north winds. They worked ceaselessly, and in a week they had carved out a cave, against whose walls they placed what stones they could drag from the riverbed. They made a room extending from the cave with the sod they cut and hauled and stacked squarely, earth up to the sun, and then they placed timbers crosswise and laid more sod down as a roof, the door being between two poles split at their tops to hold a beam. They packed the earth floor as best they could, then dragged two beds, bedding, a table and three chairs from the wagon and placed these inside. They hung two oil lamps from one of the ceiling beams, and strung a blanket over the doorway. That dank, dark, breathless place became their home. Abigail Buwell remained in the wagon.

The brothers erected sod shelters for the horses and oxen and cows, fenced in a makeshift corral with bailing wire, stringing it around poles they went distances to cut, bring back, and put into the holes they dug in the hard ground. They put up a sod leanto against one side of the house, where the stove was placed. All the while, Abigail Buwell tended the animals, herded them to decent grazing, riding the saddle horse bareback. She scanned the endless land, studied the endless sky, pushed the oxen and cows forward in search of the most tender grasses. She cooked meals and kept a washbasin near the stove; she washed clothes and spread these on top of the wagon's canvas top to dry; she kept the bucket of drinking water full and tied a dipper to it; she made a place for washing themselves in private, behind the leanto. She worked uncomplainingly and in silence, and she asked nothing of them. At night the immensity of the sky took her breath away, and the yowling of coyotes saddened her. She thought she had never been more alone in a lifetime of being nothing but lonely. And in a world without end.

By the time the Buwell brothers brought the cart and sod cutter back to the Smiths, it was deep autumn. A few days later Eugene Buwell saddled his horse and, leading a pack horse, rode off. He said nothing to her of his going, and she watched helplessly until he was no more than a speck before mounting the saddle horse and riding hard after him. When she finally gained on him, the sound of cantering stopped him. He watched her come, marveling at her lightness on the horse, at her hair flying behind her, but when she pulled the horse up before him, the creature dancing sideways, he said curtly: You could lame a horse, riding like that.

He saw the wounding in her eyes and the ferocious fear in her face. She wanted to say, You can't just ride off like this and leave me here, but she didn't, knowing that he would do what he wanted, what he must. All she managed was to swallow hard and say, instead, This is unfair.

What is?

Your going.

We need supplies.

I mean your going without me.

I'm not taking my brother either. He's got work to do here. So do you.

Then your going without telling me.

He tilted his head to the side, narrowed his eyes. I didn't think I was beholden to say.

You're beholden, she told him. He heard the catch in her voice but not the pounding in her chest; she set her mouth just so. He shifted in the saddle, studied something, nothing, in the distance.

Well. I'm going to get what we'll be needing for the winter, then. I'll be back.

When?

The Smiths say there's a supply post some five days northeast of here. Figure less than two weeks.

There was nothing more she could ask, nothing more he would say. He reined his horse around and she watched him lead the pack horse away, stop.

You've been working real hard, he said over one shoulder. It's appreciated. When he moved forward again, he did not look back. She watched him go, watched until he and the horses were devoured by the distance.

It was twelve days before he returned. Both horses were so heavily laden that he was leading them on foot, and he was bone weary, sick of the infernal wind that now blew hard and ceaselessly across the churning sea of prairie grass, ripping up thorn by the roots and swirling dust into mysterious formations, its moan constant in his ears and grating upon his nerves, its grit in his mouth, in the horses' eyes and nostrils. He had made no fire since leaving the supply post because he was unable to do so; he was tired of hardtack as sustenance; and he had nothing but pity for the two horses. His own feet were so sore that he could feel the shock of each step in his skull. In such a condition, Eugene Buwell came upon the swell of welcome water in the riverbed, crossed the stream, was relieved to find that the small dam he and his brother made had held— the water had backed up and was clear—and felt happy to approach what six months before he could never have imagined would be his home, anyone's home, lodged in one of the poorest of places on the face of the earth.

The cows and oxen were nowhere to be seen, nor was the saddle horse or his brother's mount. No smoke rose from the stove; there was no one in the wagon that stood forlorn with its frayed canvas top. Eugene Buwell called into the wind, but his voice did not carry. He ran his eye along the horizon and saw no one, nothing, as panic gripped him hard. At the supply depot he'd heard stories—not for the first time, but for the first time firsthand accounts—of the savages. Grizzled men, trading and bartering there, spoke of the savages' sudden and unaccountable appearances, their brutality, described the way they slaughtered women and children, flayed men, took scalps, killed livestock. Eugene Buwell pulled so hard on the horse he was leading that the creature stretched its neck and lay its head even with its withers to keep pace with him, and then Eugene Buwell shouted again and, to his great relief, saw his brother stumble out of the sod house. A split second later, he realized that James Buwell's head was bandaged, half his face unrecognizable, his legs unsteady.

His brother could tell him nothing. His nose was broken, his cheekbone swollen, the left side of his face discolored and distorted. He moaned when Eugene Buwell pried his mouth open to see broken teeth, worse, for he had almost bitten through his tongue; and when Eugene Buwell cried *Oh god, where is she?*, his brother spit a wad of bloody phlegm and wiped the back of one wrist against his purplish lips.

Eugene Buwell left the two horses packed and standing, their noses to the ground. He ran toward where she grazed the cows and oxen, he ran until he thought his chest would burst, until he could no longer feel his legs, until he made out the oxen, the cows, his brother's horse and the saddle horse in a far-off hollow, standing belly-deep in prairie grass with their heads down, and then he began to yell. He did not see her, and he could only imagine that she had been slashed to ribbons, violated, slain. And then the saddle horse raised its head from grazing and a figure rose from the ground—it was her—but she did not move toward him as he lunged through the tough grass. He saw that the animals were fine, the cows moving off, the oxen raising their heads, but she was crying, and filthy. She stood in the middle of a depression trampled in the grass, with a blanket on the ground, his brother's rifle, a bucket with almost no water, the remains of a fire nearby. She was still crying, and there was something wild about her, and she hit Eugene Buwell as hard as she could as soon as he was close enough. The blow to his jaw caught him off guard, and the force of it made him stagger back a step, two, raise his hand to his chin. How could you, she bawled at him, how could you give me to him?—and then he saw her split lip and swollen eye and the scratches upon her hands in another way, and something in him sickened as the wind bit into his back. He stood there rubbing his jaw before he turned wordlessly and left her where she was.

Eugene Buwell told the brother he loved more than himself to take half their possessions, half their livestock, the wagon, and move off. Which James Buwell did sullenly, working his swollen tongue so that something like words came from him. She's a lying bitch, and a whore, is what he managed to say.

For the bruised time that remained to them, grief hung like an impenetrable veil between Abigail Buwell and the man who had married her. His brother moved six hard-riding hours to the west, and Eugene Buwell did not begrudge him the wagon or the livestock. He returned his rifle to him, helped him cut sod for a winter shelter. If their relationship changed, neither of them acknowledged it.

Eugene Buwell would be considerate of her for the rest of his short life, but he would never tell her that he did not give her to his brother. By spring, there were days when he and his wife worked side by side and he thought, This is good, the land will bear, we might make a life together. But when James Buwell visited, she withdrew into herself, remained silent and distant for days thereafter, for she knew what she knew, that the derangement and brutality within James Buwell lay deep beneath his surface, like a hibernating evil, and that Eugene Buwell would never admit this. She would never say aloud that James Buwell was, for her, an amalgam of Abraham Hume and Hiram Worth; she would never tell Eugene Buwell what transpired in his absence. Her silence, and Eugene Buwell's love for his brother, would pool into the gulf separating them.

And yet. There were times she found herself casting sideways glances at the man who worked beside her, whose name was now hers, and felt a deep gratitude for his goodness. There were evenings when she was comfortable in his company and minded not at all the quick brush of their hands as they shared a meal. There were moments she was struck still by his nearness; there were times when both were tantalized. From Eugene Buwell, the man who had married her, the man who would never be her husband, she learned a quiet calm and a way of living without fear. Sometimes, leaning over the stove, she thought of the women in the large kitchen, of their tenderness with her, of their way with men, and something within her would stir and she would gaze toward wherever he was and wonder what it would be like to lie in his embrace, to be intimate in a way she had never been with a man, with desire and affection, and then she would turn back to the stove and feel its heat on her cheeks.

Time, Abigail Buwell would tell herself, they say time heals all things. And so she waited for time to work its medicine. But time stopped one day just after dawn, when the savages came.

Nineteen

This is the end, Major Robert Cutter thinks. The sounds of the town can be heard from within the fort, hawker cries and carriage clatter, strains of music from the dance halls, newspaper vendors calling out headlines, bells tolling the hour, neighing horses, cattle lowing near the slaughterhouses. There are smells too, town smells, of bakeries and spice dens and fish stores and butcher shops, of starch and soap, of boiling meat and perfume and pomade and manure and human waste, cat urine, rotting vegetables.

He has met with his superiors, and a date for the military inquiry has been set. Henry, withdrawn and sullen and oddly vacuous, has been examined by military doctors; papers have been signed and forwarded, arrangements made. Abigail Buwell is now beyond Cutter's reach: she too has been evaluated, after being taken in by some officers' wives and forcibly stripped and properly dressed, as well as placed under guard, having shown no gratitude for the women's trouble and a singlemindedness about sleeping in horse stalls.

Tomorrow's journey will be her last.

It will be, Reed Gabriel thinks, a sad occasion. He is billeted with Hastings and Cutter and the major's son in the unmarried officers' quarters, where he now sits; Cole has been told by the major's superiors to sleep elsewhere. There is nothing to be done: the major's possessions have been stored, their dinner is finished, the cognac poured. Gabriel watches Henry rip at his fingertips and pull the skin from them. Hastings is pensive. The major looks lost. Two weeks from now, Reed Gabriel will hand in his account of Constance Smith's captivity, for which he will be paid handsomely; its publication will make him famous. A few months thereafter, he will cover Robert Cutter's court-martial. From that time forward, he will be sought after in government circles, invited to grace the tables of the wealthy, and wooed by the nation's most serious newspapers.

On the steps of the long, officious brick building that stands odd and red against the stretch of manicured lawn before it and a barren, rocky hill behind, the staff awaits them. Reed Gabriel wonders if they are seen as a strange procession, the major and Hastings and a few troops in uniform, Henry in his green hat and ridiculous clothes, Abigail Buwell with her shorn head and in petticoats and dress and stockings and slippers, riding bareback on the impressive roan, himself, and the black soldier trailing them on an ornery mule. No stranger, he decides, than the men and women awaiting them, the women in white bonneted and the men in white wearing long jackets looking as fashionable as, say, butchers or cooks, the two doctors in silk vests and shiny dark coats with tails and starched collars and string ties, one sporting a monocle with a black cord and the other a colored handkerchief in his pocket.

Henry dismounts first and matter-of-factly hands the reins to one of the soldiers as if this were the most natural thing in the world, then walks over to the doctors and shakes their hands and introduces himself. When he is led away he does not so much as look in the direction of the others, or at his father. Cutter feels the bones in his feet crunch when he dismounts and lets the reins drop altogether, leaves his horse where it is, and goes over to her. Abigail Buwell looks down at him from the blue roan's back and then stretches herself along the length of its neck. The horse turns its head and she brings her mouth to one of its ears and whispers to it—Reed Gabriel will swear to his dying day that she did so—and then she places her palms very carefully on certain points of its body, neck, withers, back, before sliding off and coming around to the horse's head to press her forehead against its face and stand there, motionless, a long time. Just before she straightens to look at the horse for the last time, she thinks *I cannot let go,* and then she takes her forehead from its face and one step back, looks into the creature's eyes. Two white-clad women approach her and put their hands on her elbows. She hands the reins to the major and, for the first time since he put eyes on her, smiles at him. It is a small and beautiful smile, a tragic smile. And then she feels herself letting go, she feels winds blow through her, she is empty, she smiles her smile, and something catches in Cutter's throat and then she is gone, taken from him by the women in white. He watches her go as the blue roan stands quietly, nudges his shoulder. Reed Gabriel will understand then how painful it is to see a grown man weep. How little it takes to break a heart.

After his court-martial, Robert Cutter will find a small, rundown house with a rotting picket fence and a neglected garden on the outskirts of town, and he will move into it after making the proper inquiries and learning it is in fact abandoned. Behind the house he erects a shed for the two horses he has, a chestnut and a blue roan. Both will outlive Abigail Buwell, the roan by three days, the chestnut by thirteen years. A brindle mutt will appear one day and wag its tail and its mangy behind and eventually move onto the porch and later into the house. Cutter will never give it a name because, in the beginning, he hardly believes the dog will stay; later, some time before the dog dies from old age, Cutter begins to contemplate such notions as the meaning of naming things and the insurmountable odds against doing so appropriately. He will live frugally and keep two sets of civilian clothes, one for Sundays—a misnomered day, he ruefully observes, on which it seems most likely to rain—and the other for the remaining six. He will tend an unyielding garden and become expert in the varieties of weeds, and he will allow himself one luxury only, good cognac. Shortly after Henry is released from Clearwater Asylum and returns not to his father but to his mother's sister, Robert Cutter will begin to hallucinate a small boy by the fence and take to never leaving his house after dusk.

The past will always be with him. He will come to see it as his worst enemy and also consider it, sadly, his only companion.

Twenty

*A*h, but who can foresee the unforeseeable, my dearest Lavinia? Fate is ruthless with its undiscerning ways, our ends incomprehensible no matter what they be. If I sound bitter is it because I am finally old, unrecognizable even to myself in the mirror that was once a present from you—my eyes rheumed and my sight much diminished and my always pronounced nose now wart-sprouting, my skin mottled, my cheekbones too prominent, my ears long, my hair sparse and what strands left the color of powdered slate—or is it because my body is frail, feeble, and my mind so clouded that I confuse the days and even the time of day, that I sometimes awake at dawn only to find it is dusk and sometimes awake thinking I have slept through an entire day only to discover the sun is rising? Who could have imagined—not you, not I—that I would so often sink to my knees from weakness in the poor garden I have tended for a score of years, more, into even poorer condition, that though I am stooped I cannot bend, my teeth have gone, my hands are useless and my fingers gnarled, I masticate *soft foods like a cow, taste nothing, smell nothing. This, the indignity of old age: infirmity. We dreamed of growing old as a time of leisure, I dreamed of distinction upon retiring my rank. Instead of leisure there are only hard, empty hours and hard, empty days and empty nights, weeks, months, years; instead of distinction a summary dismissal that the officers who sat in judgment thought kind, for in the end they considered me as we consider our dear son Henry, non compos mentis, someone not to be held responsible for his actions, though to this day when I try to remember what has now become so confused and obscure it still occurs to me that, at the outpost, there were simply no actions to take.*

Instead of prison, they retired me without rank in accordance with their notion of charity and left me to rot on barely a pittance, and so I have rotted. I served them well, I served my country, I led men to and from death, I gave my all, and I was repaid not in kind but dismissed and scorned, uninvited even to funerals of brother officers, men once my comrades. I have been shunned and overlooked as though leprous, I have lived without friends save for Cole who seldom visits and the journalist who from time to time writes to me; I am without you, without Henry—no, my dear, fear not, our son is well or at least I once heard he was, he outgrew his spells of nervous anxiety the doctors said were the result of a sensitive disposition and the rigors of an unsettled childhood and a too demanding education. When he left the asylum he was lucid and impersonated no one, spoke neither Hindi nor Arabic nor gobbledygook nor claimed to have ridden upon magic carpets nor to have visited Japan and the North Pole, he wore no silly clothes and he took his leave as a gentleman. Your sister once wrote to me that he had worked his way into the ownership of a dry goods store in—which city? ah, I can't remember—a waste of his intelligence no doubt, but there is much to be said for the mundane. When I think back that, with the war looming, one could not choose the mundane I regret history itself, I regret the forces outside us that shape us only to mangle us, chew us to bits and spit out our broken spirits, leaving wrecked families and dead siblings and diseased children in their wake, rather than honor and sensibility, though at the time I believed in something larger than myself, larger than us, I believed in principles and the righteousness of dying for such, and though I read in your eyes hesitation and despair—or was it fear?—I ignored them though your eyes haunted me, I fought as a man and as an officer should until my brother died and I wept and slept on his grave not only because he was lost to me the way you would later be, but because of a promise we'd made, one undoubtedly fulfilled. For the fact that he did not return from the dead nor send a sign from the hereafter meant there was but worm meat for us, that death is final, that we the living would no more be redeemed by dying than we were by living. If one can call this continuation of breathing—the physical function of a heart beating, blood circulating, the cycles of sleep and wake, the passing of days and nights—living.

The books I've carried with me all these years are so tattered that their pages have loosened and been misplaced, I can find no continuity in the telling of stories. I find page 47 before page 12, 89 behind 105—all is haphazard, as if gremlins spring through the cracks in the floorboards at night and wreak havoc upon these tomes. I find my razor in the coffee pot, the coffee pot on the porch, the butter spoiled and rancid, potato skins in the ice box, eggs broken in the wash basin, flowers in the outhouse, halters and bridles that once belonged to my horses so long dead on a chair. I spend my days wondering whether I am the butt of pranks wrought by invisible spirits or whether I am merely a wellspring of confusion and suffer such infirmity of mind that I simply play these games of startle and wonder with myself. Your likeness, however, is always in its place, here on the corner of my writing table, your packets of letters are still tied with faded blue ribbon now so fragile I can no longer undo the knots without fearing all will turn to dust. And though it is many years since I could remember the timbre of your voice and imagine the shape of your body, I know by heart every word you ever wrote to me, I spent years copying your letters over and over trying to imagine being you, trying to imitate the slant of your script, trying to come closer, to cross the great void, that partition between us, trying to edge myself over the brink, fall into the abyss, reach you. All to no avail.

And so I have not written to you for these many, many years.

This night in another place would smell of jasmine, and sweat would drip down between shoulder blades, and the sweltering stillness would be sweet; but here there is no jasmine and the heat is dry and the earth never swelters but bakes, and there is no sweetness, though strangely enough after all this time I have come to find beauty in the lack of verdancy, come to be moved by the starkness of muted colors—brown and umber, gray, ocher yellow—of rock and soil and dry grass under skies that whiten in the heat and cloud in the cold and are always immense. But I will leave this place without regret. Yes, Lavinia, I am returning to you, I am through with the impoverished existence I have led, I will deliver this missive in person at last, and upon your gravesite which I have never seen I will place a bouquet of violets, your favorite, in a final gesture of farewell. For we will never meet, nor will I meet our dead children nor the redeemed captive I long ago wrote to you about at length—her grave is in a pauper's field—nor my beloved brother nor any of the men who died under me or who died opposing us nor any of those who perished or disappeared at my last outpost, nor Dr. Matthews, who was indeed a friend. Oh, Lavinia, this farewell will be cruel: would that I had died when I still had hope of an afterlife. When I still had hope of anything.

Hopeless as I have become, I can still be made to marvel at coincidence. As soon as I made my decision to leave this place, Cole that very day arrived and, without my saying anything of my intentions, kindly offered me an old sorrel gelding he had with him, with hooves so hard it never needs shoeing. I had not seen the man for—ah, how I lose track of damnable time—and he said little, but his farewell was so heartfelt, it was as if he knew we would never meet again. And so the sorrel and I will plod our way to where I should long ago have gone. All that is left to me is my last journey to you and our children and then to my brother. Tomorrow I will burn all, the books, this old writing table, my Sunday clothes, the bed, the garden; I will leave ashes behind me and perhaps rid myself forever of gremlins and the small boy at the fence's edge, for surely he will not accompany me. I will burn everything but your letters and your likeness and my razor and the mirror and one bridle and saddle, I will burn what little I have acquired in a lifetime—how surprisingly little a man needs *really—and be done with it, ride out into a world much changed, with my bones rattling and my teeth missing and my sight failing, cutting a figure more preposterous than Quixote and more alone, without any fight or illusions left, perhaps more deranged than Lear upon the moors and certainly without the love of a child to protect him. For no child loves me. Has ever loved me.*

Lavinia, I must ask: Would more happiness have made this life less useless? Was our allotment of just that much, and no more, the same as everyone's? I despair that you cannot answer, despair I have no answers, that the only questions that now occur to me are unanswerable. I beg your forgiveness, you who can no longer forgive. And I remain your loving husband, a former brigadier and major, and a decrepit, bitter old man.

When Abigail Buwell died, something in Robert Cutter died with her. What she suffered he never knew, though she was so thin that her skin had turned translucent but for the circle scarred upon her cheek, and beneath her skin her veins ran blue and her bones were clearly visible. Her diaphanous eyes always glowed in his presence, and toward the end her soft laughter was so quick to come and her words so unhesitating when he visited and they sat upon the chairs of the great lawn, beyond the hearing of any, that he could hardly imagine she spoke to no one else, that she withdrew into herself the way a hermit crab hides in an empty shell, that she had to be force-fed with a funnel, that she slept naked on the wooden floor rather than blanketed on a bed, that she repeatedly shredded what clothes she was given to wear, cut herself and sheared her hair when she managed to swipe scissors or a razor, bit her hands.

In the first months of her stay at Clearwater, Abigail Buwell was subjected to cures thought viable and humane. The enlightened and well-intentioned doctors believed that any being capable of reason would respond positively to reasonable treatment, and so she was given drugs to regulate her digestive and intestinal tracts, tonics to stimulate her appetite, laxatives to purge bile; she had soothing baths, was given counterirritants, cooked food, clean clothes, a room with furniture; the bloodletting, it was hoped, would arrest any disease she might have; and she was taken to chapel services and allowed contact only with the sane. But she vomited the food, tore off her clothes, ignored the furniture, spit out the drugs, became dehydrated from the laxatives, weakened visibly with the bloodletting. She ignored the chapel services and sought no contact at all. After a time, other methods were tried to bring her to her senses. She suffered ice baths and long periods of painful deprivation, blindfolded and bound, or locked in a windowless room without knowing day from night. But she responded to nothing. She bore the ice baths without her teeth chattering, seemed undisturbed by the light after being blindfolded, was indifferent to her release from a straightjacket, and was found in the same position—as composed, indeed catatonic, as ever—as when left in the locked, windowless room.

Abigail Buwell's symptoms, her condition, led her doctors to eventually diagnose irrevocable moral insanity. They concluded that her life among the savages had been so profoundly debasing as to render her incurable. They carefully read the published text of Constance Smith's captivity and went to great lengths to bring her to the asylum and interview her, which only substantiated their inclination to relate Abigail Buwell's madness to her exposure to—and eventual acceptance of—immorality, vice, and filth. Theirs was a curious assessment, given the fact the doctors were well read and believed, as was the current trend, that mental illness was curiously absent among the savages and other primitive peoples; but they managed this contradiction—of which they were well aware—by assuring one another that the noble savage should not be mistaken for the pure and simple savage.

As to their other patients, including Henry Cutter, the doctors humanely regarded insanity in its myriad manifestations—melancholy, mania, dementia—as part of the price paid for civilization, for in their day and age the pattern of greater opportunities and rewards for excessive mental action could place great strain upon the healthiest of persons. But after the first six months of Abigail Buwell's commitment, both doctors and staff stopped treating her as someone who had once been or could perhaps again become reasonable, or one strained by the worst of circumstance, for she remained obstinately unreasonable and, to them, unreasoning. If she understood the simple institutional privileges, the rewards for appropriate behavior—and she did—she never once manifested this intelligence.

After Abigail Buwell was deemed incurable, her care became barely custodial: there were the twice-daily forced feedings that finally ruptured her esophagus, weekly hosings with cold water in lieu of baths, chemical dustings for lice. They moved the furniture from her room except for a bedstand and cot, they stopped bringing her to chapel, they allowed her contact with the insane, they ignored her for the most part. The doctors and staff did not discourage Robert Cutter or Reed Gabriel from visiting her, but they were nonplussed that anyone would—in their eyes—waste time with someone so terminally insane.

When Reed Gabriel came to call, Abigail Buwell allowed him to escort her through the corridors and sat quietly beside him in the common room; when the weather was fine, he took her outdoors. She let him hold her elbow as they walked, bent her head toward him in a way that gave the impression she was listening. The one sentence she ever spoke to him, he never mentioned to another soul. Her conversations with Robert Cutter, which would have stunned her caretakers and doctors but not Reed Gabriel, both took to their graves.

Reed Gabriel was informed of her death by mail. *To our amazement,* one of her doctors wrote him, *a small packet addressed to you was found under her mattress; of course, we had no idea she could either read or write; as you know, we considered her incapable of speech altogether. Because she was our ward, we examined its contents, which are enclosed in their entirety. I am sure you will agree these fragments—I hesitate to call them poems—reveal a sadly fractured and distraught mind. Our handwriting expert confirmed our diagnosis of moral insanity, as did the autopsy.* The doctor did not write of the autopsy's details, the disfigurement to her face when they flayed the skin in quadrants from her crown, sawed open her skull, removed her brain, noted its weight (normal) and configuration (normal): that which ailed Abigail Buwell, they were relieved to confirm, was a matter of the soul and its deprivations.

Reed Gabriel did not immediately read what the doctors sent to him, and he never knew why the crude envelope she made was addressed to him: but it pained him deeply that she would speak to him from beyond the grave. For upon each successive visit—all of them random—he found Abigail Buwell more exacting only of herself, more perfectly composed and perfectly wordless, and astonishingly desirable. There was something in the way she moved that reminded him of leaves spiraling in the wind, there was a disconcerting lightness to her, a nightmarish beauty to her eyes. She watched him from the corners of these as he spoke, and he knew she understood his words, for she spoke to him that one time. He was so smitten—as much by her impenetrability as by what he came to consider her beauty—that he dared to dream she would eventually recognize in him her salvation, and he kept alive the hope that the next time he visited, or the next, she would look up from her chair in surprise and delight to see him standing in the doorway, rise, and say: I've been waiting for you.

She waited only for the end, and he felt cheated, angry, deceived. He ranted rather than mourned, he thought how unfair, how *unfair*, how like a suicide, how selfish; he castigated her, he fumed, he almost burned her scribblings unread, he cursed her as cruel, and once, just once, he heard himself cry out: Now you speak, *now*, when there is no possibility of conversation. He could hardly forgive her for stealing the privilege of all writers, for leaving her words behind, because he considered this privilege his own, not hers—and thought of her as ungrateful, outrageous, pitiless.

But Abigail Buwell did pity him. This, Reed Gabriel never knew: she pitied him for his constancy, his visits, his kindness, his patience, his transparent if harmless narcissism—for he preened, he could not pass a mirror without glancing at himself and admiring his good grooming, he sniffed his sleeve for the slight hint of scent he wore—his sweet rakishness, his persistence. She pitied him his charms, for these were wasted on her; and she pitied his gullibility and cynicism, both of which allowed him to exploit Constance Smith and a readership that wanted to be edified—that is, shocked. Which is why she once told him her truth, all she could tell him, in one sentence. Which is why what she wrote, she wrote for him: so he might know, if he wanted to know.

A week after receiving the packet, Reed Gabriel opened it and took out a torn piece of paper and read

I was not brought here to be mad,
but to die. So be it, I will
accord them this favor, it is what
they expect and, after all, nothing more
than a matter of good manners. For dying is
so simple, really, if one is courteous: excuse me,
I must now go, pardon me for this brush
I've accidentally had with life. Smiles all around

and folded the piece of paper without reading it again, exactly the way it was creased, and put it back in the packet. Over the course of several months, in between journeys and work, he would sometimes sit holding the envelope, run his fingers around its edges, open it and withdraw one snippet or another, examine the graphite letters that connected into words in a small, uneven script—the handwriting of a child, he thought—and from time to time read a fragment and then pour himself a glass of sour mash, pondering the imponderable. He moved many times, and the packet always accompanied him; but in his seventy-eighth year he misplaced it, could not find it at all, and did not know whether he was relieved or distressed.

He always remembered what she wrote. Always remembered the one thing she ever said to him: *I simply wish I had never been found.*

During the rest of her life in the asylum, Abigail Buwell remains steadfast in never again becoming Abigail Buwell. She knows she was born the day the savages kidnapped her and died the day she was redeemed, mounted upon the magnificent horse by the man who fathered her children. She remains She-Who-Was-Dreamed-By-The-Blue-Horse, the woman given this name by the savages. For it was the blue colt that led the savages to her and to Constance Smith when they tried to escape, the same colt whose breached birth almost ended its life before it even began. She had pulled the foal from its dam by reaching into the mare's slimy recesses and, grasping a leg, two, somehow twisted the thing struggling to be born until the canal allowed its passage; she guided the hind legs out, the tail, the haunches, as the mare screamed and expelled the rest of the bloody mess, and she cleared the foal's nostrils of mucus and fluid and blew into them, gave the newborn colt its life. Her breath was the first scent it smelled, her hands the first touch it felt, before feeling the tongue of its exhausted dam, before drinking its milk; and it was forevermore inseparable from her. The colt raced to her whenever it caught her scent, followed her, nuzzled her palms and her neck and ears, and sometimes lay down beside her when she watched over the horse herd, which was her pleasure.

They said the blue horse dreamed her because it would have been stillborn without her, and that it wanted to live. They said the blue horse dreamed her because blue horses, the rarest of all, have powerful magic and possess spirits not unlike that of a man or a woman of the People. Which was the word they called themselves and no others.

She too came to believe that she was dreamed by this horse, for her life among the savages had nothing if not the quality of a dream. She was punished severely for running away: she had betrayed their confidence, she had betrayed the family to whom she had been given and who had treated her well, dressed her in robes and combed and greased and braided her hair, sheltered and fed her and were content to let her look after their horses. She was given liberty, she staked their horses and saw to it that they were watered and fed, she made bands of fringe to strap about their ears and hang over their eyes so the flies would not gather in them, she carved picks from hardwood with which to clean their feet, she pulled their tails, their manes. She took the place of a dead son the family could no longer mourn, and their hearts were lightened by her presence. And so, for her deception, for her attempted escape, she was stripped and whipped and spat upon and cudgeled and tied and denied water until her tongue swelled, denied food until she knew what it is to starve, and then she was forgiven. She was tenderly washed, dressed again in robes by the family who would readopt her; her hair was greased and combed and plaited, smoke was blown into her eyes and nostrils to dispel the evil spirits that had taken up residence within her, and then she was given water and food and a fur to sleep upon. It was made clear that she was once again to care for their horses, which she did. As she spent her nights watching the herd graze with the blue colt beside her, the moons came and went, and she had ample time to reflect upon the fact that, for the first time in her life, men neither violated nor assaulted nor abused nor spurned her, that for the first time since her early childhood she was in the company of women who were tender and quick to laugh, who were so indulgent with their children that they grew without crying. She was with women who worked when there was work and who lolled unashamedly with their men when there was little to do—during those winter months spent in high ranges where the snows fell incessantly and the horses ate bark, or during times of plenty after a hunting party laden with meat returned—with women who taught her words she could never have imagined.

Their language stunned her: there was a word for the way in which a man fording a river leans forward on his horse, a word for the way a wounded hawk flies to the crag where its chicks are nesting, a word for rain that clings to juniper needles rather than drips from them, a word for her name, a word for each moon cycle and its meaning—the moon of acorns dropping, the moon of raindust falling—a word for the way a woman suffering labor pains walks to the shelter where women withdrew to suffer labor pains. And on and on. It is these words she clings to for the rest of her short life, words with no alphabet, words that died with the last of them who were murdered under the command of Colonel Harold Chapman, words that will never be spoken again—for, with her death, an entire language will be lost—words that once fell like laughter from the mouths of babes but are now dead, like the People who spoke them.

Except during the visits by Robert Cutter and the persistent if unpredictable journalist, and when jotting what she will manage to write, Abigail Buwell will never think in or speak the first language she knew. She leaves this language behind her when she enters the asylum; she drowns it within her. She can bear her life at Clearwater only by steeping herself in that other world, in her past among the People, a past no one will ever decode, imagine or decipher, and she will mourn. And if her mourning eats away at her, which it does, it also sustains her: as she thins, as she becomes skeletal, she becomes more fully herself; as she withdraws further and further within herself, she becomes perfectly impenetrable, inviolable. She imagines she is weaving herself into a chrysalis, she spins a cocoon, she feels herself enwrapped, suspended by a fragile silken thread that remains peculiarly indestructible, that neither she nor anyone else can sever, though she knows it will break.

It is only a matter of time, and she awaits patiently the fog of unreleased spirits—for which she knows the word—to descend, thick with the dead whose bodies and bones were left to putrefy on the ground, in leaves and muck, in mud or silt or sand, in bogs, rather than placed in trees or upon bowers or cliffs, anywhere the earth's slime could not penetrate them, absorb them, rot them, eternally clutch at their souls, suck their decaying bodies into itself and trap their spirits. She makes peace with her fate, which is the same as the fate of the child she willed unborn, the fate of her other child and of its father, the fate of the women who taught her their language, of their men, their children. She knows she will be buried in the earth, that her mouth and eyes and nostrils and ears will fill with soil, that her body will become the provenance of grubs and worms, ants and slugs, for the gravediggers will throw her naked, autopsied, mutilated corpse into the ground and cover it. She knows she will not hear the thud of the dirt shoveled atop her, will not see the sky, will not breathe the fetid, cool damp; she knows her spirit will not be released. She knows there is nothing to be done. And so she waits and bides her time until the fog descends and drags her spirit from her as she closes her eyes, as she starves herself, for she has no appetite to recover a life she does not want or the ability to bring back the life she does. When the moment comes and the fog of unreleased spirits finally envelopes her, she is ready.

It does not do so until one year and four months and three days after her commitment to the asylum. Eight days before the fog rolls in, Robert Cutter, whose life is shattered and whose wounds ail him, visits her. He is, as always with her, undemanding and comforting, for he is all too aware of her fragility and his own fate, which will be to survive her for many years but not the ravages of circumstance nor the punishments of time. The last time he sees her, Abigail Buwell is restrainedly animated as they wander outside and far from the lawn's chairs; she glances often at him, sometimes smiles, speaks to him in the only language they have in common. She describes with great nostalgia how she was courted by a savage of good standing, who asked nothing of her but to be his and to tether his horses well. She tells Cutter that her firstborn grew willow-like and gave her great joy, and that her life with the savages, and with the man who had courted her, was not one of deprivation but of its opposite. She speaks to Robert Cutter of these things one year and seven months and fourteen days after her redemption, and eight days before she is dropped into the earth in a pauper's grave marked only by a number, which corresponds to the name of the person she no longer was, and for years had not been.

The blue roan stops dreaming her from the moment the fog of unreleased spirits descends. Three days after Abigail Buwell's death, the horse lies on its side in the throes of colic, its intestines twisted, and dies in great pain as the light in its eyes spills into the murk.

Robert Cutter does not visit the asylum for weeks thereafter. He doesn't know how to tell Abigail Buwell that her splendid and much beloved horse is dead and buried, that he labored over the course of two days digging its grave; that he put the chestnut in a makeshift harness so he could drag the dead roan to the edge of the hole and then tumble it in, that there was an awful thud and a finality so terrible that he wept as he shoveled dirt atop this creature that remained, oddly and after two days, magnificent even in death. Robert Cutter cannot read signs, and so he pays no attention to the fog but to curse it. He does not know that when her horse stopped dreaming her, she was already gone.

He never knew what Abigail Buwell was called by the savages.

All's well that ends well, my dearest Lavinia: ah, how pithy our Shakespeare, that's what you always remarked, yes, my dear, how pithy. All's well that ends well: for years this pithy notion played havoc with me, I thought of it after battles won at great cost with tens of thousands dead, the fields strewn with arms and legs and disembodied heads and pieces of flesh unrecognizable as once human, all's well that ends well. It repeated itself almost as a refrain during our only surviving son's various recoveries after painful interludes of madness and ineptitude, after which he would slip into insanity once again; it came to mind when Colonel Chapman rode into my last and most horrid post, his men adorned with the scalps and fingers and ears and private parts of the savages. Abigail Buwell was returned to civilization and spent her redemption committed to an asylum where they said she showed neither signs of happiness nor unhappiness and had the good fortune to die peacefully one night lying upon the floor next to a cot she never slept in—they emphasized the word peacefully—all's well that ends well. How bitter I am you know, my love, how angry: What you cannot know is what has been revealed to me, that no ending ends well, it only ends, and we end facing a great void, the same void we spent our entire lives struggling to bridge, imagining a great crossing in the name of anything larger and more complex than our puny selves, pushing on no matter the consequences, no matter the brutality, no matter the circumstances, no matter the cost in labor and strife.

I burned the volumes of Shakespeare today. I burned all the books I have carried with me throughout a lifetime, I burned all the meager possessions I ever accumulated, the writing table last, I fed the fire with the mattress and bed, wash stand and chairs, a few hooked rugs, a cabinet, a chest, my military stars and pips, a set of clothes; I tore everything living from the garden and burned that as well, I burned pots and pans and porcelain and tins and cupboard doors and a bench. The books burned best: How easily words become ashes. How easily so much is turned to ash. How simple it is to disappear every trace of oneself. How easy it is to be forgotten, in the end we are all forgotten, time being the cruelest and most efficient amnesiac of all. All's well that ends well.

Once upon a time and long ago I looked out over a stockade and did not know at first what I was seeing: it could have been anything or nothing at all. Now I look at this smoldering pit of ashes which has consumed the sum total of my years except for my memories and think, as I look back from this beyond: I still do not know what it is I have seen. I can make no more sense of that which lies behind than that which lies before me.

It could be anything, or nothing at all.